THE CLAIMING OF THE HIGHLANDS

BOOK SEVEN OF THE SYLVAN CHRONICLES

PETER WACHT

Kestrel
Media Group, LLC

ISBN: 978-1-950236-12-1

eBook ISBN: 978-1-950236-13-8

Library of Congress Control Number: 2020912186

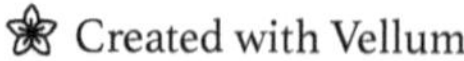 Created with Vellum

The Raptor of the Highlands

The Makings of a Warrior

The Lord of the Highlands

The Lost Kestrel Found

The Claiming of the Highlands

The Fight Against the Dark

The Defender of the Light

THE RISE OF THE SYLVAN WARRIORS

Through the Knife's Edge (short story)*

* Free short stories can be downloaded from my author website at www.PeterWachtBooks.com.

YOUR FREE SHORT STORY IS WAITING

BLOOD ON THE WHITE SAND BY PETER WACHT

This short story is a prelude to the events in my new series *The Tales of Caledonia* and is free to readers who receive my newsletter.

Sign up and get your free copy at www.PeterWachtBooks.com.

1

AMBUSH

"Steady, lads. Steady, lasses. Steady."

Nestor, a grizzled Highlander with a white beard trailing halfway down his chest, whispered his instructions to the men and women hidden among the trees, Marchers all. Trained as the warriors of the Highlands beginning at the age of ten, they were a hard people. But such a practice proved necessary. They lived in a harsh environment. The Highlands were a beautiful sight, but also dangerous. The rugged land hid untold riches -- gold and silver, precious jewels and more -- among its craggy, snowcapped peaks. But throughout their history the Highlanders had little use for the wealth that could be mined in their homeland. Rather, the people of the Highlands remained focused on a cold, stark and unforgiving reality, one of constant threats and peril, particularly from the north.

For Nestor and the other Highlanders that reality had crashed down upon them just a decade before. In a valley to the east of where the squad of Marchers now hid rose the stronghold of the Highlanders, the Crag, a monolithic rock that thrust up out of the earth and the surrounding forest. Carved from the mountain, the redoubt was a formidable sight. The Highlanders had built their fortress on top of a long-dead volcano, taking great slabs of black stone from the plateau to form its walls. During the night, the citadel receded into the darkness, indistinct in the gloom. The Crag had never fallen to an enemy. Many an army had learned that lesson the hard way, leaving behind crushed bodies and broken spirits. Until that fateful day ten years before, when a traitor among the Marchers had aided the reivers during their surprise attack on the Crag. Supported by warlocks and dark creatures, as soon as the Ogren and Shades broke through the Crag's outer curtain, the reivers grasped that they had won, and that the fate of the Highlands was sealed. Nestor and many of the Marchers standing with him now and shivering in the early morning cold had lived through that day, a day of shame and infamy. Talyn Kestrel, the Lord of the Highlands, had died that day. Refusing to escape, he fought until the very end in the Hall of the Highland Lord. His son, Benlorin Kestrel, met a similar fate at his camp in the northern peaks. Consequently, the Kestrel line had been broken, or so it had appeared.

Led by the Dunmoorian Lord Johin Killeran, who served as the High King's regent, from that point forward the reivers had assumed control of the Highlands. The High King had wanted the Highlands outright for himself, but there were still questions about the grandson. Did he die that night as well? Or had he survived the attack? A body had never been found. Therefore, according to the law set down during the time of the first High King, a decade-long regency was required. If no legitimate claimant stepped forward prior to the end of the stated time period, then the Highlands would revert to the High King for administration and rule. Although unhappy with the forced delay, it did not stop the High King, through his selected regent, from doing as he wished within the Highlands, much to the detriment of the Highlanders themselves, who reeled from the shock and loss of what had happened that fateful night and set the Highlands on a path of terror and oppression.

Nestor smiled to himself, remembering those not so long ago dark days. Hope had been lost during that desperate time and he, much like many of his people, had felt cast adrift, their thoughts only of survival, not vengeance. For with none of the other Kingdoms strong enough or willing to aid the Highlands against the expanding dominance of the High King, Killeran and his so-called Army of the Black Sword had been given free rein by Rodric Tessaril to do as charged. Enslave the Highlanders and force them into the mines so that the High King could extract the wealth that he needed to increase his power and achieve his larger objectives. For almost ten years the scheme had worked well for the High King and his sycophants. Until the boy appeared. The boy first known as the Raptor. The boy who aided the Highlanders whenever possible and killed dark creatures with ease. At first, Nestor, staying close to family in the passes of the northern Highlands, had taken the stories that had begun to spread among the peaks as no more than the fantasies of a desperate people, a people slowly being crushed under the heel of the High King. Even though the Marchers had the will to continue the fight, they didn't have the numbers to defeat the thousands of reivers that had flooded into the Highlands as part of the Army of the Black Sword and, more importantly, they had no way to defend against the Dark Magic of Killeran's warlocks.

But with time, as the stories continued to proliferate among the Highland towns and villages, and Nestor began to find evidence of the Raptor's work sprinkled among the Highland peaks – a small village saved from a reiver patrol thanks to the sharp shooting of a near perfect archer or the remains of several Ogren hamstrung and beheaded – he had started to believe, his hope returning once more. For Nestor and many others, that boy who had become the Raptor had shifted from myth to reality, in fact a new reality that held the promise of a better future for the subjugated Highlanders. The same boy who became a constant thorn in Killeran's side, burning down his primary fort and in the process reigniting the fire for freedom that now blazed in the breast of every Marcher. The boy who just a few months before had become the Lord of the Highlands. The Lost Kestrel was no longer lost. The grandson of Talyn Kestrel had returned to the Highlands to take his rightful place, and woe to any who opposed him, as the honorable Marchers had a saying: "A debt is owed."

With the return of the Lord of the Highlands, the Marchers began collecting on those debts, starting with the Army of the Black Sword, which had pushed deeper into the Highlands seeking to quell the uprising before it gained a momentum that could not be stopped. Killeran's reivers had failed miserably. What a glorious day that had been, thought Nestor, allowing his mind to drift just for a moment even as his eyes scanned his surroundings in an unerring arc, paying particular attention to the gulley that ran beneath where the Marchers hid among the evergreens. With the last of night still upon them, there was nothing but shadows to stare at among the bracken below.

Even though Ogren and Shades had been used in support of the reivers, the Marchers under the command of Thomas Kestrel had destroyed the Army of the Black Sword against the walls of a Highland village named Anselm, which was located at the very edge of one of the northern passes. Since that time, the Marchers had harried and harassed any reivers foolish enough to remain in the Highlands, driving them out or, as Nestor preferred, killing them. For the Marchers sought to pay their debts, and they owed the reivers a huge sum for the pain, misery, and death Killeran's lackeys had spawned in their homeland since the fall of the Crag.

Yet even with one victory attained, other challenges remained. Dark creatures from the Charnel Mountains continued to cross the barren Northern Steppes, seeking to gain a foothold in the Highlands for their master, who stirred once more. It was because of that threat, one that had troubled the Highlands for centuries, that Nestor and his Marchers waited patiently among the trees, bows in hand, several long, steel-tipped arrows stuck point first into the rocky soil and within easy reach. The Shadow Lord sought the Kingdoms for his own, and when his Dark Horde descended from the north the Lord Thomas and every other Highland chief, Nestor included, believed that the black-hearted bastard would seek to avoid the Breaker, the massive, granite wall to the west that ran from the Highlands to the coast and the Winter Sea. Three hundred feet in height and one hundred feet in width, the Breaker was constructed after the Great War by the Kingdoms as a way to defend against the Dark Horde, believing that the massive barrier would prevent the Ogren and Shades, Fearhounds and Mongrels, and the other terrifying, monstrous dark creatures that obeyed the Shadow Lord from threatening the Kingdoms once again. Yet Nestor scoffed at the naïve and misplaced hopes of those who had thought a stone wall would eliminate the need to defend against such an ancient evil. The Shadow Lord was not a fool. He had simply adopted a different strategy, seeking different routes into the west that would allow him to bypass the Breaker. Thus, the importance of the Highlands to his plans as an alternative path into the Kingdoms. Because of this threat, the new Highland Lord had charged Nestor and his Marchers with protecting the northern Highlands while he made his formal claim to the Highland throne during the Council of the Kingdoms.

Nestor hoped that all had gone well in Eamhain Mhacha, understanding the danger that Thomas, Coban, Oso, and the other Marchers had ridden toward. A danger that was difficult to defend against because more often than not politics hid your enemy in plain sight up until the instant you felt the dagger slide into your back. Much better to be here in the Highlands where you had no doubt about what you were fighting for and what you were fighting against.

"On my command," whispered Nestor, his eyes tightening as he glimpsed finally the movement that he had been expecting. The several dozen Marchers raised their bows in unison, the pull back on their strings barely making a sound as the biting wind swept up from the Northern Steppes, finding a path through the ravines and gullies leading up to the higher passes.

Large shapes had appeared just below the Marchers in the gloom of the early morning, the sun yet to find its way over the towering, rugged mountain peaks to the east. Bunched together, the huge creatures struggled up the slope of broken brush and loose rock, unaware or uncaring of what waited for them at the top.

"Release!"

The arrows flew through the morning mist, almost all finding a target. Roars of anger and pain echoed off the surrounding spires of rock. Below the Marchers some of the large shapes had fallen to the ground, never to rise again. But only a few, as these creatures were difficult to kill because of their armor and toughened hide, often requiring an arrow through the eye to ensure a clean kill, and to ask that of the Marchers in the dim light of the morning would have been unfair.

"Nock!"

The Marchers immediately heeded Nestor's command, pulling free the arrows they had stuck in the dirt by their feet and fitting them to the taut strings of their bows.

"On my command!"

The Marchers pulled back on their heavy bows, now seeking individual targets. The dark creatures below them had separated, their once orderly march having dissolved into a maelstrom of uncoordinated activity. Several of the beasts roared in rage and began to climb the slope toward their attackers.

"Release!"

A second flight of arrows arced through the air, all striking true this time as the monsters emerged from the grey murk in their rush to confront their tormentors. The dark creatures roared in rage as they struggled up the loose rocks of the incline, several using the broken brush to pull themselves up in order to avoid sliding back down the steep slope. Twice the size of a man, their heavily muscled bodies covered in fur, Ogren were truly hideous creatures. Their massive shoulders and upper body sometimes proved too heavy for their spines, forcing them to walk hunched over. Their chiseled, beast-like faces looked as if they had been carved from rock. Long, sharp tusks protruded from their lower lips to curl around their cheeks. They lacked intelligence, but their strength and viciousness more than made up for that shortcoming. Ogren were efficient soldiers. They enjoyed killing, and given the opportunity they ate what they killed, no matter what it was. A single person did not willingly fight an Ogren, not if they wanted to live. But the Marchers had mastered how to fight dark creatures such as these.

"Nock!"

The Marchers responded a third time to Nestor's command, ignoring the Ogren as they hauled themselves closer, several resembling pin cushions as arrows sprouted from their chests and thighs, the wounds seemingly having no effect on the enraged beasts.

"On my command!"

The Marchers raised their bows once more, sighting on individual targets, selecting the Ogren that had scrabbled closest to the Marcher line.

"Release!"

The third wave of arrows had a devastating impact at such a close distance, the steel-tipped shafts of wood tearing through Ogren eyes and mouths as the Marchers targeted where the beasts were most vulnerable. Almost all of the Ogren closest to the Marchers fell to the ground, an arrow embedded in their brains. But not every dark creature unfortunately. Therefore, Nestor judged that it was time to go.

"Retreat!"

The Marchers quickly began pulling back, following Nestor as he trotted off to the south. The Highland chief took great pleasure in the fact that they had hurt the Ogren raiding party badly with none of his Marchers the worse for wear. But the dark creatures were too many for the Marchers to stand and fight, and the beasts would be after them in an instant. In fact, he could hear several of the Ogren already pulling themselves to the top of the slope, their roars of triumph sending a shiver through his body and giving him a greater sense of urgency as the monstrous beasts began the chase.

"Come on my lads!" encouraged Nestor. "Come on my lasses! No one for an Ogren cook pot tonight."

The Marchers responded with a burst of speed. Increasing their pace, Nestor and his fighters ran across the rocky terrain, understanding the price they would pay if caught.

A TALL MAN stood unmoving within the shadows of the forest, looking out from his place of concealment among the evergreens and birch trees at the verge of a small plateau. The field of long grass funneled toward him, constricted by two large, stone outcroppings that loomed above the wood on both sides. This would do nicely, he thought. Nicely, indeed.

He wore brown breeks and a dark blue shirt that covered a slim body. Though he did not look it, he had a deceptive strength. The cloak he wore not only helped to ward off the chill, but it also swirled around him, its green and brown colors allowing him to blend in perfectly with the environment. His piercing blue eyes held an intensity that would have frightened most men and were accentuated by the sharp features of his face. The short black beard flecked with grey gave him an almost dastardly appearance. If anyone had the courage to tell him so, he would have smiled and thanked them for the compliment.

"They come," said the diminutive woman standing next to him, who wore a similarly designed cloak so that she would remain hidden among the trees as well. She had used the Talent to scan their surroundings, having expected their quarry to arrive shortly after sunrise.

"It's about time," replied the man. "I'm tired of waiting." He glanced down at the beautiful woman who had stolen his heart so long ago. No more than five feet tall, she carried herself like a giant. As she swept her dark, chestnut hair away from her face with a quick swipe of her hand, she revealed deep blue eyes. Eyes that the tall man had often gotten lost in time and time again, much to his pleasure. In his mind, saying she was beautiful did not do her justice.

A massive shadow approached from behind, only the bright yellow of its eyes visible in the gloom of the forest. The growl that emanated from its throat sounded like the rumble of thunder.

"Yes, I know you had a part to play in putting this all together, Beluil," said the tall man, turning toward the wolf as it stepped out of the murk. The wolf stood as tall as a pony. Covered in a thick, black fur, he was invisible in the night, except for the streak of white fur that crossed his eyes. "Are you and your packs ready?"

Beluil growled once more, stretching his jaws in anticipation of what was to come and revealing his sharp teeth in the process.

"Then off with you, you big furball. We'll meet in the center."

Beluil dashed back into the trees straight away, lost from sight in less than a second.

"I'm glad that wolf is a friend," said Catal Huyuk, the hulking warrior stepping forward to stand next to his companions. He stood a head taller than most men, and his dark brown face disguised his age. His leathery skin showed him to be a man who had spent most of his life in the outdoors, and that he wasted little time in towns or cities. His long black hair was held back from his face by a knot of leather at the base of his neck. He was dressed in the leathers of a woodsman with a huge sword strapped to his back and a wickedly curved axe hanging at his waist instead of the expected bow and quiver of arrows. "Because I would hate to be his enemy."

"Yes, indeed," replied Rya. "Our grandson has a habit of acquiring dangerous friends."

"That's why I like him so much," rumbled Catal Huyuk. "He keeps things interesting and fun. Makes you feel alive."

"Fun?" asked Rya Keldragan, eyebrow raised quizzically.

"What could be more fun than killing dark creatures?" replied Catal Huyuk.

"It's time," said Rynlin Keldragan, ending the banter around him, his gaze fixed on the far side of the field. "They're only a few hundred yards from the entrance and coming fast."

"Good," said Catal Huyuk, who pulled his battle axe free. Even the largest of men would struggle to use the heavy weapon effectively, yet the Sylvan Warrior flipped it from one hand to the other as if it were no more than a child's toy. "I haven't been in a good fight in days."

NESTOR CURSED as he ran through the forest, ignoring the branches that scraped at his face and body. He had started out leading his Marchers through the fractured and jagged terrain as they sprinted from one copse of trees to the next after their ambush of the Ogren raiding party. But that hadn't lasted long. The younger and faster Marchers had sped ahead, and he had urged them on.

Now he was the last one, and he had larger things to worry about. Much larger. A handful of Ogren had closed in on him since the chase began, the foul beasts now no more than a few hundred feet behind and coming fast. The rest of the dark creature raiding party followed just seconds behind, ravenously pursuing their prey, pushed on by hunger and rage. Roars blasted through the small forest, the Ogren calling to one another as they continued to hound the Highlanders.

Peeking quickly over his shoulder to gauge his distance from the closest Ogren, the veteran Marcher stumbled on some loose rock, tumbling to the ground and slamming into the base of a fallen tree. Nestor hauled himself up rapidly, thankful that he hadn't injured anything except for his pride, but also realizing that his clumsiness had cost him greatly. The five Ogren that had raced ahead of the other dark creatures approached in a line, having caught up to him. The beasts bellowed in triumph as they brandished their short swords and axes, strings of spittle hanging from their curved tusks. Nestor pulled his sword from its scabbard across his back, relieved that it was still there after his tumble. There was no point in running. He'd never make it now. The Ogren were too fast. Better to die like a Marcher.

One Ogren charged forward, wanting the kill for itself. Nestor set himself, preparing for the attack and hoping that he could put up a good fight at least for a time. If he could delay the Ogren, even for just a couple minutes, then perhaps the time earned would aid his Marchers in their escape. The Ogren raised its battle axe above its head, thinking to bring it down on top of his smaller opponent and split him in two. Raising his sword in a two-handed grip, Nestor sought to deflect the blow, but he knew with some regret that he had little chance of success, the dark creature's blow too powerful.

At the last second, Nestor ducked down, hearing the distinctive thrum from behind him as three arrows in rapid succession streaked through the space he had just been occupying. The first arrow struck the beast in the chest, the second in the thigh, but those only enraged it. It was the third, driving through its cheek into its brain, that finished the job. The massive beast crashed face first to the ground, dead before it hit the rocky soil. The other Ogren watched in disbelief, then bellowed in anger and rushed forward.

A tall Highlander stood above Nestor, offering a hand. Nestor gladly accepted it and quickly regained his feet.

"Come on, old man," said Aric. "We're almost to the plateau. Once there, it's just a straight run across. Can you do it without falling?"

Not bothering to reply, though several pointed comments crossed his mind, Nestor ran through the forest, dodging trees, rocks and other obstacles that sought to take him down, until finally breaking out onto the wide stretch of grassland that he saw narrowed just ahead between two rocky outcroppings. Aric stuck close to his heels, apparently wanting to make certain that Nestor didn't have any more problems during their attempted escape.

Blasted children, Nestor thought. Stronger. Faster. Thinking they knew more than you. Much too confident. Not understanding the value of experience. The Highland chief pushed the thoughts from his mind. Yes, he was old. But he could still fight and lead. And he'd need to thank Aric once they escaped the Ogren. The young stripling had saved his life, and for that he owed him a debt.

· · ·

"THERE THEY ARE," rumbled Catal Huyuk, pointing to the two Highlanders sprinting through the long grass and striving for the trees at the far side.

"The Ogren are gaining," said Rya. "They're not going to make it."

Nestor and Aric didn't bother to look behind them. The Marchers were well aware of the danger that pursued them. Four Ogren were no more than one hundred feet behind them and gaining with every step, the beasts' long strides allowing them to make up the ground in seconds. The remainder of the Ogren raiding party, almost five dozen in all despite their previous losses, followed after them, intent on the chase and not paying attention to their surroundings.

"They don't need to make it," said Rynlin. "They just need to get a little farther. We need the last of the Ogren into the gap. Otherwise, the trap fails."

"Marchers to the ready," Catal Huyuk ordered. Nestor's Marchers, all of whom had made it safely across the grassland into the small forest at the far side, stepped to the edge of the wood. Bows in hand, an arrow already on the string, they placed a half dozen arrows each into the soft earth in front of them, ready to launch on command. Nestor and Aric were agonizingly close, but it was too late. They weren't going to reach the safety of the trees by just a small margin. The Ogren were only a dozen feet behind them now.

"They're through the gap," confirmed Rya.

"Now!" shouted Rynlin.

He and Rya stepped forward, seizing hold of the Talent and allowing the natural energy of the world to flow through them. Several other Sylvan Warriors followed them out from the trees. Maden, almost as tall as Rynlin, wore a sword at his hip. Though it appeared as if his features were carved from granite, he always had a ready smile, and he wore it now as balls of white energy danced across his hands. Gavin of Ferranagh, a short man with a long, white beard that he looped in his belt to keep out of the way, emerged next. Followed by Brinn Kavolin, an extremely tall, slender man. He had a sharp, angular face and dark brown hair that continually threatened to fall into his eyes. Right behind him came the twins, Elisia and Aurelia Valeran from Kashel, the only difference between the two being the color of their hair, Elisia's a midnight black and Aurelia's a shocking white.

Just as the lead Ogren was about to stab his sword into Nestor's back, a bolt of white light shot over the Marcher's head and blasted through the chest of the pursuing Ogren. Nestor had ducked the blow he felt coming, sliding through the grass and then tumbling past the men and women who stepped from between the trees and faced the onrushing Ogren. Once again Aric helped him to his feet, and they watched in astonishment and delight as more bolts and balls of white energy slammed into the charging dark creatures, blasting through their wide chests and leaving a sickly smell of burning meat to drift on the wind.

"Release at will!"

Catal Huyuk's craggy voice cut through the commotion. The Marchers lined up behind the Sylvan Warriors released their first flight of arrows, and then another, followed by another. The men and women of the Highlands each sent a half-dozen shafts into the sky in less than a minute. The arrows flew through the air in an almost continuous stream, the flow thick and heavy, forcing the Ogren to halt their attack. Most of the arrows found their target, slamming into the Ogrens' heavily muscled bodies, although few found their killing mark. But that was not the intention. The Marchers simply wanted to cause confusion among the Ogren, and they swiftly did, as the huge beasts, many with two or three shafts protruding from their chests or legs, looked around uncertainly, not sure whether to continue their attack or seek to escape.

The decision was made for the slow-witted Ogren when a howl echoed off the two rocky outcroppings. A massive black wolf, a stripe of white across his eyes, sprinted at the head of more than a hundred wolves that streamed through the gap leading onto the plateau, their shining eyes intent on their prey. Launching himself into the air, Beluil slammed into the back of an Ogren, forcing it to the ground. Before the dark creature could bring its short sword to bear, the rusty blade stuck beneath its chest, the black wolf tore into the beast's throat with his sharp teeth. The growls and howls of the wolves added to the almost overwhelming din as they broke off into groups of three or four and tried to separate the Ogren, nipping at the back of its legs and seeking to bite into a calf or hamstring. Once disabled and on the ground, the wolves could easily finish the task or leave it to their allies, as the Marchers, having dropped their bows and pulled their swords, charged into the melee, Catal Huyuk leading the way as he cleaved an Ogren's head from its shoulders with the first swing of his giant battle axe.

In just a few minutes, it was over, the bodies of the Ogren scattered across the trampled long grass of the plateau. Marchers and Sylvan Warriors walked among the dark creatures, ensuring that none survived.

Rynlin watched the entire exercise with a grim smile, knowing that the lack of mercy was necessary. He was pleased. The trap had sprung exactly as planned with none of the Marchers, Sylvan Warriors, or wolves seriously injured. Smiling in satisfaction, a shriek above him pulled him from his thoughts and his gaze to the sky. A large raptor circled above. Dipping its wing, the large kestrel glided across the battlefield screeching in triumph, then tilted its wings to catch the wind coming through the gap between the two rocky promontories, which had served the purpose of the Marchers and Sylvan Warriors so well by guiding the Ogren toward the defenders of the Highlands. Rynlin watched the raptor sweep past. Its strong wings, spanning seven feet, propelled it higher into the air. The white feathers speckled with grey on the bird's underside blended perfectly with the sky. When visible, the raptor was a dangerous predator. When hidden, it was deadly, shooting down through the thin air like an arrow, its sharp claws outstretched for the kill. Much like he and his allies had just done, Rynlin thought.

"What should we do with the bodies?" asked Nestor, coming to stand next to Rynlin. The grizzled Marcher looked none the worse for wear despite his struggles of the morning, though he did appear a little winded.

"We'll burn the bodies," said Rynlin. "If your Marchers could help us move them into a pile, it won't take long."

"Give me a moment to take some of the heads," said Catal Huyuk, as he strode past them toward a dead Ogren lying in the grass just a dozen feet to their front.

"Why does he want the heads?" asked Nestor.

"As a warning," replied Maden, the tall Sylvan Warrior wiping black Ogren blood from his sword onto the grass. "Catal Huyuk is a quiet man, letting his axe do most of the talking for him. But he still knows how to make a statement."

"A man after my own heart," replied Nestor. "We need to have him visit the Highlands more often."

2

———

UNEXPECTED SHADE

The young Marcher stood in the shadows of the early morning, concealing himself behind a tree, his senses attuned to the sounds and movements of the forest waking around him. He could tell that something was not right. He could feel it in his bones. Danger lurked in these woods, and it was stealthily approaching the Marcher camp. But what it was, the Marcher didn't know for sure. Kylin Stonebreaker, better known as Oso, stepped silently from behind his tree and glided to another, not making a sound. A bear of a man, still he could pad through the Highland thickets and forests like a mountain lion with no one the wiser.

Oso nodded to his right, catching Coban Serenan's gaze. The veteran Marcher, burly and stout with grey hair and a mustache that hung below his chin, hid behind a tree as well. The craggy-faced warrior flicked his eyes to the gap between the two birch trees. They could both sense it. Darkness approached. Something evil. Slowly. Quietly. The two Marchers waited patiently, muscles tense, ready to spring, though not feeling the need to rush. Time seemed to drag on, every passing minute feeling like an hour, and still the stench of wrongness came closer.

After several more minutes passed, and concluding that the evil was almost even with their position, Coban leapt out from behind the tree, swinging his sword in a deadly arc. The clash of steel on steel broke the quiet of the early morning. Coban immediately jumped back as his opponent twisted his grip, allowing the Highlander's blade to slide off his own so that he could lunge forward with the speed of a snake's strike. Coban barely escaped, the tip of his adversary's sword sliding past his side with just a finger's breadth to spare.

The veteran Marcher slowly stepped back from his opponent, his gaze never leaving the black sword that tracked him, knowing that a single scratch from that blade would mean an excruciating death. The Shade followed after as if there was nothing to fear, its sinuous, graceful movement almost mesmerizing. Stories of the dark creature that crept toward him played through Coban's mind. Supposedly a Shade had once been a man who, in accepting the gifts and dominion of the Shadow Lord, had been corrupted by Dark Magic in service to his master. The Shade's white, faintly translucent skin gave it a ghoulish cast, its long, greasy, dark hair hung down his forehead, almost covering its milky white eyes. For a moment Coban thought it might be better to die from a touch of the Shade's corrupted blade, preferring not to be a casualty of the dark creature's more sinister habits. Shades no longer ate like a normal man. Instead, for sustenance they drank the spirits of their victims, leaving only desiccated corpses in their wake.

The Shade lunged forward once more, Coban parrying the strike and returning the attack with a backhanded blow. The Shade recovered unnaturally fast, catching Coban's blade with its own. But the Shade failed to stop the second blade that sliced through its neck. The dark creature stood there for a moment longer, not realizing it was dead until its head slid from its shoulders and its body crumpled to the ground.

"Took you long enough," muttered Coban, breathing heavily, though more from the tension of the situation than from the exertion expended.

"I was just waiting for the right moment," protested Oso.

"If you had waited any longer, I'd be the one lying dead in the dirt."

A disturbance in the air behind them made both Coban and Oso turn quickly. A second Shade stood in back of them, sword raised above its head prepared to strike. But the creature never completed its swing. Rather it was held in place by the sword protruding through its chest. The two Marchers jumped back quickly as the Shade fell toward them, sliding off the blade and falling to the ground next to its partner.

Thomas Kestrel, not too tall but able to capture the attention of all around him with a presence that demanded respect, stepped out of the shadows. He swung the Sword of the Highlands down in a two-handed stroke, cutting off the Shade's head in a single swing.

"Just wanted to make sure," Thomas said, pushing his long, sandy brown hair from his face and revealing his brightly glowing green eyes. "Maybe next time you two could focus a bit more on what's going on around you rather than arguing like two old men with nothing better to do."

Thomas bent down, using the Shade's cloak to wipe the blood from his blade. Then, upon sheathing his sword in the scabbard on his back, he walked deeper among the trees, ignoring the two Marchers who had kept their gaze down, somewhat embarrassed by their failure to identify the second Shade and not knowing what to say. But they were certainly thankful that Thomas had been there to eliminate this dark creature that could have taken their lives with ease.

The Lord of the Highlands, recognized as such by the Kingdoms just the day before, continued to walk through the forest until he came to a small glade. He was on edge this morning, but not because of the dark creatures so intent on killing him and his Marchers. He was used to it by now, an all too frequent occurrence and a hazard that could not be avoided. He grasped hold of the Talent, using the natural magic of the world to search around him one more time. Confirming that there had been only two Shades trying to sneak into the Marcher camp, he released the Talent and strode to the top of a small hill.

He closed his eyes, allowing the early morning sun to warm him after a cold night. He and his fighters had accomplished a great deal since leaving the Highlands. Appearing unexpectedly at the Council of the Kingdoms, they had thwarted the High King's plans. Just the look on Rodric's face when King Gregory of Fal Carrach had declared him the Lord of the Highlands had made the arduous journey across Dunmoor to Armagh worth it. But though he had been recognized as the Lord of the Highlands, thereby ending the ten-year regency administered by the High King, there was still more to do. So much more. As he did every day, he wondered if he had the strength and the wherewithal to do what needed to be done. Thomas opened his eyes once more, realizing that whether he did or not, it didn't matter. His grandmother's favorite saying played through his thoughts: *"You must do what you must do."* And so, he would.

A screech to his left drew his attention. In the tallest tree at the edge of the clearing, Thomas stared into the sharp gaze of the kestrel. Why the large bird had left the Highlands, he didn't know. But he could suspect. The raptor peered at him intently, its orange and white feathers sparkling as the sun's rays illuminated the bird. The raptor perched on a thick branch majestically, its sharp talons digging deeply into the wood.

For several minutes, the two surveyed one another, Thomas almost losing himself in the sharp gaze of the bird that held a special place in the hearts of the Highlanders. He knew this kestrel. Their paths had crossed before, most recently when he visited the Roost, the tallest tower in the Crag. And before that when Rynlin and Rya had taught him how to use the Talent in order to shape change so that he could take on the trials to become a Sylvan Warrior. After he had assumed the form of a kestrel himself, this kestrel had stayed by his side as he had flown among the peaks of the Highlands for the first time. There were other times as well that he remembered encountering a kestrel similar to this one, and he had no doubt that he and this kestrel were connected in some way. Staring into the raptor's sharp eyes gave him a feeling of calm, filling him with a fortitude and sense of purpose that had proven difficult to find this morning. Until now. It was almost as if this majestic bird, knowing of the challenges to come, sought to share its strength with him. As Thomas continued to stare at the kestrel his confidence began to grow. Then with a shriek that tore through the early morning, the kestrel launched itself from the branch into the sky. But rather than fly east toward the Highlands, Thomas watched the imposing raptor instead head west toward the fortress of Eamhain Mhacha.

Thomas tracked the raptor until it was no more than a speck in the sky, then turned when Oso walked out from between the trees.

"Thank you for what you did back there," said Oso, coming to stand next to him. "You're right. We should have assumed there was more than one Shade."

"A lesson for all of us, Oso. Never assume. But if you do, assume the worst."

Oso nodded, agreeing with his friend, and grateful for the gentleness of the rebuke.

"You seem a bit distracted. Is there anything I can do?"

Thomas smiled, glad for his friend's support. "No, Oso. Though I appreciate the offer."

"Worried about today, I take it."

"A bit, yes. I'd rather take on the Dark Horde than deal with what's to come this afternoon."

"It'll go well, Thomas. The other Kingdoms have acknowledged you as the Lord of the Highlands. They can't take that away from you."

"Yes, I know. Nevertheless, although I may have been acknowledged as Lord of the Highlands, I assume there are several rulers who have yet to accept that fact. Therefore, I expect that today's visit to Eamhain Mhacha will be more dangerous than killing a couple of Shades."

3

DECISIONS

Kaylie sat on the windowsill of her chamber, looking out over the shimmering Heartland Lake. Her sharp, smoky blue eyes tracked a heron as it glided over the gentle waves, searching for the best place to seek its morning meal in the shallow water by the shore. Pushing away the strands of her long, black hair that the gentle breeze spun before her face, she enjoyed the solitude and quiet with which her day had begun, knowing that would all change in just a few hours.

She did not particularly like staying in the Keep of Eamhain Mhacha, finding the ancient, stone citadel oppressive and disheartening. The palace of the High King rose above the city and overlooked the Heartland Lake, while the city itself had its own wall that continued along the road leading to the fortress, protecting anyone making the short journey between the two. The port jutted out into a small bay, with the city on one end and the cliff on the other. A sea wall ran the length of the bay, except for a small opening that allowed ships to pass through. An additional section of the sea wall could be swung into place to close the gap, effectively sealing the port and fortress from attack.

The citadel towered over the bay. The cliff rose five hundred feet from base to top. The walls of the fortress added several hundred feet more. In the shape of a perfect circle, three concentric walls protected the main portion of the castle. The first outer curtain stood a hundred feet tall, with the second and third of the same height behind it. If invaders actually made it past the first wall a grass-covered space between that and the second wall awaited them, and again between the second and third. The children living in the bastion often played there, unaware of the land's true purpose. The soldiers of Armagh had dubbed the immaculately groomed lawns between the walls the Killing Fields. There was no beauty associated with the fortress, only a strict, deadly functionality.

No, she definitely did not like visiting the capital of Armagh. Nevertheless, she did enjoy the view. Kaylie's thoughts drifted to yesterday's fateful afternoon. Her eyes had barely left Thomas as he went through the process of being declared the Highland Lord. Physically he appeared much the same. Unassuming, yet with an obvious strength and determination, a purpose rare in someone so young. Even with the Marchers arrayed behind him, many frighteningly imposing, everyone's gaze had remained fixed on the charismatic, intense Highland Lord.

She could only imagine what scars had been added to his body and his psyche since she had last seen him balanced on the edge of the Tinnakilly parapet. Kaylie still blamed herself for his capture and subsequent torture, despite Rya's claims to the contrary. She remembered leaving Thomas after he won the archery contest at the Eastern Festival, walking back to her chamber with a smile on her face, pleased that she was to meet with him again the next day.

But after that the only memory she had was kneeling in the mud in the Tinnakilly courtyard watching Dunmoorian soldiers, followed by Lord Chertney, taking a beaten Thomas to the dungeon. Ragin Tessaril had stood above her, crowing about his success and thanking her for her help in his capture. She didn't know how they got there, or what had happened, yet she immediately felt responsible. Rya had explained that someone strong in Dark Magic, likely Lord Chertney, had manipulated her mind and her perceptions, compelling her to do as he wished. But the guilt had entrenched itself within her, becoming a part of her that she couldn't seem to let go.

Relief had flooded through her upon seeing Thomas stand in front of the High King, making his claim for the Highland throne. Observing him, she saw the toughness in Thomas, how what he had gone through had helped prepare him for this moment. Yet she felt shame as well for what had occurred, and she still did not know how to make it up to him. In fact, she doubted that she ever could. Moreover, she feared that he wouldn't want to speak to her, blaming her for what had occurred during the Eastern Festival.

Jealousy had also taken hold when she saw Corelia Tessaril, daughter of the High King, openly appraise Thomas, as if she were examining an item at auction, as something to acquire. She didn't know if she were more afraid of what would happen to Thomas if Corelia got her claws into him, or if Thomas actually demonstrated an attraction to the Armaghian princess. Just thinking about it made her blood boil.

Her confrontation with Corelia yesterday afternoon during the ruckus following the declaration of the Highland Lord only increased the intensity of her anger. Corelia's knowing smile and then her predatory expression appeared before her every time she closed her eyes. But worst of all, she remembered word for word what the Princess of Armagh had said when Kaylie had asked Corelia if Thomas would be interested in her: "I'm absolutely certain. I have much to offer him, Kaylie. Much indeed. More, in fact, than you."

Those words had stung deeply and much to her annoyance

had burrowed under her skin. She was stronger than that. But what was she to do? Stay to the side, afraid of how Thomas might view her? Or take a risk that might prove more painful than she could bear?

An ear-splitting screech ripped through the early morning silence, breaking her train of thought. Kaylie followed the sound to its source, watching in awe as a massive kestrel settled on the ledge of the tallest tower of the Eamhain Mhacha fortress. Its orange and grey feathers sparkled in the early morning sunlight, its razor-sharp claws digging into the stone as if the majestic raptor could never be dislodged. Kaylie was entranced. The bird's proud gaze suggested that the raptor had made the palace of Eamhain Mhacha its own, much like Thomas had done the day before. Confident. Never backing down from a challenge. Direct. Kaylie decided that she would adopt the same approach. She didn't know if she could take the pain of possible rejection, but she decided that it was worth the risk.

4

NAGGING DOUBT

Rodric shoved the doors to his private chambers open with all his strength, the large oak slabs slamming into the stone walls and startling the guards standing on the other side.

"Out!" he screamed.

The High King and ruler of Armagh was not a tall man, nor was his frame very imposing. That's why ceremony and protocol were so important to him. He did not look like a king, and he knew it. Therefore, he made sure that everyone remembered exactly who he was at all times. The dark purple cape he wore over his blue breeches and snow-white shirt concealed his gaunt physique, but it could not hide the feverish, unsettling gleam in his eyes. With his coarse black hair and ruddy complexion, his features could only be described as plain, and some thought even that was too generous. No one would ever voice their opinions out loud, of course. If overheard, the consequences would be severe, probably deadly.

The guards rushed to obey, relieved to leave the High King as he stopped in the center of his suite clenching his fists in frustration. Malachias followed him into the large room, closing the doors quietly behind him. His long black robes revealed skeletonlike fingers spotted with age, and with his cowl pushed back his bald pate reflected the sun's rays now finally breaking into the chamber, the brightness of the glare only surpassed by the glower of his hypnotic, black eyes.

Chertney had arrived at first light. He stood before them now, disheveled and weary. His black cloak and silk clothes were torn in a dozen places, the many darker stains suggesting the spilling of blood. Having escaped from the trap he had set for the now Lord of the Highlands, which had instead closed on him and the dark creatures under his command, Chertney had taken a roundabout way back to Eamhain Mhacha, not really in a rush to catch up to the boy who had beaten him so easily. Not only had the boy defeated him, humiliated him in fact, but learning of the Highland Lord's strength in the Talent had cowed him. Chertney reluctantly acknowledged that even with his own exceptional strength in Dark Magic, he could never vanquish the boy in a fair fight. The boy was simply too strong. That fact gnawed at him, tunneling into his heart and leaving a sliver of fear that seemed to spread the more he thought about his weakness. Seeing the small smile that crept onto Malachias' thin lips put him into an even fouler mood, forcing him to struggle that much more to maintain his already erratic self-control.

"I will leave you two to your own devices," said Malachias in a raspy voice that sounded like steel sliding across stone. "I have my own tasks to accomplish."

In a swirl of black mist, Malachias disappeared. Chertney cursed under his breath, realizing that because of the events of the last few days, because he had failed to stop the boy from making his way to Eamhain Mhacha, Malachias likely had gained the advantage over him in their competition to serve as the right hand of their master. For a split second, a shiver of fear ran through Chertney, an unfamiliar feeling for him. The power that Malachias had just demonstrated was beyond him. Did the Shadow Lord already know what had occurred along the Corazon River? Had his master already gifted Malachias this new ability in Dark Magic as a result? And, if so, what was the penalty his master would require him to pay for his negligence? Try as he might to forestall it, the cold uncertainty of doubt settled within him. His master was not known for his mercy. He was known for pain and death.

"How could you have let that boy live?" demanded Rodric, taking a moment to compose himself before turning his full ire on Chertney. The High King was so consumed by anger that he didn't even realize that Malachias had gone. "He was supposed to die in the attack on the Crag. A boy. Just a boy. And you failed to kill him then as you did now. Every time you've faced him, you've failed ..."

Before Rodric could finish his thought, he felt himself lifted off the ground, dangling in front of Chertney, who held him easily with one hand by the throat. Their noses almost touched as Chertney's black eyes bore into Rodric's.

"The boy was not my responsibility," hissed Chertney, his rage, at the boy, at Rodric, at himself, finally getting the better of him. "I took the Crag as commanded. Killeran was to kill the boy. He didn't. Make sure you affix the blame in the right place."

"Of course, Lord Chertney," squeaked Rodric obsequiously, both terrified by the power that burned behind Chertney's eyes and jealous of it as well, desperate to make it his own. "You're right. My temper simply ran away from me. My apologies. My deepest apologies."

Chertney dropped Rodric, stepping back as the High King fell into his carpet. He rubbed at his throat where Chertney's tight grasp had constricted his breathing.

"But that boy, Lord Chertney. Everything we have planned, everything our master has planned, hinges on that boy."

"Don't worry, Rodric, leave the boy to me. I'm sure our master will provide whatever help we need."

However, not for the first time Chertney began to experience a nagging uncertainty, the seeds of doubt having been planted. He had received assistance from his master before, in fact he had commanded several hundred Ogren and Shades just a few days past. But the boy and his allies had destroyed his dark creatures to the very last beast. Once again, he had failed to stop the new Highland Lord. He had failed to carry out his master's wishes. Boy he might be, nevertheless he was also a formidable opponent. As a result, Chertney's nagging doubt was becoming a gnawing dread. If Chertney could not defeat the boy, what was he to do? More important, if his failures continued, how much longer would his notoriously impatient master allow him to live?

5

DANGEROUS OPTION

Lord Chertney drifted down the barely seen steps, ignoring the skittering of the rats that scurried in front of him in the blackness. He hadn't bothered to get cleaned up or find new clothes after the harrowing events of the past week. His mind was on what was to come, and his thoughts of how it could all play out terrified him. Muttering to himself, his fears bubbling to the surface, he continued reluctantly but inevitably down the musty staircase. He felt at home in the inky dark, brightened only by the torches intermittently dispersed along the path that led into the depths of the keep. After several minutes he finally reached his destination, a lone storage room at the very bottom of Eamhain Mhacha's fortress, trickles of water from the Heartland Lake, which lay just on the other side of the rough stone, seeping through tiny cracks in the wall and forming a large puddle in the center of the floor.

Summoning his Dark Magic, Chertney wove his hands in a circular motion. In moments, a swirling black disk as large as he was taking shape in front of him. He spun the black disk faster and faster until the billowing coal-black mist achieved a remarkable clarity, revealing an enormous, dimly lit circular chamber mostly hidden from view by an ever-present gloom.

"The Highlands have a lord once more. You have failed me again, Lord Chertney."

The quiet whisper traveled through the swirling darkness, only two blood-red pinpricks visible in the darkness. The emotionless voice sent a spike of terror up Chertney's spine.

"No, master," started Cherney, before quickly correcting himself. "I mean yes, master. But there was a complication."

Chertney stumbled through a quick retelling of his efforts to stop the boy, crafting the story to place as much blame on Malachias as possible and suggesting that the dark creatures had failed rather than him, ending at the acknowledgement of the new Highland Lord by the rulers of the Kingdoms. Done, he tried to keep his body from shivering uncontrollably as he gazed into those two fiery depths. The silence that followed taxed his nerves, a cold sweat drenching his back.

"You disappoint me, Chertney. I am tired of your excuses, of your talk of complications."

The soft words felt like a dagger being thrust into his heart.

"I'm sorry, master," Chertney stammered. "Next time I'll ..."

A bolt of fire burst in the base of Chertney's lower back, then quickly traveled up his spine and then out into his limbs. He collapsed to the hard stone, rolling in the cold water as he sought desperately to escape the burning torment that consumed him.

"Remember, Chertney, that's just a taste of what's to come. The price you will pay for continued failure. For I will not kill you. No, that would be too kind, Chertney. Instead, I will bring you close to death and leave you there, allowing the pain you just experienced to stay with you for a millennium, a never-ending reminder of the cost of your incompetence."

The pain continued to increase. Chertney felt as if every particle of his body was turning to ash. Then, just as quickly as it had started, the fiery agony disappeared. Chertney slowly uncurled himself, lying on his back in the cold water, his limbs floundering as his nerves still sparked uncontrollably in remembrance of that all-consuming fire.

"Be happy you'll have a next time, Chertney. Next time will be your last time. But we will worry about that later. For now, we must adjust our plans and take advantage of this opportunity. You have failed to remove our problem. But perhaps another skilled in the arts of silent killing can take care of our problem once and for all."

"But the Nightstalker will have no effect, my lord," gasped Chertney, struggling to get the words out as his nerves continued to fire wildly. "Every creature we've sent after the boy has fallen short."

"This is not a Nightstalker, Chertney. This is something else. Something worse. Something the boy will not see coming, and he will not be able to defend against it."

Turning his head in the pool of water, Chertney saw the silhouette of the creature, a shadow in the swirling portal that slowly coalesced into its form. Chertney pushed himself out of the puddle and stumbled back, terrified, as the assassin stood in the swirling disk of black. It was a terror from the past, a terror even the dark feared to hide, a creature so savage and menacing that the world of men had hunted them to extinction, or at least they thought they had.

"The boy has been lucky against the Nightstalkers. Let's see what this Lord of the Highlands can do when he faces a Wraith."

6

DARKER PRESENCE

"What's the matter, Thomas?"

Oso had approached his friend quietly before, oftentimes trying to sneak up on him in order to test his own abilities. But despite his best efforts, Thomas had always known the large Highlander was there before he could spring his surprise. This time, however, Thomas hadn't bothered to acknowledge him, standing there in the small glade without making a move, staring at the walls of Eamhain Mhacha, which rose into the sky a league distant, as if he hoped to see through the stone.

"Dark Magic," replied Thomas, finally coming back to himself. "In the keep. Very strong Dark Magic. I've never felt its like before."

Thomas and the Highlanders had made their camp beyond the battlements of Eamhain Mhacha, preparing for that evening's feast. Although by law they should be safe within the walls of the Armaghian citadel, accidents had been known to happen before the conclusion of the Council, and none of the Marchers trusted the High King or his servants. So better to find a place they could defend more easily. They had located a fringe of forest that extended several leagues, giving them the cover they desired and several avenues for escape. Moreover, Thomas felt more at home among the trees, preferring the liveliness of the world around him compared to the mutedness of living within a manmade stone structure.

Oso's eyes widened, his heart beating a little faster at Thomas' words, remembering when he had first met Thomas. Killeran and his warlocks had captured him and many of the Highlanders from his village. Thomas had rescued all of them from their fate, captivity and an opportunity to die in the mines. All of them except Oso, who had fallen victim to the Dark Magic of the warlocks. But instead of leaving Oso to his inevitable doom, Thomas had stayed and fought, losing his freedom for a time in Killeran's Black Hole but gaining a life-long friend in the process. That experience had fixed a deep-seated fear of Dark Magic within Oso. The thought of not being able to defend himself against such an evil petrified him. To hear from Thomas that something more powerful could be felt emanating from Eamhain Mhacha, where they would be going later that afternoon, set his nerves on edge. Bad enough they were walking into a lion's den. Knowing that a Dragas might live there as well didn't help.

Thomas continued to stare at Eamhain Mhacha. He had used the Talent to probe the Dark Magic, but did so delicately, just pushing at the edges, not wanting to be found out. He recalled the time he spent in Tinnakilly's dungeon, Chertney trying to break through Thomas' mental defenses with his Dark Magic. He guessed it was Chertney now as well, as some of the Dark Magic felt similar, but he had detected a darker, more powerful presence with him. One that was there, but not really there. One that he was not yet ready to face.

Thomas turned away from Eamhain Mhacha, facing to the northwest. Though he couldn't see it, he could feel it pulling at him. Tugging gently but insistently. Blackstone, and before that known as Shadow's Reach. Some day in the future he would find himself there, if he survived, facing an enemy he knew he could not defeat, having no choice but to engage in the fight he was destined to lose. Not yet though. Not yet.

"I'm assuming that even with this new discovery we're still going." Oso failed to keep his lack of desire to return to the Armaghian capital from his voice. They had done what was necessary the day before. He saw no practical need for attending today's event, something he had already discussed with Thomas.

"We have no choice," his friend replied. "We must show the High King and the other monarchs that the Highlanders are strong and unafraid. We must show them that we are no longer a Kingdom to be trifled with."

Oso grunted his disapproval, but he knew that continuing his previous argument would do no good.

Still focused on the presence he had sensed in the citadel, Thomas tried to push his dark thoughts from his mind, but he failed to turn his attention away from this more immediate concern. Before he could return to the Highlands, he was required to attend the feast as the Lord of the Highlands, so he really had no choice in the matter. But he would be ready when he entered Eamhain Mhacha, come what may, come whatever the darkness offered him.

7

STORIES

Since the time of the first High King Ollav Fola, each Council of the Kingdoms ended with a feast, giving all the attending monarchs a final opportunity to confirm whatever agreements they had reached and maintain the amity expected of dignified kings and queens. Unfortunately, though the High King hosted the banquet with such noble purposes in mind, it often dissolved into a last chance for the rulers of the various Kingdoms to slight their enemies a final time without the threat of a knife in the back before returning to the safety of their own lands and people.

As was the tradition, the leaders of the Kingdoms sat at a massive head table, Rodric in the middle as the host. Much to Gregory's pleasure Sarelle sat next to him, but much to his chagrin she was next to the High King as well, who spent quite a bit of time trying to tempt the beautiful Queen of Benewyn. Gregory took some small bit of comfort in the exasperating looks Sarelle gave him from time to time as she easily fended off Rodric's clumsy advances. All Gregory could do was have the servant pouring the wine continue to fill Rodric's cup, the High King more than happy to drown himself in drink. The

King of Fal Carrach hoped that eventually the boorish High King would simply pass out.

Gregory glanced beyond his daughter who sat on his other side, thinking that the Highland Lord was the lucky one, having been placed at the very end of the table. In his opinion, Thomas Kestrel had the best seat of all, away from the distractions of Rodric and the other rulers intent on gaining as much attention for themselves as possible. The young man seemed to be enjoying a quiet though lively conversation with Rendael of Kenmare, who likely regaled him with tales from the past. Some said that Rendael could weave a tale better than any storyteller in the land, yet it appeared that Thomas was holding his own in that regard with the kindly king.

Kaylie Carlomin repeatedly peeked around her father to the far end of the table, trying to catch Thomas' eye, just to get a sense of where she stood with him. But despite her frequent attempts, he was either fully engaged with Rendael or doing a very good job of ignoring her.

Despite the conclusion she had reached that morning while taking strength from the kestrel that had visited Eamhain Mhacha at first light, she still wavered, not sure whether she should demonstrate some backbone and simply apologize or take the way of the coward and avoid Thomas at all costs. The latter option didn't appeal to her as she glanced quickly to her left, eyeing Corelia, sitting on her father's left, who stared boldly down the table toward Thomas. There was no way to misinterpret her intentions. Clearly, the Princess of Armagh wouldn't hesitate to take Thomas aside. In fact, she'd likely take great pleasure in doing so.

Knowing her father had been good friends with Talyn Kestrel, she turned to him as she sought to delay her decision just a little bit longer.

"What do you know of Thomas, father?"

His daughter's question didn't surprise Gregory, knowing

that she remained inordinately curious about him. He chose not to think about what that could mean for his daughter, and for him.

"I don't know much. Only what I can recall before Talyn and his family were murdered." Gesturing to the new Highland Lord, "Young Thomas over there escaped from the attack on the Crag somehow, which knowing Talyn doesn't surprise me. He always had a trick or two up his sleeve and a knack for getting out of tight situations."

Gregory took a sip of his wine, grimacing as Rodric moved his chair even closer to the Queen of Benewyn. He'd gladly stick a blade in the High King, but the rules of the Council still governed. Sarelle winked, pleased by Gregory's obvious frustration. Gregory continued his story, knowing that Sarelle could hold her own with the visibly inebriated Rodric.

"Thomas' father was Benlorin Kestrel, an excellent warrior and strategist, a handsome young man who was very much like Thomas, not just in terms of his looks, but also his single-mindedness, his stubbornness. I should have recognized it when the Fearhounds attacked us at the edge of the Burren."

"You were focused on other things at the time, father," Kaylie said, trying to offer some consolation.

"True," he replied. "But it still bothers me. If I had put this puzzle together earlier, perhaps we could have prevented what happened in Tinnakilly. Ahh, too late now. The focus needs to be on the future."

Sighing in frustration, Gregory returned to his story.

"Benlorin fell in love with a girl named Marya. He met her in the Highlands though she wasn't of the Highlands. She wasn't of royal blood either, at least that I know of, but nevertheless he loved her and made her his wife."

Gregory signaled to a servant, motioning for the attendant to refill Rodric's cup. Sarelle mouthed her thanks as she moved her chair closer to Gregory, seeking to escape Rodric's hands, which had an uncomfortable habit of finding hers even though she thought that she'd been clear that she expected the High King to demonstrate the appropriate decorum.

"At first Talyn wasn't thrilled with the match."

"He didn't like Marya?"

"No, he did like her, and he grew to love her like the daughter he never had."

"Then what was the issue?"

"He didn't tell me much, but from what I gathered he was worried about Marya, thinking that his son wasn't the best fit for her. Benlorin was extraordinarily intense, driven, seemingly striving to achieve some unachievable standard he had set for himself. Whether this was simply a result of who he was, or the challenge of having to compete with his father's success, or a combination of both, I don't know."

"What happened?" asked Kaylie, clearly enthralled by the story.

"Nothing. Talyn spoke with Marya, just to let her know of his concerns about his son. She told him not to worry. That she could calm him and help him see life from a different perspective."

"Talyn accepted that?"

"He did. He loved that girl. He would have done anything for her."

Kaylie looked at her father. She knew him too well. "What are you not telling me?"

Gregory hesitated, but then realized that with all the time that had passed, there was no cause to hold anything back.

"I also heard stories that Marya was different."

"How so?"

"Strange things happened around her. Some said she could talk to animals, even control the wind. Things like that. Some even claimed that she was a witch, but Benlorin ignored the whispers and Talyn accepted her into his family without hesitation. From what I remember, the new couple was happy and content. Unfortunately, Marya died giving birth to Thomas. Benlorin was very gentle to his wife and an excellent husband, but he loved her so much that he couldn't deal with her death, and that's when Talyn's fears became reality."

"What do you mean?"

"Benlorin blamed Thomas, his son, for Marya's death and wouldn't have anything to do with him. Benlorin was a very strong man, a great warrior, but as a father he was extraordinarily weak. It fell to Talyn to raise Thomas."

"How very sad!" exclaimed Kaylie.

"Aye, but Talyn loved the boy, would do anything for him. When some in the castle claimed that the boy could do the same strange things his mother could, Talyn put a stop to such rumors quickly. Thomas likely had a very lonely childhood while he lived in the Crag, but he did have a loving and protecting grandfather."

Gregory grimaced again as he watched the High King continue to bother Sarelle, his eyes turning a darker shade as his anger began to grow. Kaylie smiled as her father's discomfort and concern became more apparent.

"Sarelle seems to be in the need of assistance," she said, giving her father a nudge. "Perhaps a walk?"

Gregory nodded at the suggestion, turning his attention to the Queen of Benewyn and the struggle she endured with the High King.

8

A CHALLENGE

The feast dragged on for hours, many of the attending lords and ladies already well in their cups, others stuffed to the breaking point by the platters of exotic dishes that emerged from the kitchen in what seemed like a continual stream.

Through it all, Coban, Oso and the other Marchers sat at their own table at the back of the hall, turning away the delicacies. Although the Council was supposed to be a time of peace, Coban and his Marchers remained vigilant, their eyes tracking anyone who approached, their expressions less than welcoming. They'd eaten their fill, barely touched the wine, and spent the remainder of their time watching Thomas and those circling around him for any threat.

Their young lord handled himself well in the company of the Kingdoms' various monarchs, yet Coban felt a prickle of concern along the back of his neck. He had caught Rodric's daughter, Corelia, measuring Thomas quite a bit since the feast had begun. Knowing her reputation and knack for creating and taking advantage of intrigue, he worried that much like an octopus, if she got her tentacles around Thomas, he would be lost. Yes, Thomas had proven himself in battle many times over, but he had never faced an opponent quite like the Princess of Armagh.

Oso, on the other hand, focused his attention on Kaylie Carlomin, who also spent a great deal of time glancing toward Thomas and trying to catch his eye. He knew the cause, and the large Highlander certainly sympathized with the Princess of Fal Carrach, much preferring her demonstrating an interest in Thomas rather than Corelia, but he didn't know what Kaylie could do to rectify what had happened. Sometimes you simply couldn't escape or move beyond the past.

The raucous celebration quieted when Rodric stood at his place at the head table.

"My friends," declared the High King, his words heavily slurred by drink. "I welcome you to the final night of the Council of the Kingdoms, the traditional feast and ball."

A smattering of polite applause broke out, though many attendees remained focused on their food and wine. Rodric peered around the assembly, nodding to his allies or those he wished to bring to his side, ignoring those who opposed him or had failed to accede to his demands. Then his gaze settled on the new Highland Lord, dressed in what the High King assumed was considered finery in the Highlands, just a cleaner pair of brown breeks, brown boots, and a dark blue shirt, compared to the elaborate, colorful robes, extravagant dresses and jewels, and immaculate uniforms that saturated the gathering.

Rodric smiled to himself as he turned his gaze toward the Marchers sitting in the back of the room, dressed very similarly to Thomas, so much so that to his eye these Highlanders came across as no more than country bumpkins, better left to their wilds rather than being set free in cultured society. Perhaps he could play this to his advantage. Yes. Yes, indeed. An excellent opportunity that he could not ignore to embarrass Thomas

Kestrel and these Marchers, thereby allowing the other assembled rulers to reach the conclusion on their own that the Highlanders had no place in the world he sought to create. The world he sought to rule. These uncultured, unsophisticated ruffians simply didn't belong here and, much like a pest, should be exterminated.

Having decided on the course of action he would take, Rodric shifted his focus back to Thomas, who stared at him with little expression on his face, revealing nothing of what he might be thinking. From what Rodric had learned, the boy had grown up in the forest, so based on that and his clothes, he couldn't be too knowledgeable about the ways of the royal court. Yes, this could be the perfect way to make a fool out of him. Besides, knocking this particular opponent down a peg could only help him.

"It is the custom for me, as High King, to lead everyone to the dance floor." Rodric glared at Thomas, his gaze challenging. "However, on this special day, in which the Lord of the Highlands has returned to our august company, I think it would be more appropriate if the young Lord Thomas Kestrel led us in the first dance."

Thomas' sharp eyes remained locked on Rodric, showing no emotion, apparently unperturbed by the suggestion. Gregory leaned down to whisper to Kaylie as tension wove itself throughout the room.

"Remember that the first dance at this feast is the Dance of the Kings and Queens. Rodric is simply trying to embarrass Thomas and show everyone here that he doesn't belong."

"I would be honored," replied Thomas, rising from his seat. "Unfortunately, I have no one to dance with."

Kaylie knew that the prescribed dance was incredibly intricate, requiring several dozen set poses and movements to be conducted flawlessly to the rhythm of the music. When she was a young girl, she felt that all she did was train to perform this dance, which she found to be more difficult to learn than her work with Kael to master the sword. She was about to rise and try to help Thomas with the dance so that he wouldn't appear the fool when a voice broke through her thoughts.

"It would be a pleasure, Lord Thomas."

Corelia Tessaril elegantly rose from her chair and glided gracefully toward the newly proclaimed Highland Lord, every eye in the room on the Princess of Armagh. Thomas accepted her hand and walked her to the middle of the chamber, which had been cleared for this very purpose. He couldn't help but notice how her silk dress shimmered in the firelight and clung to the curves of her body. He found the beautiful woman distracting, almost intoxicating when he caught a whiff of her perfume. And he struggled to keep his thoughts from going any further, knowing that she was also exceedingly dangerous.

As Thomas escorted Corelia to the dance floor, Kaylie stared in disbelief, her eyes turning to daggers. Her disappointment showed as she was forced to watch the Princess of Armagh grasp Thomas' arm tightly as they walked through the crowd, Corelia leaning in close to Thomas to say something in his ear. Gregory leaned down to whisper to her once again.

"Don't let your irritation show," her father instructed. "She can use it against you if she sees it, and she will see it. Next time be quicker. Don't get angry, get even."

Kaylie glanced at her father, embarrassed because he had noticed her reaction, but then realized the truth of his words. She forced herself to regain her composure as the musicians began to play the music for the Dance of the Kings and Queens.

"For hundreds of years only royalty learned this dance," Rodric taunted. "As the Lord of the Highlands, I have no doubt of the young Lord Kestrel's lineage and his ability to lead us in this dance."

Rodric snorted then laughed after he finished his pronouncement, obviously thinking that there was no way a boy reputedly raised in the forest would have knowledge of the intricate steps required.

"Do you know this dance?" asked Corelia, outwardly calm but suddenly a bit nervous, as she was rethinking the alacrity of her decision making. This was a chance that could benefit her in the future, but not if it ended with her humiliated due to her partner's unfamiliarity with what was required.

"We're about to find out," grinned Thomas.

The gracefulness that Thomas had displayed many times in battle became readily apparent on the dance floor. That and the fact that he did indeed know the complicated moves demanded of the dance. As Thomas twirled Corelia across the chamber, Rodric's smile fell from his face as he realized that his attempt to demean the boy had turned against him. In fact, many of the young women, watching the Lord Kestrel's movements and skill, quickly became entranced with the young Highland Lord, clearly viewing him as more than just someone who had wandered in from the wilderness.

As the dance came to an end, the applause loud and deafening in the chamber, Corelia stared at Thomas breathlessly. Her face showed both surprise at what she had just experienced, but also intrigue and a touch of infatuation. She realized that there was more to this new Highland Lord than she had expected. Her calculating mind never stopped working as she continued to think about how she could turn Thomas to her advantage.

"You surprise me, Lord Kestrel," said Corelia, her face flushed a rosy pink from their exertions. She pulled Thomas in close, her hands resting gently on his shoulders. "Where did you learn to dance like that?"

"I had a very good teacher," replied Thomas, doing his best to ignore what Corelia's low-cut gown revealed.

"Who?"

"My grandmother."

"Your grandmother is a queen?" Corelia sounded incredulous, still trying to fathom how someone raised as Thomas had been could have any inkling of what was required in a royal court.

"No, but she learned during a time when there wasn't much difference between a lady and a queen."

Corelia didn't understand his reply, her confusion plain. Nevertheless, her interest in this new Highland Lord increased tenfold. With a smoldering look, Corelia was about to try to sink her first lure into him. But she was too slow as Thomas caught her off guard by speaking first.

"Princess, it was truly a pleasure, and you are a magnificent dancer. Thank you." Thomas smiled at her, and much to her surprise his grin quickly pierced her calculating heart. "Yet it seems that there are several others who would like to dance with you, and though it pains me, I would feel a great deal of remorse if I prevented you from dancing with these other admirers. Hopefully, later this evening, we could dance again."

Thomas bent at the waist, took her hand and kissed it softly, then backed away from a now crowded dance floor filled with other couples until he was lost in the mix.

It took Corelia a few moments to regain her senses as she watched him move to the edge of the crowd and back among the Marchers. She didn't know if she was more shocked by how much she enjoyed dancing with Thomas or how smoothly he had extricated himself from her grip. Placing her weight on one leg, she continued to watch the Highland Lord, arms crossed, one foot tapping, deep in thought, realizing that this boy would be a much more formidable prospect than she had expected.

"When next we meet, Thomas," she whispered to herself. "You will not escape me so easily. Perhaps next time I'll surprise you."

9

———

HIDDEN MEANING

Rodric's face turned a flaming red, the vein in his forehead throbbing dangerously, as he watched Thomas dance with his daughter Corelia. No matter what he attempted, nothing seemed to take that blasted boy down a notch. And why was that foolish girl trying to help him? She should know better than to involve herself in a matter such as this. Unless she had her own machinations in the works. He pondered that for a few minutes, wondering what his daughter might be contriving, before gazing around the chamber. He noticed Killeran seeking to entertain several ladies in a corner, though it appeared that they received his attentions half-heartedly at best. Rodric motioned angrily to the Lord of Dunmoor for him to disengage himself.

Killeran, his large nose once again leading the way, reluctantly approached. He had expected this conversation ever since the boy declared himself the Highland Lord, and as a result he had done his best to avoid the High King since he had arrived in Eamhain Mhacha. His strategy had worked, until now.

"For ten years he was in the Highlands. For ten years! And

you couldn't even kill a boy." Rodric grabbed Killeran's arm roughly, pulling him away from the other revelers to a quiet place along the back wall of the chamber. "Then Chertney gives you an army of Ogren and some Shades and you still can't kill him! A whelp and a few Highlanders routed you. I should kill you now for your incompetence."

Killeran cringed against the stone, his face turning white at the vehemence of Rodric's castigating whisper. He tried to stammer out an apology, but the High King cut him off.

"But not yet, no matter how much your death might be deserved. The Highlands will be mine, one way or the other." Rodric's voice dripped contempt, the throbbing vein on his forehead threatening to explode. "The Lord Thomas has much to do to rebuild his country. There will be much going on. He will be distracted. That's when we'll strike."

Killeran had trouble following the conversation, his face revealing his obvious confusion. Rodric seemed to be talking to himself more than him. Rather than seeking clarity, Killeran chose to remain silent, not wanting to push the High King over the edge.

"And this time, Killeran, if you fail you will die. I'll give you to the Ogren. They're always hungry, especially for pompous, incompetent bastards."

Rodric released Killeran's arm, turning away.

"Meet me in my chambers tomorrow morning. We'll discuss your next, and perhaps final, assignment then."

Killeran stood there for a moment, puzzled, watching the High King wade into the crowd, his small stature quickly swallowed by those standing around him. What was Rodric talking about? Usually he picked up hidden meanings quickly. It was a necessary trait to survive and excel at Dunmoorian politics. Maybe all the wine he had been drinking in anticipation of this encounter had dulled his senses. With the boy now the Highland Lord, the only way to gain control of the Highlands would be to ...

Killeran smiled, his drink-muddled thoughts finally breaking through the fog. Now he understood what Rodric planned. He had pulled it off once before with the grandfather and father, so why not again? It might actually be fun, he thought, ignoring the inconvenient memories of all that he had suffered because of this upstart Highland Lord, and how many times he had barely escaped dire circumstances with his life, not contemplating the fact that eventually his luck just might run out. No, if he was interpreting the High King correctly this would give him a chance to get even with the boy who had done such a good job of embarrassing him and threatening the plans he had laid so long ago, plans that now teetered on the verge of destruction. The Dunmoorian Lord began to laugh, his nasal twang catching the attention of the people around him.

To hell with them. He stared back defiantly at anyone brave enough to turn in his direction. To hell with them all. Rodric. Chertney. The whelp.

"I'll get what's coming to me," he whispered to himself. "One way or the other."

Killeran wandered back into the crowd in search of another glass of wine. If he had to deal with Rodric in the morning, he would have some fun tonight.

10

A NEW PAWN

Ragin Tessaril wiped away the drops of sweat that regularly stung his eyes. He had no wish to attend the feast, yet despite making that fact known, his father still felt the need to order him to stay away so as to save him the embarrassment of revealing his injury. Or in terms of how he interpreted his father's order, to reveal that he was less than what he had once been. Though whether his father felt shame for him or for himself, he didn't know. And he really didn't care. Instead, he had trained for hours, hacking at the various wooden figures designed to help swordfighters hone their skills, seeking to channel the rage that ran through him like a deep-flowing river, knowing that his tormentor was within easy reach but that he could do nothing about it. He resisted the urge to scratch at the jagged scar that ran down the right side of his face. The wound had healed, but it still festered within him, leaving him bitter and angry.

That one moment in time, up on the battlements of Tinnakilly, had changed his life drastically. When he had captured the boy, he was on top of the world. Favored by his father, having gained in Rodric's eyes in his constant, relentless competition with his sister, respected by his father's underlings, yet in seconds it had all changed irrevocably. His power, his appearance, his prospects, his personality. The life he had become accustomed to, the life that he had deserved, had been taken from him by one lucky strike by a woodland boy.

He knew in his heart that he would get another chance at the new Highland Lord, to pay him back for what he had taken from him, and when he did, he wanted to be ready. He wanted to show that upstart that luck had won him the day the first time they had dueled. But the second time they met, the boy would discover that his luck wouldn't be enough.

"It wasn't luck. You'll never kill the Highland Lord with a sword. His skill with a blade surpasses yours no matter how much you hack at these pieces of wood."

Ragin spun around, sword poised to strike, searching for the source of the voice. A shape stepped out of the shadows that wrapped around the edges of the training room. Tall and gaunt, skin pulled tightly over his bones, and wearing gray robes that revealed liver-spotted, skeletal hands. The most memorable aspect of the figure approaching the Prince of Armagh were the eyes, the black, malevolent eyes that sent a shiver through Ragin's body.

"You said as much yesterday," stated Ragin bitterly. "Who are you to say so, Malachias? What skill do you have with a blade?"

"I am a man who understands the desire for revenge, the necessity of it, how the need for revenge burrows into your heart until you can think of nothing else," Malachias replied in his raspy voice. "And I stand by what I said. Train all you want. You'll never kill him with steel."

Ragin's rage at being criticized withered, replaced by fear. He sensed a power in this man that both terrified him and excited him at the same time.

"Then how?"

"I see it in you now, Ragin. The boy took more from you than your good looks on the battlements of Tinnakilly. Your hatred of the new Highland Lord grows every time you think of him. Every time you see him. Every time you hear of him and his latest exploits."

Ragin was unnerved that this Malachias had hit so close to the mark. That he could read his very thoughts.

"So what if it does?"

"I wouldn't fault you, after the gift he left you." Malachias gestured to the scar that marred Ragin's once handsome visage. "Yet every time you think of him, you hate yourself just a little more as well. You hate your weakness. He's too strong for you. Not only with the sword, but also the Talent."

"The Talent?"

Malachias gestured toward Ragin. In an instant, he couldn't move his body, arms tight to his sides, legs pressed together. It felt like his head was caught in a vice. He could only move his eyes to track Malachias as he began to pace the room.

"You didn't know? Yes, your rival seems to have many skills that most people don't know about. This Highland Lord has some ability in the Talent. He can harness the power of nature. So even if by some miracle you could compete with him with a blade, you'd still be at a disadvantage. You would be vulnerable. As you are now."

The sweat began to pour off of Ragin as he realized he was at Malachias' mercy. Though he struggled against his invisible bonds, he couldn't convince any part of his body to move. Malachias stepped in front of him, his height placing the Prince of Armagh in an unwanted shadow.

"But as you can see, and as I have said, I can help you. I can give you a way to negate his Talent. I can give you a way to destroy him." Malachias leaned in close, his face just a finger's breadth from Ragin's, his foul breath, smelling like an open grave, wafting over him. "You need only decide. But beware, my young Prince of Armagh. For if you want to achieve power, real power, a power that only a handful in all the Kingdoms have the ability to employ, there is a price that you must pay. Are you willing to pay that price?"

11

A DANCE

Thomas walked through the crowded chamber, the lords and ladies parting in front of him, many offering their good wishes. Some because they truly were pleased to see him take the throne of the Highlands; others hoping to curry favor at a later date. He approached Gregory and Kaylie, who had just finished speaking with Rendael, King of Kenmare. The old king had guided Sarelle away from Gregory so that he could speak to the Queen of Benewyn on his own about some proposed trade agreements.

"King Gregory," said Thomas, inclining his head as a sign of respect. "Princess, you look beautiful this evening."

Kaylie could only whisper a thank you as she tried to hide the blush that she felt spreading across her cheeks. She still struggled to look Thomas in the eyes because of the shame that burdened her.

"You are full of surprises, Thomas. In fact, just today I believe you've tweaked Rodric's nose at least three times. That's a feat that most men can't lay claim to no matter how hard they may try."

"I do what I can, King Gregory," chuckled Thomas

nervously, still a bit uncomfortable standing next to Kaylie. He wanted to blame her for what had happened in Tinnakilly, but the more he thought about it the more he had realized that it had all been beyond her control. His grandmother had been insistent in that regard, and he had no reason to doubt her. "I was hoping that in the months ahead we might discuss some matters regarding Fal Carrach and the Highlands. Before the death of my family we had excellent relations between our two Kingdoms. I would like to make it so once again."

"It would be a pleasure, Thomas. Fal Carrach has stood with the Highlands in the past. It will do so in the future."

"Then we will speak on it later, since this is supposed to be a celebration," said Thomas, thankful for Gregory's support and recognizing the importance of the statement the King of Fal Carrach had just made.

Thomas turned toward Kaylie. Finally she had the courage to look at him directly, catching the sparkle in his green eyes.

"Princess, we have run into each other several times, but we have never had the pleasure of a dance," said Thomas with a grin, his manner disarming and welcoming. "Would you dance with me, Kaylie?"

Her breath caught as he said her name. "Of course," she replied, the smile that crept on to her face adding to her beauty.

Yet before Thomas could guide Kaylie to the dance floor, Killeran blocked their path, glass of wine in hand, his large nose reddened by the many drinks he had already imbibed.

"Impressive dancing, boy," said Killeran rudely. "Who taught you that in the forest? The animals?"

Killeran snickered loudly, his lame attempt at a joke seeming even funnier to him because of the drink that now impaired his senses.

Thomas simply stared at Killeran, no expression on his face. Gregory had seen that look before on other men.

Dangerous men. Men who in less than a second had come up with a dozen painful ways to kill you.

"I see that when you work on improving your manners, you shall have to work on your sense of humor as well," replied Thomas in a clipped tone. "For one who tries to appear so worldly, so successful, I find it quite revealing that you fail so frequently and on such a massive scale."

Gregory hid a laugh at Thomas' barbed response. The Lord of Dunmoor did, indeed, have an extremely poor record of accomplishment during the last few years, helped along in large part by Thomas himself. His failed regency in the Highlands having come to an ignominious end, and less than flattering stories of what had occurred in that rugged Kingdom sticking to him like a dog to a bone, his once promising future had been cut apart piece by piece.

Clearly Killeran did not appreciate the reminder. His face turned beet red, his anger, never far from the surface, threatening to boil over.

"I missed several opportunities to kill you during the last few years," replied Killeran in a quiet hiss. "Next time I shall not fail."

"Delude yourself all you want, Killeran." Thomas smiled wickedly. He stepped forward so that he was no more than a nose from the Dunmoorian Lord. If anyone who knew his grandfather Rynlin Keldragan had seen his expression, they would have said Thomas was simply a younger version of the imposing Sylvan Warrior, the resemblance uncanny. "You're not smart enough to figure out how to kill me, and you're too much of a coward to face me yourself now that I'm no longer in chains."

Kaylie reminded herself to breathe, a space having opened up around Thomas and Killeran, almost everyone in the hall looking on with interest, captured by the growing tension. Gregory stood there silently, understanding that Thomas purposely goaded Killeran, and understanding the result if Killeran foolishly drew his dagger. Though he knew he should not, he was actually quite enjoying the drama.

"I'm surprised you're still alive, Killeran," continued Thomas. "Last time I saw you, my Marchers had crushed your reivers and you were running with your tail between your legs. You didn't have the courage to stand and fight. I would have thought that after your failure in the Highlands, Rodric would have gotten rid of you by now. Or if not Rodric, the master you and he truly serve."

Thomas' final comment gave the King of Fal Carrach pause, his mind moving down a path that worried him. But he acknowledged that he could not ignore the insinuation, hearing the truth in Thomas' words. Nevertheless, worrisome though it might be, that was a matter for another day as there was nothing to be done about it now.

Gregory didn't doubt that Thomas could kill Killeran if given the chance. Glancing over his shoulder, the King of Fal Carrach saw that the Marchers had moved to the edge of the crowd now, appearing to watch the conflict of words casually, but he could tell that they were ready and willing to jump into the fray in an instant. In fact, their intense, hungry looks suggested that they would welcome the opportunity to have a private word with the former regent of the Highlands them-selves, away from prying eyes, about all the pain and misery he had wrought in their homeland.

Thomas obviously would welcome the chance as well. Standing there apparently at ease, he looked more like a moun-tain cat ready to spring on his prey. Remembering how well Thomas handled a bow, Gregory reminded himself that this was a very dangerous young man indeed.

Glimpsing the movement at the back of the crowd, Killer-an's instinct for survival finally forced its way through the haze of wine that had clouded his judgment. He realized that he had placed himself in a precarious position. Forcing down his anger and embarrassment, he sought to extricate himself from the situation he had unwittingly created. To that end, he adopted a pleasant tone and smiled condescendingly.

"Perhaps another time, boy. Tonight's feast is a time for a different type of conquest." He turned to Kaylie, who was taken aback by the Dunmoorian Lord's leer. "Princess, would you care to dance?"

Kaylie replied immediately, barely able to keep the scorn from her voice. "I already have a commitment."

She reached for Thomas' hand and began walking toward the dance floor, bringing Thomas with her as she sought to end the confrontation. But Killeran, his mind still muddled by wine, stupidly grabbed Thomas' shoulder.

"I'm sure the young lord would not mind yielding to his betters and allow me the privilege," said Killeran smoothly.

The condescension on Killeran's face did a poor job of hiding the anger that struggled to break through. Yet when the Dunmoorian Lord saw Thomas' expression he concluded in a moment of clarity that he had misjudged the situation badly.

Thomas' hard stare and intense, green eyes sent a shiver down Killeran's spine. The look reminded him of his first encounter with the boy. Then the boy appeared to be no more than a ragged Highlander who was trying to free his people from Killeran's encampment after his warlocks had taken their village. They had dueled, and Thomas had quickly gotten his steel to Killeran's neck. What he had initially laughed off as luck, Killeran now realized was skill, a skill that he did not have. To fight this boy would mean his death, and a quick one at that.

For the first time he also noticed that the Marchers watched their exchange with great interest, seemingly at ease among the crowd that had gathered around them. But they stood ready to defend their lord. In fact, the ferocity of their gazes, the way they balanced on their toes ready to rush to the aid of their lord, indicated that they would be pleased to become enmeshed in the spectacle Killeran foolishly had initiated.

"Lord Killeran, we have known each other for a long time, yet each time we meet your timing is always a bit off," said Thomas. "You are right, though. I would, of course, yield this dance to my better. However, since I do not include you in that category, I will have to refuse."

Thomas shook off Killeran's hand and calmly walked to the dance floor with Kaylie. Most of the people who had sidled closer to watch the drama had gone silent, listening to the conversation. Several now chuckled at how this new Lord Thomas had so easily made a fool of the arrogant Killeran.

The laughter almost put Killeran over the edge, his hand moving to the hilt of his dagger. Gregory stepped next to Killeran and placed a large hand over Killeran's, not allowing him to draw the weapon.

"I wouldn't, Killeran. I don't doubt that if you went after the Highland Lord, it is the last thing that you would do. Granted, that wouldn't bother me in the least. But Thomas will have to kill you another time. You'll just have to wait a little longer and have faith that when you die the last face you will see will be that of the Highland Lord." Gregory stepped back, releasing his hold on Killeran. "Then again, who am I to tell you what to do. It's your funeral."

Killeran seemed to come to his senses then, glancing around and noticing that now not only did the Marchers surround him, but also several Fal Carrachian soldiers. Their faces were grim, focused, ready to take the next step if necessary, all obviously hoping to do so, the rules of the Council be damned.

Coban stepped forward, his expression murderous. "Lord Thomas isn't the only one with a claim on you, Killeran. If the Highland Lord doesn't get you, you can expect a Marcher to come calling sometime soon. Very soon. A Highlander always pays his debts, and we owe you quite a lot."

Killeran's face turned white. Dropping his hand and muttering curses, he stalked from the hall, pushing his way through the crowd and not caring who stood before him.

"A dangerous snake," said Coban, who came to stand next to Gregory.

"Yes, he is."

"There is only one way to deal with a dangerous snake, my lord."

Gregory turned toward him, remembering Coban from his visits to the Crag.

"You're right. There is only one way. You take the head. The difficult part is making sure it's done at the right time."

Coban looked at Gregory for a moment, a predatory smile splitting his face.

"Lord Talyn always remarked on the wisdom of Gregory, King of Fal Carrach. I see that like his aim with a bow, his opinion of others never missed the mark."

Slapping Gregory on the back, Coban followed the Highlanders as they slipped away through the crowd.

12
____

POINT TAKEN

When the music began, an awkwardness settled over Thomas and Kaylie, neither looking at the other. Thomas didn't know what to say; Kaylie didn't have the courage to say what she wanted to say. After taking a few turns around the dance floor, Kaylie at long last discovered the fortitude she needed.

"Thomas, I'm sorry. I really am. You probably hate me, but I don't know what happened in Tinnakilly. It's as if the time when you were taken was wiped from my memory. I never intended for you ..."

"Kaylie, enough." She looked at him with some consternation, surprised by his smile rather than the scowl she had expected. "You've apologized once before, and once is all that's required."

"But I ..."

"Kaylie, truly, there's no more need to apologize. What's done is done. Clearly there was more going on than either of us suspected. Let's speak of other things."

True, Thomas didn't want to rehash what had been an extremely painful experience for them both. But the more he thought about it, and the more Kaylie tried to explain, the more he felt certain that his grandmother was correct. Chertney had been in Tinnakilly at the time, as evidenced by his efforts to break Thomas mentally after his capture. He could very easily have used his Dark Magic against Kaylie as well, making her an unwitting pawn in Ragin's scheme. Thomas simply added that experience to the debt he owed the silk-clad servant of the Shadow Lord but knowing as well that he'd have to wait for a time before he could collect on it. Of course, the confrontation with Chertney and his dark creatures on the way to Eamhain Mhacha was a good start in that direction.

"I'm sorry, Thomas. It's just that I feel that I failed you badly and..."

Thomas cut her off, wanting to move on to a different subject. "So, Kael Bellilil tells me that you're well on your way to becoming Fal Carrach's Swordmaster. Do they even allow royalty to do that?"

"And why not?" replied Kaylie, thankful for the change in topic. "Who's to say what a princess can or can't do?"

"Point taken," grinned Thomas. "What's your preferred weapon?"

"The rapier," she replied with some pride.

"A good choice. Kael said you were exceedingly quick with a blade. The rapier's lightness would play to that."

"Perhaps after the Council you'd join me in the training circle," said Kaylie with a glint in her eye. "We could find out which one of us is quicker with a blade."

Thomas chuckled, enjoying Kaylie's bravado.

"An appealing challenge," Thomas agreed amiably. "I'd welcome the chance."

For a time, silence settled over them. But unlike the oppressiveness of when they first started dancing, it instead felt comfortable. Shifting her gaze from the people around them, Kaylie peeked at Thomas again, realizing that he had been staring at her. Uncertain but pleased, she sought to restart the conversation.

"Do you know a woman named Rya?"

"Indeed, I do," Thomas replied. "Tough but fair, very demanding. Always thinks she's right."

"How do you know her? Did she teach you how to use the Talent?"

"And how is your training going in the Talent?" asked Thomas, ignoring her questions. "Your father knows?"

"He does," replied Kaylie. "I think it's going well, at least based on what Rya says."

"How did you come to have Rya as your instructor?"

Over the next several minutes, Kaylie explained all that had happened in Ballinasloe, starting with the assassination attempt on her father, Kaylie's role in thwarting it thanks to Rya's help and guidance, the exposure of the Dinnegans as traitors, and finally finishing with some of what she had learned during her last few lessons.

"You're rebuilding the Crag," Kaylie said.

Thomas gazed at her closely. "You've been searching the Highlands."

"Yes," replied Kaylie gleefully. "How did you know?"

"A few weeks ago at the Crag I sensed a presence that brought you to mind. Now I know why."

"So, the next time I search out the Crag, you'll know it's me?"

"Yes, everyone's unique presence has a different feel. Now that I know yours, I'll know it's you."

"Can you teach me how to do that?"

"Of course, if Rya doesn't teach you before me."

"You know, you never answered my questions. How do you know Rya? Was she your instructor in the Talent?"

"She was," Thomas replied. "One among several, in fact. I'm assuming she's as difficult and obstinate as always?"

"Yes, she is," Kaylie laughed, not realizing that Thomas continued to hold something back. "When she sets a task for you, she won't let it go until you've completed it."

The conversation continued as they glided across the dance floor, touching on various topics. As one dance blended into another Kaylie came to realize that she did most of the talking. Thomas kept up a constant stream of questions and didn't offer much in return. A part of him remained closed to her. The last time they had been together he had been much more open. Kaylie was disappointed, but she understood why. She was simply relieved that Thomas had forgiven her. It felt as if a huge weight had been lifted off her chest, and she hoped that with time the connection she had experienced with Thomas before would return.

13

DEEPER MEANING

Gregory watched Kaylie dance with Thomas, a small smile escaping. Many young men had sought his daughter's favor. Most, such as Ragin Tessaril and Maddan Dinnegan, because they saw her as an avenue toward greater power or wealth. The fact that she was a beautiful, accomplished, intelligent young woman didn't register with them.

But Thomas was different. He seemed to like her for her and didn't care that she was his daughter. That pleased him quite a bit, and it clearly pleased Kaylie. And seeing how the new Highland Lord handled himself, here at the Council and previously atop the hillock with a bow in his hand, delighted him even more. There was a hardness to the boy, one that was necessary and would likely serve him well for what was to come, but also humility and kindness. Comprehending everything that Thomas had gone through and what the young man had become, he looked forward to working with him as Lord of the Highlands.

"Would you care to dance, King Gregory?"

Focused on other things, the question caught Gregory off guard, and he was barely able to keep himself from jumping.

Turning his head, the beautiful Sarelle Makarin stood so close to him that he could feel her breath on his ear. She smiled at him, her eyes sparkling. The Queen of Benewyn in her clinging silk gown definitely had caught the attention of the King of Fal Carrach.

"Thank you for the offer, my lady. But I'm not a very good dancer."

"Neither am I," replied Sarelle, reaching for his hand and pulling him from the crowd. "So, we should be perfect for each other."

Gregory wondered if there was a deeper meaning to what Sarelle had just said. Nevertheless, he couldn't find fault in her logic. Besides, the chance to get a little closer to the Queen of Benewyn appealed to him. He liked the feel of her hand in his own.

As the dance began, Sarelle leaned tightly against Gregory. He learned quickly that Sarelle had lied. She was a much better dancer than he was. Put him on a battlefield, and he could demonstrate the grace of a warrior. Put him on a dance floor, and he had two left feet. But for some reason, he didn't care. He was having too much fun and was thrilled to have Sarelle in his arms.

"Kaylie seems to have taken quite a liking to the young Highland Lord," said Sarelle, her eyes tracking the couple as they danced not too far away.

"She has."

"Do you hope her interest is returned?"

Gregory didn't need any time to think of how to respond. "I do. There's something about the boy that appeals to me, but I can't put my finger on it."

"I had the same feeling," replied Sarelle. "It seems that Thomas isn't here for himself. He's here for his people, putting their interests above his own."

Gregory nodded in agreement, realizing that Sarelle had put into words what he had been thinking.

"The mark of a good ruler."

"Yes, if he survives."

"True." Thomas had worn a target on his back for a decade, ever since the fall of the Crag. With him being proclaimed the Highland Lord officially, that target had only grown larger. Gregory was certain that the High King's desire to remove the new Highland Lord had only increased after yesterday's humiliation. "Perhaps there is something we could do about that."

Sarelle grinned mischievously. "I do love intrigue, Gregory." She pulled the King of Fal Carrach against her, her words spoken softly and close to his ear. "We should talk about what you have in mind later when our discussion would benefit from some needed privacy."

Gregory flushed at Sarelle's words and was glad that she couldn't see his reaction. Just as there was something about Thomas that intrigued Kaylie, there was something about Sarelle that piqued Gregory's interest. He didn't know what it was, but he meant to find out.

After several dances in which Gregory and Sarelle didn't feel the need to speak, they both decided it was time to exit the floor. Gregory reluctantly released his hold of her, something that Sarelle noticed, which sent a delightful quiver through her.

"You dance wonderfully, Gregory. You should do it more often."

"Perhaps I will. If I can find the right partner."

Gregory stepped back and bowed, kissing her hand.

Sarelle stared at him, somewhat surprised, not only by his action but also by what he had said. She didn't think his comment referred solely to dancing. Sarelle was used to being the predator in her relationship with Gregory, but at the moment she felt like the prey. And she liked it.

14

————

MARCHER METTLE

Rodric's already foul mood worsened as the feast continued. Every attempt to embarrass this upstart Highland Lord had failed miserably. How could a boy purportedly raised in a forest learn a dance reserved for royalty? Who could have taught him?

Because of this boy, this whelp who didn't know when he should just lay down and die, his plans for the Highlands – a ten-year design – were in ruins. Yet no matter what he tried, he could not gain the upper hand. Another scheme began to form after he scanned the crowd, and he felt the need to try one more time, to show all those who had gathered here in his citadel that these Highlanders were no better than rabble and didn't deserve a chair at the Council of the Kingdoms.

If he couldn't embarrass the boy directly, maybe he could humiliate the new Highland Lord in another way. His eyes had settled on the Marchers sitting at a table at the back of the room. Perhaps he could use the boy's soldiers instead to make his point. As the music died, he walked toward the Highlanders, stopping in front of the Highland Swordmaster.

"Your lord has done well on the dance floor this evening,"

acknowledged Rodric, speaking loudly enough for everyone in the hall to hear. "But I haven't seen any of you out there with him, helping to uphold the honor of the Highlands."

Coban stared daggers at the High King, knowing his goal. None of the Highlanders knew the dances of the nobility. Why would they?

"We would be honored, Rodric," replied Thomas, who had come up behind him on silent feet.

The High King jumped at the voice. Rodric had the unsettling thought that if the boy had wanted to slip a dagger between his ribs, he could do so before Rodric even realized that he was a dead man. The Highland Lord smiled arrogantly at him, which only served to irritate the High King more.

Pulling Oso and Aric aside, Thomas spoke to them briefly. They nodded and hurried out of the chamber. He then motioned for the Highlanders to follow him to the dance floor. They did so reluctantly, almost dragging their feet, knowing the High King's intention and realizing that there was little they could do to avoid the likely embarrassment that was to come next.

"Thomas, we can't dance like this," whispered Coban. "We'll make fools of ourselves. That's what Rodric wants."

"Don't worry, Coban. Just do what I do. Rodric suggested that we dance. He didn't suggest how we should dance."

A space opened up on the dance floor as Thomas and the Highlanders approached, everyone in the ballroom watching them expectantly. With a sharp movement of his hand, Thomas gave the command to form a battle line. The Marchers instinctively obeyed. The musicians raised their instruments, about to begin playing, but they hesitated when Thomas turned toward them.

"My friends, you and your fellows have played wonderfully all evening. I think you deserve a rest. If you would allow us, we would like to provide the music for the next few minutes."

"What are you doing, Thomas?" hissed Coban, his face flushing as he felt the eyes of everyone in the chamber on him and not wanting to be the center of attention.

"Trust me, Coban. Rodric wants to see us dance, and we shall. But we will dance to the music that we know."

It was then that Oso and Aric ran back into the chamber, Aric carrying a small drum and Oso the set of pipes that Anara had carved for him. They settled themselves on the musicians' platform behind the line of Marchers. Thomas nodded to Oso, and he and Aric began to play an old song about a Highlander in love with a woman who rejects his multiple requests to marry, often in hilarious fashion.

The rhythm of the song was designed to get the blood flowing, and it certainly worked with the Marchers. Knowing the tune, and smiling with delight, they allowed their instincts to take over. Their feet pounded on the dance floor, serving as an additional instrument to the pipes and drums played by their two compatriots. As the music increased in pace, so did the Marchers, beginning to weave among themselves in an intricate pattern. Everyone in the chamber watched in rapt fascination, never having seen the like. Many in the audience began to clap in time with the music, their feet tapping as well.

For several minutes the Highlanders cast their spell on those watching them. Then in a flash Thomas shot forward, his hand outstretched. Too late, Kaylie saw that Thomas was coming directly toward her. A bolt of fear shot through her as she realized that he was going to pull her into the dance. But then she observed Corelia trying to get in front of her and in Thomas' path.

A quick spark of anger burned away her fright. Kaylie stepped forward, blocking Corelia's advance. Grasping her hand, Thomas pulled Kaylie out on to the dance floor, the Marchers dancing around them in a circle that constantly changed direction and size. Caught up in the moment, the pace and excitement of the Marchers energized her. She loved every minute of the dance, allowing herself to be lost within the rhythm and flow.

The clapping of the crowd grew in intensity, many whooping and hollering as the tempo of the dance quickened. Gregory was one of them, tapping his foot, clapping his hands, and cheering his daughter on. He didn't notice Sarelle as she slipped up beside him.

"This young Highland Lord certainly is intriguing. So full of surprises. What do you see?"

Gregory waited a moment before answering, watching the dance come to an end and yelling his approval with the rest of the audience.

"I see his grandfather."

Sarelle nodded. "So do I."

"And I see something more," said Gregory. "It seems like Thomas is carrying more than just the weight of the Highlands on his shoulders. Danger, perhaps? An added strength? Maybe both. I'm not entirely sure."

Gregory looked down at Sarelle, noting the slightly worried expression on her face, as if she hadn't yet reached her own conclusion.

"Whatever it is, though, I like it."

15

———————

ALL SMILES

After several more Highland dances, many of the participants began to exit the chamber, making for their beds or other pleasures that could be experienced in the privacy of their rooms. Thomas escorted Kaylie back to her father, her hand still tightly held in his.

"Thank you for allowing me to dance with Kaylie, King Gregory. It was truly a pleasure and made what could have been a rather dull event much more exciting."

"You're quite welcome, Thomas. I hope we will be speaking again soon. There is much our two Kingdoms need to work out." The intent of Gregory's words left no doubt of what would be discussed.

"We will. I just need to clean up a few things in the Highlands first. Then we can address some of the larger issues plaguing the Kingdoms."

Thomas was certain that Gregory knew what he meant. Turning to Kaylie, he inclined his head and brought his lips to the back of her hand.

"Princess, thank you. Tonight wouldn't have succeeded without you."

Kaylie's eyes narrowed as she sensed Thomas using the Talent. She looked down as an object slowly took shape in Thomas' palm. In just a few seconds Thomas held a red rose in his hand, which he gave to Kaylie.

"Thank you for indulging me this evening."

As Thomas turned and walked away, Kaylie called after him.

"Will I be seeing you again, Thomas?" A note of worry had snuck into her voice.

Thomas looked at her quite seriously for a moment, then grinned.

"I expect you will, Princess. Perhaps more than you would like." Bowing to her deeply, he walked out of the chamber.

Kaylie smiled at Thomas' last comment, but it turned into a grimace when she saw the grin on her father's face.

"Why are you smiling, father?"

"No reason," he replied, trying to control his good humor. "No reason at all."

Unfortunately his attempts to hide his mood failed. As he escorted his daughter back to their rooms, she fixed him with a hard glare that only made him grin that much more.

16

BLACK WIDOW

After taking his leave of Gregory and Kaylie, Thomas paid his respects to Sarelle, who seemed intent on continuing her conversation with Gregory, Rendael and the other rulers friendly to the Highlands, before heading down to the stables. Coban, Oso and the other Marchers should already be there, preparing to depart. Though the Council of the Kingdoms was put forward as a time of peace, no Marcher wanted to spend the night behind the walls of Eamhain Mhacha and within easy reach of the High King.

The evening had been an exercise in many things for Thomas. Patience. Perseverance. Self-control. It was also an opportunity to begin confirming who among the Kingdoms' monarchs he could trust, who he could trust to stab him in the back, and who would side with Rodric when the High King attacked the Highlands. And the High King would attack. Thomas had no doubt of that. It was simply a question of what excuse Rodric would concoct to do so.

As Thomas walked silently down the halls, he mused at how nice it would be if he were to run into Killeran right then. Quiet and dark within the keep, much could happen with no one the wiser. A sense of danger that sent a spark of warning up his spine forced his thoughts back to the present and stopped him in his tracks, his hand automatically grasping the hilt of his dagger. He sensed someone in front of him, his sharp eyes catching the shape of a person hidden in one of the many dark alcoves that dotted the hallway.

"Show yourself," said Thomas sternly.

The figure hesitated just a moment before emerging from the gloom into the dim light. The torches set into the wall sconces were few and far between, casting irregular and distracting shadows across the stone. Thomas' hand stayed on his dagger. He remained wary, remembering the darkness he had sensed earlier in the day in Eamhain Mhacha that he had not been able to identify. As the shape walked into the trembling light, he knew who it was by the sway of its hips.

"So forceful," said the woman in a silky voice, stepping close to Thomas to reveal her luxurious gown and long, blonde tresses, her hands clasped demurely in front of her. "You need not be afraid of me."

"I don't know, Corelia. For their own safety, most men likely should fear you."

The High King's daughter let loose a rich, throaty laugh. Looking at her, he could believe the stories he had heard. How she gained whatever she wanted, no matter the cost, and no matter at whose expense. Judging by her calculating gaze, obviously she was trying to determine how he fit into her world. How she could use him to attain her goals. The question was, what were her plans for him and was she acting alone?

"You are a remarkable person, Thomas," she said, circling him slowly, taking in everything about him. "From accused murderer to vanquisher of the Makreen to Lord of the Highlands in just a matter of months. And you walk these halls unafraid, even though you nearly killed my brother in a duel, unconcerned that perhaps the High King would view this as an opportunity to take his vengeance on you."

"I have no doubt that your father will seek to take his revenge," said Thomas. "In fact, I hope he does. Your father and I have unfinished business. And your brother got what he deserved. Some would say he is lucky to still be drawing breath."

Thomas' words set Corelia's eyes blazing, but not in anger. Rather his certainty and lack of fear only stirred her excitement and her interest in him. Was Thomas an obstacle or an opportunity? She couldn't decide which. Perhaps he was both.

"True. Very true. I cannot disagree." The Princess of Armagh continued to circle. "You have much to offer a woman, Thomas. Smart, handsome, an excellent fighter. You know I, too, have talents."

She stopped right in front of him, stepping close again. He felt her breath on his cheek as she leaned into him, her voice smoky. If he leaned forward just a tiny bit, their lips would touch. No matter how much he may have desired it, he understood the danger of that happening.

"You are the Lord of the Highlands," continued Corelia. She brushed her fingers lightly across his arm, outlining the corded muscle in his forearm. "I am the Princess of Armagh. Together we could be so much more."

Thomas stood there as still as stone, looking Corelia in the eye. He noticed the way her hair curled at her shoulders, the swell of her breasts, how her gown hugged her body. A truly beautiful woman, yet also extremely dangerous. She was smart, cunning and could seduce a man easily with her charms. Then when she gained what she desired, leave him in the street with a knife in the gut.

"I will think on it, Princess."

Thomas gently freed his arm and began walking down the hallway, eager to reach the stables and his friends, and more than a little uneasy by his reaction to Corelia. Despite his worries, he couldn't help but feel the light touch of attraction.

"By all means, Thomas. Remember, though, that my father wants you dead and the Highlands for his own. If we work together, I'm sure we could eliminate that threat. We both could gain what we want."

Thomas stopped and turned to look back at her. Corelia stood there calm and collected, but the image she presented didn't match her words, which had taken him by surprise. He understood what she implied but had never thought she would take such a risk.

"I will think on it, Princess."

Corelia stared after Thomas, even after the darkness consumed him. She was getting closer, she thought, pleased with herself. Convincing Thomas to trust her would take time. And then she could do what she did best.

17

SHOCKING SURPRISE

Thomas strode briskly down the dimly lit hallway, remembering that he had a few more turns to make before he reached the stables and his Marchers. He wanted to leave Eamhain Mhacha as soon as possible. After all that had happened during the evening, and his unsettling experience with Corelia Tessaril, he needed to get outside the stone and into the cool night so that he could think about how to handle the challenges ahead for him and the Highlands.

As he approached the courtyard that led to the stables, he found it odd that no one was about, especially on an evening such as this one with so many revelers in the citadel. Yet the only sound he heard were his boots striking the stone of the walkway. It reminded him of what it was like in the forest when quiet descended, the songs of the birds and the skittering of the smaller animals coming to a stop. Silence in a forest meant only one thing. A predator was on the hunt.

Stepping into the courtyard, Thomas touched the hilt of his dagger, taking some comfort in the action. It was the only weapon he had brought into the keep with him because of the Council restrictions. But knowing that he had at least that blade at hand helped to settle his nerves somewhat. Maybe it was his recent encounter with the Princess of Armagh that made him feel as he did now. He was on edge, his sense of awareness heightened as he took in everything around him, his eyes peering into the darkness. The feeling that something was off continued to nag at him. It would certainly make sense. The Princess of Armagh had a way about her that could make even the strongest, most confident man uncomfortable. She had clearly done so to him with barely a touch. Speaking with Corelia rarely was direct. Instead, interactions with her tended to involve insinuations and suggestions, allowing the other person's mind to wander onto whatever path she placed before them. Obviously, she enjoyed the game she played. But Thomas did not. He didn't have the patience for her games. He likely acquired that preference from his grandfather, Rynlin, who had little tolerance for anyone not willing to say what was on their mind.

"A word, my young Highland Lord."

Thomas halted in the middle of the courtyard, his hand ready to pull the dagger from its sheath. His unease grew. He had used the Talent to sense all that was around him as he made his way to the stables, yet he had not identified the figure who approached him now from a shady alcove. Something wasn't quite right, but he didn't know what it could be. He allowed his hand to drop from his dagger's hilt as the woman stepped into the moonlight.

Sarelle Makarin, Queen of Benewyn, stood before him. Her dark green dress accentuated her green eyes and set off her auburn hair. A beautiful woman, but also a ruthless negotiator. She had to be as her Kingdom relied on trade for its independence and economic success.

"Queen Sarelle," said Thomas, offering a slight nod of his head, somewhat perplexed. He had left the throne room well before her and at the time she had been engaged in a discussion with Gregory and several others. How had she gotten to the courtyard before him? "I didn't expect you here. Last I saw, you were talking with King Gregory."

Sarelle offered Thomas a dazzling smile, though her silence before responding dragged on for an unnaturally long period of time, as if she needed to figure out what to say. The prickle at the base of Thomas' neck had begun to spread down his spine. The premonition of danger increased with each passing second, but the cause of his growing alarm continued to tease him.

"Indeed, I was, Lord Kestrel."

Sarelle's eyes bore into his, staring deeply, though the warmth that he had seen in them when he spoke with her earlier in the evening had disappeared. There was a hardness lurking there now, and a faint touch of black appeared to flicker in the very center of her pupils. Was it just a trick of the shadows and the few torches lighting the courtyard?

"Are you all right, Queen Sarelle?" Thomas took a step back. His sense of unease was growing. Corelia had made him feel uncomfortable. But Sarelle sent a shiver through his body.

"Quite fine, Lord Kestrel." Sarelle stepped forward, closing the gap that Thomas had opened. "I simply wished to speak with you privately."

Thomas took another step back, and once more Sarelle followed. Thomas stepped back once again, trying to put some distance between them, but Sarelle matched his movement. It seemed as if they had started a strange dance.

"About what, Queen Sarelle?" asked Thomas, his hand naturally drifting back to the hilt of his dagger. He had not known Sarelle very long, but this was not the behavior he had expected from her.

Sarelle stopped her advance, the light leaving her green eyes for a moment, the pupils shifting fully to black, before returning to their original color.

"About what? About what? About what?" Sarelle repeated Thomas' words as if she didn't understand their meaning. As she continued to follow him around the courtyard, her movements became jerky, almost like a puppet.

"Are you all right, Queen Sarelle?" Thomas asked, not having any idea what was going on. The woman standing before him now clearly was not the same as the one who had spoken with him just a quarter hour before. "Do you need help with something? Perhaps a physick?"

The Queen of Benewyn stood frozen in place for several long moments, seemingly in a daze. Thomas' discomfort increased, his fingers itching to pull the dagger, his senses telling him that danger was close, but he couldn't locate the source.

In an instant, Sarelle came back to herself. "I do need your help, young Lord Kestrel."

"And what help do you need?" Thomas took another step back, Sarelle following once more, their strange dance beginning again.

Sarelle grinned wickedly as she lunged blazingly fast toward Thomas, her left hand shooting forward. "I need you to die!"

Thomas ducked and rolled away, the Queen of Benewyn's fingers elongating into a claw that swiped the air where Thomas had been standing just an instant before. Rising to his feet, he leapt backward, Sarelle's other hand now transformed into a razor-sharp claw, sweeping toward him from his other side. The Queen of Benewyn continued her advance, Thomas giving ground but having little space to maneuver, the courtyard limiting his options.

Thomas raised his dagger and blocked one of Sarelle's claws as it slashed toward him. As the steel of his dagger struck, it felt like he had dragged his blade across a rock. No wound appeared on Sarelle's forearm. Thomas dodged backward quickly once more, avoiding Sarelle's other claw as he struggled to control his shock. Sarelle maintained her relentless progress toward him, her green eyes now replaced by black orbs that reflected the light of the moon. He didn't know what type of creature sought to kill him, but Thomas understood now that it wasn't the Queen of Benewyn.

"You have nowhere to run, boy," screeched the woman who tracked him. "Nowhere to hide. My master wants you dead, and dead you will be."

The creature lunged forward faster than the eye could follow, slashing with her claws, Thomas barely escaping from her attack as he danced around the courtyard. She moved faster than a Shade, Thomas calling on all his training to defend himself. Each time his dagger deflected a claw, his arm stung as bolts of numbness shot through him.

Cursing himself for a fool, Thomas realized that he had been cornered against the courtyard wall, his hand finding the rough surface of the stone. He looked desperately for a way to get by his attacker.

"You can't escape me, boy," the woman cackled, claws moving sinuously between them. Poking. Prodding. Searching for a weakness. "There is no hope."

Thomas couldn't contain his surprise as his attacker shifted in front of him, a black mist settling over the creature and then quickly dissipating to reveal Rendael, the King of Kenmare, in the place of Sarelle. Its transformation complete, the creature lunged forward again, its right claw slicing through Thomas' shirt but missing the skin by a hairsbreadth. Instead, the hardened talon dug deeply into the stone wall, the old bricks crumbling from the thrust. Thomas spun away, finally gaining some room to move.

The creature crowed in delight as it pulled its claw free. The old king slashed with lightning speed, its claws a blur as it sought an opening in Thomas' defenses. As Thomas regained the center of the courtyard, sweat dripping into his eyes, the King of Kenmare stared at him with a hungry look in his black orbs.

"No one can defeat me. Because no one knows how I will come for them."

Once again, a black mist swept over the King of Kenmare. This time when the mist evaporated, Thomas remained rooted in place by shock. His best friend, Oso, stood before him, an evil grin lighting up his face.

"My master will be pleased," the creature hissed. "He will reward me when I bring him your head."

The creature, now in the form of the bearlike Marcher, resumed its attack, faster and faster, its claws snatching at Thomas' face, chest, neck, any piece of him that the creature could slice into in search of his blood. Thomas dodged desperately out of the way, seeking to avoid those razor-sharp claws that came at him faster than humanly possible. Realizing that his dagger would offer little defense, Thomas kicked out with his right leg, catching the creature in the chest and slamming it back against the courtyard wall where it slid to the ground, giving him just a few seconds to think.

The creature still resembling Oso pushed himself up off the cobblestones unharmed. Screaming in fury, the shapeshifter launched itself through the air, claws outstretched. Having no other options, Thomas took hold of the Talent. Infusing his dagger with the natural energy of the world, the steel shined a bright white as Thomas gripped the tip of the blade and threw it at the dark creature. He dove out of the way just in time as the thing that had appeared to be Oso screamed in agony and crumpled to the cobblestones, the brightly glowing dagger sticking out from its chest.

Thomas approached cautiously, the Talent at the ready just in case. Oso lay on the uneven stones unmoving, his black orbs staring up at the nighttime sky. The creature's face flickered back and forth between that of Sarelle Makarin, Rendael of Kenmare, and Oso, faster and faster, until all that Thomas could see was an amorphous black mist.

"You only delayed the inevitable," a scratchy voice whispered to Thomas. "You can't escape me, boy. I will be back. You can't escape ..."

Thomas watched in horrified fascination as the creature's body began to transform as well, shifting between the various bodies it had revealed until finally, with a barely audible gasp, his attacker dissolved into a black mist that merged with the shadows.

Still wary, Thomas extended his Talent to well beyond the keep of Eamhain Mhacha. But he found no sign of any other dark creatures or any feeling that resembled the one attached to whatever he had just escaped. Then again, he had failed to identify this dark creature, so who knew what waited for him in the shadows. The next time he saw Rynlin or Rya he would have to ask them about whatever this thing had been, because he had never heard of a dark creature having the ability to shape change as this one had done. And he had absolutely no doubt that he would be facing this creature again. He may have survived this latest attempt on his life, but he knew that he had not killed whatever it was that had attacked him. He had simply won a temporary victory.

Pushing his dark thoughts to the side, Thomas walked to the stables, exhausted. The Shadow Lord was getting agitated. Understandably Thomas had become more than just a nuisance. Shades attacking the night before, whatever this thing was trying to kill him this evening. All the better for him if he could take advantage of the Shadow Lord's nervousness, assuming he lived long enough.

18

AT WHAT PRICE?

A gentle zephyr drifted through the open window of Corelia's lush chambers. Discarding her extravagant gown, she stood in her shift, enjoying the cool caress of the breeze on her body as she gazed up at the stars. The events of the evening played through her mind once more. Thomas making good on his claim for the Highland throne had troubled her father greatly as it destroyed the High King's decade-long plan for dominion in the Highlands. She felt little remorse or concern for her father. This new Lord of the Highlands could be of use to her, and that's all that mattered.

He intrigued her. She found the fire in his green eyes quite appealing. There was a spark, a fire, a purpose there that she believed matched her own. But how to make use of him? She was an excellent judge of character and an accomplished strategist, knowing when she should manipulate or cajole, praise or criticize, and often doing so with great success and much to the chagrin of many a lord and lady in the Kingdoms. Yet she sensed in Thomas a strength she had not encountered in any of the others she had tangled with. A strength that both attracted her and made her pause. There must be a way to win his favor.

If she could, a whole new world of options would open up before her.

"There is a way, Princess. A very simple way."

Corelia whipped around at the sound of the grating voice, eyeing a tall bald man, rail thin, wearing dirty grey robes. His gaze captured hers, invading her very core.

"How did you get in here, Malachias?"

Her initial reaction was to reach for a robe, feeling naked under this intruder's piercing eyes, but deciding against it. Instead, she attempted to demonstrate her strength and stood in front of him with a feigned confidence. There was something about this man that terrified her. She required every ounce of her concentration and toughness to keep her body from trembling.

"How I got in here isn't important," the man said. "That I am here is important."

He began to pace the room slowly, his steps gliding silently across the carpet. But he kept his distance, not wanting to make the Princess of Armagh skittish. He knew her curiosity and desire for the upper hand would work to his advantage if he managed the next few minutes deftly.

"Why is that?"

"I thought you should know about your brother." Malachias stopped pacing, not offering any more in the way of detail. He wanted Corelia to ask for the information he could provide, as he knew she would.

"What about my brother?"

"He and I have reached an agreement of sorts. One that might give him an opportunity to regain the power he has lost since his terrible injury."

Corelia stared intently at Malachias, forcing herself to look into his eyes, but unable to maintain the contact for very long. The liquid pools of black beckoned, but in a way that horrified her. Her skeletal visitor knew her weaknesses. She and her brother had been competing ever since they were young children, understanding that their father eventually would pick a successor. They had fought to earn his favor, both doing so with regularity, and just as often falling out with their father and losing the ground they had gained at the other's expense. As a result, a game had ensued between the two, but a game with telling implications. Malachias could give Ragin an advantage that she could not compete against.

"Why are you here?"

Corelia's control wavered, her hands beginning to shake as her anxiety intensified. She had heard the stories that swirled around Malachias and who he truly served. And she understood the risks and rewards of aligning with him. So, she had to handle this conversation carefully, or it could prove fatal.

"To help you, of course."

"Help me? Why? It seems that you've already taken up with my brother."

She didn't need to ask about what help could be provided. Corelia sensed that Malachias knew exactly what she fancied, that if he really wanted to, he could discover all of her desires and secrets in an instant. She also knew that he would charge a steep price for any assistance he gave.

"Because you have an interesting desire, Princess. But to achieve it you need a stronger ally."

"You?"

"Me, yes," he said in a whisper. His hypnotic eyes locked onto hers. "And the master I serve."

Corelia's breath caught in her throat. She knew to whom he referred, but she feared to say the name openly.

"What do I desire?"

"It's quite obvious, my dear. Power. Over everything and everyone. Even if you are to beat your brother to the Kingdom, Armagh will never satisfy you. You need more. So much more."

"You told me what I want, Malachias," her interest in his

words getting the better of her fears, her common sense. "You have yet to tell me why you want to help me obtain it."

"Clever girl." Malachias chuckled softly, the sound resembling a saw scraping through wood. "Because what you want serves my purpose as well."

"And what purpose is that?"

Corelia's shaking increased. Giving in to her weakness, she leaned back against the windowsill to steady herself, crossing her arms across her chest in hopes of appearing calm though she felt anything but.

"To place the new Lord of the Highlands under my thumb, of course."

"Why?"

"So many questions, Princess. You don't seem to understand that this isn't a negotiation. And there are consequences regardless of whatever you decide." Malachias' gaze burned into her. "This new Lord of the Highlands, this boy, impedes my plans, yet he has a great deal of power that could prove useful to the task my master has set for me. Some would like him removed from the game. I, on the other hand, would like to play him, at least for a time."

Malachias took a step toward Corelia. She cringed, realizing she had nowhere to go. Seeing her reaction, the tall man stopped so close that his fetid breath burned Corelia's nose and throat.

"We view people in much the same way, Princess. As pieces to be played on a game board. Furthermore, in this game, we both have the same design. Rather than taking the Highland Lord off the board, as your father Rodric would prefer, we want to use him. And I have no doubt that he can be used, to great effect in fact. But enough questions, Princess. Do you want my assistance?"

"I won't dispute your assessment. But my participation depends on what you offer."

"Quite the negotiator," chuckled Malachias. "And much shrewder than your brother. It's really quite simple, Princess. I offer a way for you to gain the new Lord of the Highlands, or rather I should say a way to control him. Once you control him, we can do with him whatever we want. I have every expectation that he would fit into your plans quite nicely. Then you wouldn't have to rely solely on the Dinnegans. With their recent fall from grace, who can measure the real value of such an alliance now?"

Malachias leaned in closer to Corelia, his shadow falling over her. She cringed again involuntarily, hating her weakness. He extended his hand, and the glint of the light on the metal he held within his grasp captivated her.

"I'm sure you can figure out some way to get close to him, Princess. When you do, simply put this around his neck."

He held in front of her a necklace made of a strange, black metal interspersed with onyx that shined like glass. A darkness emanated from the finely woven chain even with the bright light in the room eliminating any shadows.

"Once he wears this, he is yours to command, Princess. No matter how much he might want to resist, he won't be able to. He will do whatever you desire. Moreover, once fixed in place, the chain can never be removed."

"And what do you want of me if I accept this gift?" Corelia asked.

Malachias had mentioned consequences regardless of what decision she made. She remained wary and worried about the price she would have to pay, but her calculating gaze revealed her obvious interest, and her willingness to perhaps take a risk.

"The price would be you failing to achieve your objective, Princess. Simple as that."

Malachias grinned at her. It may have been a trick of the light, but for just an instant his teeth appeared to be sharpened points.

"As I said, Princess. It would serve my designs as well. It is your choice. Take my help or not." He dropped the black necklace on a small table as he turned toward the door. "But you would be a fool not to accept my aid."

Corelia glanced at the necklace laying on the table, captivated by the dark gleam of the metal and onyx. When finally she broke her gaze away from the shining, black metal, she looked around the room in surprise. Malachias was gone, yet the door remained undisturbed. Her shivering intensified, attacking her entire body. She closed the shutters and threw on a robe, yet her eyes never left the black necklace.

She licked her lips in anticipation. Should she accept this gift? What were the consequences that Malachias had not mentioned? Was it worth the risk to obtain all that she desired?

As her mind struggled to find the dangers hidden from her, the dangers she knew that her frightening visitor had not revealed, Malachias' words continued to play through her mind: *You would be a fool not to.*

19

SCRUBBING POTS

The dark gloom of the early morning still covered the land, yet the Marchers were already well on their way to breaking camp, not wanting to be anywhere near Eamhain Mhacha now that the Council of the Kingdoms, and its guaranteed peace, had come to an end. Almost all the horses were saddled, breakfast done, and the final tasks about to be accomplished so that they could return to the Highlands by the fastest, safest route, as all remembered the challenges faced just a few days before as they dodged Ogren raiding parties until they had no choice but to fight their way through the Armaghian countryside. The Marchers hoped to avoid a repeat of that experience on the way back to the Highlands so that they could focus their attention on matters closer to home. Besides not trusting the High King, they still needed to eliminate the small bands of reivers that remained in their homeland, or at least make the intruders see their error in crossing into the Highlands.

Thomas had been wandering through the small forest the Marchers had chosen for their hidden camp for more than an hour already. He had said that he wanted to scan their surroundings before they began their journey. Oso assumed that he simply wanted some time to himself, because if Thomas wanted to get a sense of what was around them he could use the Talent and gain a glimpse of what was occurring for hundreds of leagues in any direction.

"Help Aric and the others clean the breakfast pots, Oso," ordered Coban. "We need to be ready to go as soon as Thomas is back."

"Why me?"

"Because if you don't, I'll tell Anara you were dancing with a young, beautiful woman with blonde hair in the court of the High King," replied Coban with a grin. "She'll eat you for breakfast."

"I was just dancing," protested Oso. "So was everyone else."

"Doesn't matter," said Coban, nodding his head sagely. "The only thing she'll care about is you. Besides, I'm sure that Anara can do quite a bit with that dagger of hers besides whittling."

"All right, all right." Oso headed down toward the stream where Aric and a few other Marchers had already started working on the pots. "I assume that I'll be doing this all the way back to the Crag?"

"Smart boy." Coban walked off chuckling to himself.

"Wonderful, just wonderful," Oso mumbled under his breath.

20

A GOOD SIGN

The sun had barely touched the horizon, yet the sailors on the *River Dancer* already were making their final preparations to untie the river barge from the dock at Eamhain Mhacha. King Gregory had been very specific when arranging passage with Burnley, master of the craft. He wanted to be away from the city at first light after the previous night's feast. There was a bonus in it for Burnley and his crew, and Burnley wanted that bonus. His goal was to be at the eastern shore of the Heartland Lake before Eamhain Mhacha awoke, which he could accomplish if he maneuvered the *River Dancer* into the swiftly running current of the Corazon River in the next few minutes.

Burnley, who looked more like the retired soldier that he was than a ship's captain, stalked the decks of the craft much like a Swordmaster would his training ground, yelling instructions to his crew as they pulled on and readjusted lines, moved cargo out of the way, and tied everything down before they slipped their lines. The *River Dancer* was one of the largest barges in the Kingdoms, which was why Gregory had hired him. It carried his fifty men, horses and gear comfortably.

Perhaps most important to the King of Fal Carrach, the

River Dancer had served first as a troop carrier before becoming a river barge, thus Burnley's love for the old vessel. Burnley could beach the front of the barge, then lower a gangplank that ran across the front of the ship so that armored riders could charge off onto the land or into the surf. The *River Dancer* hadn't been used in that way for quite some time, but Burnley had assured Gregory that it still could perform such a service if circumstances warranted. Burnley hoped that their journey wouldn't require it, but he kept that possibility in the back of his mind. The King of Fal Carrach seemed to suspect that some danger might be just over the horizon. So he'd be ready, though he had no desire to fight. He'd left the military for a reason.

As sailors slipped the *River Dancer's* lines free from the dock the large barge swiftly caught the current. At the aft of the vessel, a metal chain linked two massive rudders placed on each side of the craft, allowing the helmsman to guide the barge into the center of the river.

With only a few fishermen out on the water in the early morning, the sailors didn't have to worry about any other ships getting in their way, and Burnley exhorted them on as they lay into their tasks. Having spent years on the river, they knew their craft. In a matter of minutes Eamhain Mhacha was a speck in the distance and the *River Dancer,* true to its name, skimmed across the water like a dancer across the stage despite its great size.

Kaylie sat near the bow of the craft, watching the landscape speed by. It was going to be a beautiful day, the breeze already strong as the sun began to shine brightly down on her. She reveled in the freedom she felt, yet she couldn't help but think of the fun she had experienced during the feast the night before. That's where her mind was when her father approached, as Gregory was finally satisfied that they were well on their way and free from Rodric.

"He was different than the last time we spoke," said Kaylie

of Thomas, thinking back to their picnic in the forest before Ragin had led a troop of soldiers to capture him.

"Much is different since you last spoke to him," agreed Gregory.

He continued to scan the shorelines of the river. Even though the *River Dancer* benefited from the strong current, the Corazon River tightened in places to the point where enterprising bandits, or perhaps a more dangerous enemy, could leap the distance between the barge and shoreline and land on the deck. True, it was unlikely to occur with fifty armed, vigilant soldiers on the barge. But who was to say what was or was not possible?

"I know, Father. You're right. And there was always a hardness to him, a wariness. But there was also an openness, at least before Tinnakilly, but not anymore. Do you think he'll let me back in?"

"It could just be a matter of time, Kaylie," sighed Gregory. "But the fact that he danced with you is an important step."

"Why do you say that?"

"Much has changed for Thomas," continued Gregory, turning his gaze from the landscape to look at his daughter. "Think about what he's been through, not just in Tinnakilly, but for the past ten years, to say nothing of the snippets coming out of the Highlands. If the stories are to be believed, and if what my scouts say is true, Thomas and his Marchers have been engaged in a war for the last few months to clear the Highlands of Killeran and his reivers, as well as a swarm of Ogren. That is no easy task. So, the fact that he opened himself up, even if just a little bit, and chose to spend time with you last night, I take as a good sign."

Perhaps her father was right. Perhaps it was just a matter of time. Not allowing her impatience to get the better of her was going to be her primary challenge. Kaylie looked at her father for a moment longer before he turned his attention back to the swiftly passing shoreline.

21

PURSUED

Gregory had enjoyed the last few days on the Corazon River and, after the excitement and intrigue of the Council of the Kingdoms, relished the so far uneventful trip to Ballinasloe. The *River Dancer* truly was a marvel. At night, Burnley steered the barge onto a sandy beach, allowing the horses to be taken off, fed and watered, and then set loose to wander in a glade or in a temporary stall the sailors built in a matter of minutes. Then in the morning, with the sun barely in the sky, they would head back onto the river. Nevertheless, worry continued to plague the King of Fal Carrach. As each day passed his sense of foreboding only increased, yet he couldn't determine the cause, and his mood had infected Kael and his soldiers, all of whom peered regularly at the passing shore expecting trouble to appear at any moment.

Perhaps it was their location. They had made good progress, reaching a point in the river where they were only a few leagues from the southern border of the Clanwar Desert. As the *River Dancer* skimmed through the water, the river itself had tightened and would remain something more akin to a narrow canal for many leagues. At certain points the barge, which since leaving Eamhain Mhacha had enjoyed as much as a half-mile if not more to either shoreline when running through the middle of the river, would no longer have that luxury. The *River Dancer* would need to slow and make its way carefully as the shore at some places ahead would be no more than five to ten feet clear on either side.

Gregory scanned the western bank once again. Off in the distance through the trees he thought that he could see the beginnings of the Clanwar Desert, massive sand dunes rising hundreds of feet toward the sky. It was a harsh and dangerous land. As a result, the Desert Clans were not always the most reasonable of people. But the inhabitants of the desert had little interest in the river traffic. No, Gregory's primary concern remained Rodric and the King of Dunmoor, since they now traveled through Loris' Kingdom as they made their way back to Fal Carrach.

He feared that his worry was about to become reality as Burnley trotted toward him with a frown. He held out a spyglass which Gregory grasped quickly.

"To the southwest, my lord," said Burnley. "A large group of riders, at least a few hundred, all dressed in black. No marks, no insignia, no flags."

Gregory raised the spyglass to his eye. Burnley was right. Though still more than a league or more off, he watched the several hundred black-clad men, which at this distance appeared more like a smudge than individual figures, gallop toward the river.

"Can we outrun them on the river?"

"No, my lord," replied Burnley. "Not here. The shorelines are too close, and we'll need to slow to manage the bends without running aground. If they're after you, I'd guess we have no more than an hour, maybe less, before they're on us. And there's more, King Gregory. Take a look at the leader. Haven't seen one of these since my time in the service."

Gregory raised the spyglass to his eye again, scanning the group once more. They were easier for Gregory to pick out as they galloped closer. The men rode stiffly in almost perfect alignment, as if their decisions and actions weren't their own, reminding him of the skirmish on Dinnegan's estate. Their unnatural precision suggested that they were puppets rather than men. Then he found the cause and confirmation for his suspicions.

"Kael!"

Kael Bellilil, Swordmaster of Ballinasloe, loped down the deck. Taking the spyglass Gregory handed him and looking in the pointed direction, he cursed in disgust.

"A Shade," he said simply. The black-robed creature with the milky white eyes riding at the head of the approaching soldiers was unmistakable.

Kael's thoughts immediately turned to the next step, already understanding that on this part of the river remaining on the barge with the Shade and his bewitched men fast approaching was a death wish. He shifted his gaze farther down the northern shore of the river but found nothing that he liked. This close to the Clanwar Desert the forest was gone, replaced by a dusty plain that led to the very edge of the sand dunes. Although the river would offer some defense from the Shade and its men, it would only be for a short time because of its narrowness. The outnumbered Fal Carrachians would have no good options for defending themselves once the dark creature made its way across the river with its troop of soldiers. The Swordmaster turned his attention to the southern shore, scanning his surroundings until he found what he wanted.

"There, my lord," said Kael, handing the spyglass back to Gregory and pointing to the southeast.

"A good spot," said Gregory, giving the spyglass back to Burnley. "Can you beach us as close to that as possible?"

Burnley looked through the spyglass, estimating that the

small knoll was about a league from the river. His soldier's eye recognized it immediately as defensible, at least for a time.

"Yes, within a mile or so. Get your men ready."

Kael strode off barking orders, his men responding instantly to his commands while Gregory went off to find Kaylie.

22

ATTEMPTED ESCAPE

Burnley cursed in disgust, whipping back around and pulling the spyglass from his eye.

"They're coming fast, my lord. No more than a couple miles behind us now. We need to do this as fast as we can."

"We'll be ready," replied Gregory.

Gregory and his men could sit their horses four across on the barge. All the Fal Carrachian soldiers were prepared for what was to come next. Horsemen good with bows and cross-bows had found places in the back of the barge so that they would be the last off the craft. Kaylie sat her horse next to her father. Gregory had made it clear that she was to stay next to him no matter what as they made their escape. Kael would lead the rear guard.

"Remember, my lord. As soon as we feel the first touch of sand under our keel, we'll drop the ramp. Then off you go as if you're charging into the Dark Horde itself. We'll raise the ramp and hopefully get back into the river before those black devils reach us."

"I expect they'll stay focused on us," said Kael. "But we'll do what we can to keep them off you if any try for your barge. Just make sure that if you get away you remember us when you find a place to land. We'll fight as long as we can, but how long we can hold is anyone's guess."

"On my honor," replied Burnley, the old soldier finding himself again.

"That's good enough for me," said the grim-faced Swordmaster.

Kael began repeating the commands he'd already given multiple times to the men lined up behind him, the soldiers nodding their understanding, unwilling to risk the wrath of the Highlander.

"Get ready, King Gregory!"

Burnley stood at the front of the river barge, hand on the lever holding the ramp in place. He stared into the river as they skimmed toward the southern shore. He saw the sand passing swiftly beneath him now, rising closer and closer to the hull. At the first touch of resistance between sand and keel, Burnley slammed down on the lever and the front ramp of the barge dropped down into the shallow water.

"Out! Out! Ride, you bastards!"

Gregory, Kaylie and the first few lines of soldiers leapt off the barge, galloping through the shallow water and onto the shore. The remaining lines of soldiers followed after, Kael turning his horse and taking with him the six men at the back of the troop to serve as a rear guard.

Kael was impressed that Burnley had already extricated his barge from the sandbar and was on his way once more, the *River Dancer* gliding around the twists and turns of the Corazon River. It looked like the former soldier would get away cleanly, as the black-clad riders showed no interest whatsoever in the barge. Less than a quarter mile away, the Shade and its troop bore down on Kael and his men.

23

A DRINK

Burnley had done a better job than hoped for in picking his spot to land. In just a few minutes the Fal Carrachians reached the knoll, which appeared steeper than expected as they approached. It rose one hundred feet into the air, the beginning an easy, gentle slope, yet the climb became much more difficult as its incline steepened toward the summit. Gregory urged his men up, his daughter staying right next to him as instructed. As they neared the summit, several of the soldiers had to drop from their saddles and lead their horses by the reins because of the difficulty of the slope.

Reaching the top, Gregory examined his surroundings, pleased that Kael had selected this location for their defense. Some long-forgotten people had lived here at some time in the past, the remains of stone walls and huts standing atop the hillock. Even better, a stone ring wall that reached to his waist ran the length of the crest. Though the wall had collapsed in places, it would serve as an excellent defensive fortification. He immediately put his men to work, ordering them to pull as many stones as possible from the huts and interior walls to fill the gaps in the ring wall and raise it where possible.

Kaylie and a few soldiers took charge of the horses, finding space in the center of the summit to create a makeshift line to hobble them. When she finished her task, she came to stand by her father. Gregory continued to bellow orders to his men as they began work on strengthening their fortifications, but the skirmish below them drew the bulk of his attention.

Kael and his men had done an excellent job. Although heavily outnumbered, the archers and crossbowmen had stopped the charge of the black-clad men, which clearly angered the Shade. Each arrow or bolt a Fal Carrachian soldier released took one of the attacking black-clad men off his horse. As a result, even the Shade struggled to maintain control of his pawns in the confusion that followed. After every volley, Kael had his men trot back closer to the hillock, slowly but surely, until the Fal Carrachian rear guard was almost to the base of the knoll.

"Archers to the wall!" yelled Gregory.

Instantly a dozen soldiers ran up to the ring of stones, bows out, arrows placed point first into the soft ground so that they could be drawn as quickly as possible.

As if sensing that Gregory was ready, after the next volley, Kael turned his men away from the Shade and its soldiers, yelling at them to gallop for the top of the hillock. They were more than happy to do so. The Shade, sensing an opportunity, drove his men forward, seeking to prevent Kael and his soldiers from disengaging. But Gregory was ready.

"Archers, release!"

A cloud of arrows flew into the sky, raining down into the black-clad men chasing Kael and his soldiers.

"Archers, release!"

Another swarm of arrows fell from the sky into the Shade's lackeys, and then another, and another. The aerial assault quickly halted the Shade's attack, as Kael and his men reached the hillock's summit, their horses leaping the ring wall.

Thanks to Gregory's quick thinking, all the soldiers gained the safety of the tor. Except for one. A young man lay at the bottom of the hillock dazed, his horse stepping wrong and rearing, then throwing the Fal Carrachian soldier from his saddle. Kael, having dropped down from his horse, tried to vault the ring wall to go to the soldier's aid, but Gregory placed a strong hand on his shoulder and held him back. It was too late. Despite several archers desperately trying to keep their attackers from their friend, the Shade swept in on his horse, unconcerned by the falling arrows. Reaching down the servant of the Shadow Lord grabbed the soldier by the back of his shirt and dragged him out of range of the Fal Carrachian bows.

"It's too late, Kael," Gregory sighed in frustration. "There's nothing we can do for him."

The Shade leapt gracefully from his horse to stand above the soldier, then leaned down as if to kiss him.

Kaylie watched in horrid fascination. "What's it doing?"

"Feeding," answered Kael, pounding his fists into the stone wall in frustration, his face red with rage.

All the Fal Carrachians observed, their resentment at not being able to help their comrade palpable, their anger growing. In a matter of seconds, the unfortunate soldier resembled a withered, dried out husk, his life stolen from him.

"What did it do?"

"The Shade drank the man's spirit," replied Kael, resignation in his voice, admitting reluctantly that Gregory was right to keep him from his suicide mission but still feeling ashamed of having to leave the young soldier to his fate. "To Shades, our spirits are like food. It gives them sustenance."

Gregory turned toward his daughter, seeing the hard look on her face. He was glad that he would never have to fear for Kaylie's backbone.

"The sun's almost down, my lord," said Kael, changing the subject.

Gregory looked up, watching the sun touch the western horizon and begin to sink beneath it.

"That's good. That should buy us some time. I doubt they'll attack in the dark. That would give us an advantage." Gregory turned toward the small camp his men had already started to construct. "Nevertheless, set a strong guard, Kael. Rotations every two hours. In the meantime, we'll continue to strengthen the wall."

24

CHANGE IN PLAN

Thomas and his Marchers had made good time upon leaving Eamhain Mhacha. Worried by the threat of a possible attack, they stopped only a few hours every morning and evening. During the night they walked, not wanting to chance an injury to their horses and to give their steeds a chance to rest as well. Coban sent outriders to the four points of the compass to give them additional eyes, even though Thomas' skill in the Talent was all that they really needed. But Thomas let it go, knowing that it made his Swordmaster feel better even if it really wasn't necessary.

They followed the northern shore of the Corazon River, the rising dunes of the Clanwar Desert visible just a few leagues away. Dusk was approaching, which meant it was almost time to call a halt for a few hours so that the men and horses could eat and rest before they continued through the night.

As he had done at this time the last few evenings, Thomas grabbed hold of the Talent, filling himself with the natural power of the world. He extended his senses and began to circle for leagues around them to ensure no enemies lay in wait or approached. Everything was as it should be until he turned his search to the southeast and farther down the river. It felt wrong, as if the land itself was being corrupted. Having experienced this feeling many times before, he abruptly stopped his horse.

"Thomas, what ..." exclaimed Coban.

"Patience," said Oso, walking his horse next to them. "He's found something, which can't be good."

Thomas pushed his senses farther toward the southeast. In his mind it was like he was a kestrel soaring through the sky, and with his Talent he easily homed in on the cause of the disturbance. Fires dotted a small hillock, its summit protected by a chest-high ring wall.

Black-clad men surrounded the base of the tor, sitting in the falling darkness, not bothering with fires, barely moving. It appeared strange to Thomas until he located the Shade, standing still as a statue, staring up at the top of the hillock, apparently waiting for the sun before launching his attack on the outnumbered defenders.

Turning his attention to the summit, he saw the defenders warily staring out into the darkening gloom, expecting an attack, not certain they were safe until morning. He shifted his focus to one of the small fires. Kael walked toward the growing flames, Gregory and Kaylie waiting for him. He was shocked to see them there, remembering that Gregory had said that they would be traveling back to Fal Carrach by river barge. He processed the gravity of the situation immediately.

"South of the river, about ten leagues down the shoreline, a little more than a mile from the bank," said Thomas, returning to himself and startling Coban in the process, the Swordmaster cursing softly under his breath as a result. "A Shade and several hundred men."

"What are they doing out here?" asked Oso. A fair question, they all thought.

"Hunting would be my guess," said Thomas. "They've trapped Gregory of Fal Carrach and his party."

"He only brought fifty soldiers," said Coban.

"And his daughter is with him," offered Oso, knowing where Thomas' heart lay, even if his friend refused to admit it to himself.

"Yes," answered Thomas simply.

"Gregory is a friend and ally," said Coban, his voice steely. "Marchers always help their friends."

"Yes, we do," said Thomas, his mind already focused on the task at hand. "Oso, tell the Marchers they have one hour to eat and sharpen their weapons. Then we ride."

25

SLEEPLESS NIGHT

Gregory sat by the small fire, staring into the flames, his daughter next to him. His dark mood threatened to get the better of him. Kael had just left to check the defenses one more time. But Gregory wasn't worried. The men knew what they were about and what they were up against. Those positioned at the ring wall would remain vigilant, those seeking to get some rest wouldn't. He didn't hear the expected sound of snoring coming from his soldiers at this late hour. Rather the scrapes of blades being sharpened, of steel being drawn against a whetstone, dominated.

Kaylie had been quiet ever since the death of Linas, the Fal Carrachian soldier taken by the Shade. Yet his daughter didn't seem to be afraid. Rather she appeared resolved. Committed to what they expected would occur on the morrow. To what would be required of her.

"What are they, father?"

"The Shade's men?"

"Yes. They felt wrong. As if they're not all there. They don't seem human."

"I don't know that they are human anymore," replied

Gregory, stoking the fire with a stick and earning a brief flare from the flames. "I'd never come across them until we assaulted Dinnegan's manor and now once more, but I've heard tell of men who have pledged themselves to the Shadow Lord, placing themselves in his service but not realizing the consequences of doing so."

At the mention of the Shadow Lord, a hope-stealing cold took up residence in Kaylie. She had read the histories and heard the stories but looking down from the hillock's summit made it all a bit too real for her.

"And when they do realize what they've done, the mistake they've made, it's too late," continued her father. "They're not warlocks. They haven't been given Dark Magic. They're more like puppets, compelled to do as the Shadow Lord, or one of his minions, commands. They can't fight the compulsion. If that Shade down there told them all to walk off a cliff, they'd do it without question whether they wanted to or not."

Kaylie mulled her father's words, beginning to realize the enormity of the challenge before them. They had less than fifty soldiers. The Shade commanded several hundred. No matter how well the Fal Carrachians fought, the numbers would determine the result of the battle that was all but certain at sunrise. It was pure mathematics. And the numbers did not favor the Fal Carrachians.

Gregory saw the look in her daughter's eyes, the realization coming to her. He wished he could comfort her; tell her everything would be all right. But he couldn't. He wouldn't. He didn't want to lie. Searching for even the smallest of positives, he knew that if they escaped this trap it was a lesson she would remember always.

Kaylie turned her gaze back to the fire, brooding as the flames danced at the touch of the wind. There had to be something they could do. But what? Even with her learning the Talent, she knew that she couldn't take on the Shade and such a large force with any expectation of success. Startled, Kaylie looked over her shoulder, expecting to catch a glimpse of someone just beyond her peripheral vision. But no one was there. It had felt as if someone had been watching her from afar. Someone she knew, perhaps. For some reason her thoughts drifted to Thomas. Could it be?

"The odds are slim, but we still have a chance," said Gregory. "Perhaps Burnley will find aid in time."

"And if he doesn't?" Kaylie didn't want to hear the answer, her fear beginning to take hold, though she kept it from showing, or at least she hoped that she did.

"Then we fight until we can't fight anymore," her father said grimly as he stoked the fire with a stick, the disturbed flames capturing the anger and the beginnings of resignation in his eyes.

26

QUICK CIRCUIT

The Marchers trotted their horses along the southern bank of the Corazon River. They had made good time during the night, thanks to Thomas finding a shallow ford to cross the river, which gave them a few additional hours to spare. It was still early morning, still dark. The sun wouldn't rise for another hour or so. The Marchers could see the hillock just scarcely visible off in the distance, a few small fires still burning at its top, the light flickering inconsistently as a fog had formed during the night and drifted off the river to envelop the surrounding countryside in a white mist.

Shades and Ogren had trespassed in the Highlands for centuries. Of all the Kingdoms, because of their homeland's proximity to the Charnel Mountains, the Marchers had a long history of fighting the Shadow Lord's monstrous servants. They took pride in their ability to do so, honing their strategy and tactics over the centuries so that they could neutralize the advantages the dark creatures so often exhibited.

In fact, it was widely said that a Marcher would go well out of their way if there was an opportunity to kill a dark creature. They knew that the Shadow Lord could feel the death of each of his minions; some said it felt like a painful prick. Whether true or not, the Marchers didn't care. They took particular satisfaction in making the Shadow Lord feel that pain by eliminating his creations whenever given the opportunity. Hard fighters from a hard land with an even harder duty.

Thomas had believed that Shades generally did not have an ability in Dark Magic, but he had run across a few now that did, such as the one he had killed at Anselm. So he chose to release his hold on the Talent just in case, not wanting to make the Shade aware of his presence as he approached the hillock then hopped off his horse just a few miles away, handing the reins to Coban.

"We have about an hour before the sun rises," said Thomas. "I'm assuming the Shade will attack at dawn. So, I'm going to get a little closer and see what I can see."

Oso made to go with him, starting to slide down his saddle, but Thomas stopped him. He appreciated the assistance, but it wasn't necessary.

"Thank you, Oso. But I can go faster on my own."

Oso seemed a little put out by the statement, but the large Highlander couldn't disagree with his friend and reluctantly nodded his head in agreement.

"Coban, you know what to do. Assume the fight begins at dawn."

"We'll be ready," he replied. Coban turned his horse and Thomas' away from the knoll, giving orders through hand signals and whispers as his Marchers set up a makeshift camp.

As the Highlanders began to prepare for their attack, Thomas continued forward, jogging through the high grass toward the hillock. He slowed his pace as he drew closer, his sharp eyes constantly scanning for any danger. The light fog hid many of the features of the land. He understood now why the Shade had waited until morning to attack. The sides of the hill, though an easy slope to begin with, gradually became much steeper and were littered with rocks and other obstacles as they increased in height. Definitely not terrain to assault in the dark.

Thomas made a quick circuit of the camp at the base of the hillock. The Shade acted the fool, not in the least worried that an assailant could come at it from behind. All the Shade's attention, including that of its black-clad soldiers, remained concentrated on the hillock and their prey on the summit. Then again, why should the Shade even worry about an attack out here? Who in their right mind would willingly confront a Shade?

As Thomas quickly worked his way back to his Marchers, he had the feeling that he was missing something. It didn't feel right, as if the evil he felt from the Shade was stronger, but he couldn't put his finger on it. He would do what he could to prepare, but he locked the unsettling concern away in another part of his mind as he strode silently through the tall grass and shifted his focus to the surprise he had planned for when the sun began to rise.

27

FINAL PREPARATIONS

Thomas trotted back into the Marcher camp. His fighters were checking their gear, their saddles, their horses' hooves to make sure all was ready. He found Coban talking quietly with Oso and Aric.

"Everything ready, Coban?" asked Thomas, sneaking up behind the Swordmaster out of the first flush of the morning.

"Dammit, Thomas!" hissed Coban, having nearly jumped out of his skin. "You're the Highland Lord, yet you still feel the need to act like a boy!"

"Sorry, couldn't resist."

Both Oso and Aric chuckled, though softly. They didn't want to risk Coban's well-known wrath.

"What did you find?" asked Oso.

"One Shade and several hundred men likely pledged to the Shadow Lord. Kill the Shade and the men will be easy pickings. Until then, they'll be an effective military force, fighting to the death."

"Any defenses?" asked Aric.

"None. The Shade is focused on the hilltop. They have no

sentries in place. Just a few groups on the perimeter to ensure that those on the hill remain there."

"Then let's get a move on," smiled Coban. "We can use this fog to our advantage. No one's going to want to miss the fun."

28

RIDERS

Gregory and Kaylie peered out over the ring wall, now chest height, the Fal Carrachian soldiers having scrambled to strengthen the barrier during the night. Still not high enough, thought Gregory. But it would have to do with time running short. Nevertheless, it would make the job of their attackers that much more difficult. He and his daughter looked down at the base of the hillock. They could only pick out indistinct shadows and movement. Dawn approached, and a misty fog wafted across the land from the river, hiding some aspects of their surroundings and revealing others as a result of a capricious wind.

"We're ready, my lord," said Kael, striding up to the wall out of the murk. "Or rather as ready as we're ever going to be."

They stood there in silence for several minutes, not moving, the soldiers guarding the barrier seemingly having turned to stone. The unnatural stillness of the morning had infected them. They were startled out of their false solitude when the Shade stepped out of the white mist at the bottom of the knoll, his rigidly moving men forming into several ranks behind him.

Kaylie saw the grim expression on her father's face, remembering their conversation from the night before. She knew that they didn't stand a very good chance with the odds stacked against them because of the Shade's overwhelming numbers. Even with their enemy attacking uphill, if what her father said was true these men, no matter the reality on the battlefield, would not stop until they achieved the goal set for them by the Shade, or death took them first.

"Father, what's that?"

A slight ridge rose about a quarter mile beyond their attackers. Riders had appeared, though she couldn't tell how many, their horses perhaps no more than specters as the fog drifted on the breeze. The white mist did an excellent job of concealing them. For a moment, they would be visible, the next hidden.

"What?"

"On the ridge to our front. I thought I saw riders."

"I don't see anything," said Kael. "But you have the younger eyes, Princess."

"It's this blasted fog," grumbled Gregory.

His attention remained fixed on the Shade below. He expected it to signal its men forward at any moment.

"It could be their outriders," said Kael, pointing to several points on the compass. "The Shade placed a few of his men to the west and north of his main host so that we couldn't sneak down the hillock and try to attack them in the flanks."

Kaylie peered in those directions, identifying the two squads of five men each set exactly where Fal Carrach's Swordmaster had said. These black-clad men, too, were focused on the hillock, intent on making sure that their prey didn't break free.

She leaned back from the ring wall, startled. She had been observing the small group of outriders to the west. She had counted five, but in this fog, she could have been mistaken. Now she could only make out three. She looked again. Now only two. A few more seconds passed, the mist trailing across the land, shapes becoming indistinct or disappearing entirely as the fog shifted, the wind playing havoc with her ability to identify anything in the swirling mist. Now none. It had to be the fog playing tricks with her eyes.

Kaylie turned to the north, the enveloping silence that came with the fog eerie, almost ominous. She located the group of outriders placed there by the Shade, picking them out despite the shifting mist. Five all together. Then four. Three. Zero. They had disappeared, horses and all. One second they were there, the next they were gone. What was going on?

She looked back to the ridge, the riders she had seen just minutes before visible again, but no longer standing still. They had begun walking their mounts toward the hillock. Yet they made no noise. She didn't hear the tell-tale jingling of the horses' bridles and the pounding of their hooves on rough ground. The fog had to be muffling their approach. It appeared to her as if a ghostly band of fighters had begun their charge though at a glacial pace.

"Father ..."

"Not now, Kaylie."

Gregory watched the Shade begin to walk his horse up the hillock's lower slope, his men following. The King of Fal Carrach drew his sword.

"Get ready, men!" bellowed Kael. "Remember, if they try to leap the wall, aim for their horses' bellies!"

"Father!" yelled Kaylie, grabbing his arm to capture his attention. "Look to the northwest!"

Irritated by the distraction, nonetheless he glanced in the direction Kaylie pointed. The thick fog was beginning to weaken as the sun showed its first touch of color in the east. And then he saw them. Riders, maybe thirty in all. Yet how could they be so quiet?

About halfway to the Shade and its men, one of the riders

unfurled a banner, though Gregory couldn't determine what it revealed. It was then that the riders increased their pace, urging their horses from a walk to a trot.

"Kael, can you make out …"

"I'll be damned," said the stoic Highlander, putting both hands on the ring wall and leaning forward to make sure his eyes hadn't betrayed him.

A smile broke out on his face. As the riders increased their pace, the banner caught the air and snapped open behind its bearer. Kael could see it clearly now. On a field of white appeared three mountain peaks and a kestrel streaking down from the sky, claws outstretched. The symbol of his homeland.

"It's the Highlands, my lord. The Marchers attack."

29

DESPERATE MELEE

Coban had strung the Marchers along the top of the small ridge facing the hillock while the fog, which helped to mask their arrival, was thick and heavy. The Shade had set outriders to his south and east, not because it was worried about an attack from behind, but rather it feared that its prey trapped on the knoll might try to escape.

A smart move, perhaps, but an incomplete strategy. Thomas took advantage of it immediately, letting loose a handful of Marchers who quickly and quietly removed those outriders from the battlefield. When those Marchers returned, using hand signals, Thomas had his fighters step their horses off the ridge and begin their approach at a walk. The swirling mist and damp ground helped to hide the noise, that and the ruckus that came from the Shade and its men as they prepared to launch their assault.

Halfway there, Thomas increased their pace. His Marchers drew their swords, a few preferring war axes. Aric unfurled the banner, allowing the wind to catch the large white expanse, the three peaks and the kestrel shining brightly as rays of the morning sun began to break through the fog.

Thomas and his Marchers pushed their horses into a gallop, their targets still unaware of what approached from behind them. Sensing the coming clash, their steeds strained to go faster, their hooves pounding into the wet turf.

One of the black-clad men finally turned as the thundering hooves of the charging horses overwhelmed the din of the black-clad men trying to force their mounts up the increasingly steep incline of the knoll. He shouted a warning, but it was too late.

Raising their blades into the air, the rising sun shining brightly off the steel, Thomas and his Marchers roared as one, "For the Highlands!"

The Marchers took the Shade and its men completely by surprise. The battle that had once been an assured victory for the dark creature instead became a desperate melee. The High-landers, only thirty fighters in all, drove deeply into the black-clad men, swords biting into flesh, axes cleaving helmets and arms. The speed and surprise of the attack gave the Marchers the initial advantage.

But as they drove into their opponents, their enemies' larger numbers slowed the charge. Under normal circumstances, such an assault likely would have broken the men. But the compul-sion placed on them by the Shadow Lord, and controlled by the Shade, forced them to stand their ground and fight, not allowing them to run as they normally would.

Thomas quickly realized the dilemma his Marchers faced, having expected it. Eventually the larger host they had attacked would turn the tide simply with its numbers. There was only one way to break them. Thomas knew that in order to kill a bloodsnake, you had to take the head. The same held true in this case. Thomas needed to kill the Shade.

Locating the Shadow Lord's minion at the fringe of the battle, Thomas began to fight his way through the opposing force, Coban and Oso taking positions at his sides to protect Thomas from attacks on his flanks. Several Marchers joined the wedge as he progressed through the black-clad men. Slowly, ever so slowly, Thomas and his protectors hacked their way toward the Shadow Lord's servant.

30

SHIFTING SKIRMISH

Gregory, Kael and Kaylie watched in amazement as the small force of Marchers crashed into the Shade and its men. Kael was laughing, unable to contain his pleasure at seeing the Highland banner unfurled once more.

"How could they have known?" asked Gregory, though Kaylie had a suspicion, remembering that brief touch of being watched the night before.

"They're Marchers, my lord," answered Kael. "The Highland Lord has a knack for appearing when he's needed."

"Mount up!" yelled Gregory, seeing how the attack had become a stalemate despite the obvious skill and ferocity of the Marchers. The Highland warriors held their own in the middle of a larger opposing force. But they had found advancing further through the ranks of the Shade's soldiers more difficult now that the initial shock of the assault had worn off.

The Fal Carrachian soldiers hurried to obey, running for their steeds. They quickly brought their horses in line with Gregory's a short distance from the ring wall. Kaylie followed with her own, staying a few feet behind her father. The battle at the base of the knoll consumed the King of Fal Carrach's focus, so she wanted to take advantage of the distraction before he told her to stay on top of the hillock.

"We ride for Fal Carrach!" shouted Gregory. "We ride to the Highland Lord!"

Touching his heels to his horse's flanks, the large animal easily jumped the hastily rebuilt stone barrier followed by the soldiers of Fal Carrach. Kael rode next to Gregory, seeking to protect the king, and Kaylie followed right behind, her own sword in hand.

She could see Thomas clearly now in the middle of the fray, fighting his way through the confused skirmish toward the Shade. She guessed his intentions, but she was worried. She had seen what the Shade had done to the soldier the day before, draining the spirit from him. She couldn't bear to think of the same thing happening to Thomas.

31

───────

A DEBT PAID

With Coban, Oso and several other Marchers taking positions to his right and left, Thomas fought his way through the black-clad soldiers, driving a wedge into the host that his accompanying Highlanders savagely expanded. Much to his surprise and pleasure, a space opened up in front of Thomas that gave him a clear path to the Shade, and he sought to benefit from it as he urged his horse forward. The Shade saw him coming and attacked instinctually, forcing its own horse into a charge, corrupted black steel poised above its head.

Sensing the approaching Shade, Thomas' horse leapt forward, reaching a gallop in seconds. Thomas raised his own blade to shoulder height, which would give him several options for defending against the Shade. As the two combatants met, Thomas parried the Shade's strike with a controlled, back-handed swing, silvery sparks clattering off the steel. Disengaging, Thomas and the Shade quickly turned their horses, preparing once more for the charge.

Taking hold of the Talent, Thomas infused the steel of his blade with the power of nature, knowing that it would help him in his duel with the dark creature. The steel blazed an almost blinding white as he once again charged at the Shade. This time, though, as the Shade raised his sword to swing down, Thomas ignored the attempted strike, sliding to the side of his saddle so that he was parallel to the ground that rushed by and swinging his sword at the Shade's mid-section, his glowing blade slicing through the dark creature's hip.

The Shade tried to turn its horse, but weakened by Thomas' strike, which almost took its entire leg off, the Shadow Lord's servant slipped off its saddle to the ground. The dark blood seeping from the wound stained the trampled grass a midnight black.

Thomas jumped down from his horse, approaching the Shade on foot. The dark creature raised its sword, trying to defend itself despite its grievous wound, but Thomas easily parried the blow. Thomas then raised his sword above his head and swung down in a vicious arc. The magic-infused blade sliced through the Shade's neck without any resistance, the dark creature's body slumping to the flattened grass as its head rolled several feet away.

At just that moment when steel bit into flesh, the feeling that had bothered Thomas that morning of a greater evil hidden within that of the Shade sent a shock of warning through him. He twisted around swiftly, sensing the danger behind him. A beast that resembled a Nightstalker, though lacking wings, stood poised to strike, its massive, midnight-black frame blocking the sun. The demon extended its claws as it sought to drive a scaled fist through Thomas' heart. Thomas tried to bring his sword up to block the blow, but he knew that quick as he was, he couldn't do it in time. The demon was faster than any dark creature Thomas had ever faced.

Right before the dark creature's scythed hand plunged into Thomas' unprotected chest, a sword point appeared in the beast's chest. Then again, and again, and a final time as the blade pierced the dark creature's heart. The demon roared in pain as it fell to its knees, its life seeping out through its back and chest onto the long grass. Not wanting to take any chances, Thomas swung his sword again, slicing cleanly through the dark creature's neck, its head tumbling to the ground to come to rest near that of the Shade.

"Thank you, Oso."

Thomas sought to control his breathing, the excitement of the last few minutes getting the better of him. Centering himself once more, he thought about the Dark Magic he had just confronted. Somehow the Shade's death had released this demon, which would explain why the evil of the Shade that Thomas felt the night before had differed from previous encounters. He would need to talk with Rya and Rynlin about this and what it could mean. The Shadow Lord was either growing more desperate, more powerful, or both.

"It's damn hard killing one of these things," said Oso, smiling sheepishly. He was never one for attention. "I was afraid I wouldn't be able to get my steel through this thing's armored back. But once done, it was easier to do a second time. And then a third and a fourth, of course."

"You know that debt you've been harping about since we first met?" asked Thomas.

"Yes."

Highlanders took their debts seriously, as it was a strict part of their culture. When one Highlander saved another's life, they commonly said, "A debt is owed," and that debt would remain in place until it was repaid. When Thomas had first met Oso, he had saved his life, and Oso had invoked the saying. At the time, Thomas, still living with his grandparents on the Isle of Mist and not having yet revealed his lineage to the High-landers, didn't understand fully the significance of the words. But now he did.

"A debt is paid."

Thomas raised his sword to his forehead then inclined his

head toward Oso. The large Highlander responded in turn. Kaylie broke the solemnity of the brief ceremony as she galloped up and jumped from her horse, sword in hand.

"Do you have any idea how dangerous that dark creature is?" demanded the Princess of Fal Carrach, striding up to Thomas as she pointed her blade at the decapitated Shade. She didn't seem to care about the Nightstalker, or whatever the other creature had been. "Any idea at all? Charging at that thing like you don't have a care in the world, and then that second beast appearing out of the mist? You could have been killed."

At first startled by Kaylie's verbal dressing down, which continued unabated as the seconds passed, Thomas stood there in stunned silence as the petite princess questioned his ability to make decisions. To care for himself. Essentially, to function on his own without the help of a nursemaid. Thomas looked to his friend for help, but Oso was trying his best not to laugh. Searching for some way to extricate himself, Thomas was pleased to see that the battle was over.

Gregory had led his men in a charge down the hillock, catching their attackers unaware. The shock of that assault, and the death of the Shade, quickly turned an evenly matched skirmish into a rout as the Marchers and soldiers of Fal Carrach eliminated their foes and met in the middle of the enemy force. Many of the black-clad men had dropped their swords and sprinted for the perceived safety of the river once they had been released from their compulsion when Thomas killed the Shade. But escape was a futile hope. Neither the Fal Carrachians nor the Marchers were in the mood for mercy.

Not knowing what else to do in the face of Kaylie's onslaught, Thomas smiled broadly. "A pleasure to see you this morning, Princess." He bent down to wipe the black blood of the Shade and the other dark creature off his blade in the dew of the grass, hoping that the tactic of agreeing with Kaylie, something that he had done when a target of his grandmother's wrath, might defuse her anger. "You're right. I should have been more careful."

"Well met, Thomas," said Gregory, riding up on his horse. Her father's appearance prevented Kaylie from continuing her tirade. Despite Thomas' apparent remorse, she still had several choice comments that she wanted to share with him. "My thanks for your assistance. Without you and your Marchers, I doubt we would have left that hillock alive."

"We were happy to help, King Gregory."

"My Lord Kestrel, you seem to have a habit of surprising people," said Kael as he rode up as well, inclining his head as a sign of respect.

"I've always felt it's better to keep people on their toes. I wouldn't want them to think I was predictable."

"I don't think anyone would describe you as predictable," muttered Kaylie, staring daggers at Thomas.

"As I said, it's a pleasure to see you, too, Princess," said Thomas smoothly, though his eyes suggested something quite different.

32

A REVELATION

After caring for their wounded and thrilled that none of their fighters was seriously injured, Gregory and Thomas decided to ride together toward the east, combining their forces for protection. Although they sent out scouts, none of the Marchers worried, knowing that Thomas would keep a sharp eye for leagues around through his use of the Talent, not realizing that the Princess of Fal Carrach could and would do the same.

For Gregory, it was an opportunity to catch up with Coban, having first met the Highland Swordmaster when he visited Talyn at the Crag. And for Kael it was a chance to spend time with Oso, Aric and the other Marchers, learning more about what was happening in his homeland.

With their numbers increased, Thomas thought that he might have an opportunity for some peace and quiet on this final leg of their journey. However, that wish almost immediately disappeared as Kaylie nudged her horse next to his as they followed the Corazon River toward the Inland Sea.

"Good afternoon, Princess."

"You know, you don't have to keep calling me that. You didn't the last time we spoke in Eamhain Mhacha."

"True, but at the Council you weren't berating me for killing a Shade."

Kaylie blushed, the color seeping into her face, still a little embarrassed by her reaction to Thomas charging at the dark creature. She feared that she had come across as an overbearing lover.

"I'm sorry about that," sighed Kaylie. "I've seen what a dark creature like that is capable of and didn't think it wise for one man to attack it alone."

"Apology accepted."

Thomas clearly wasn't in a talkative mood, but Kaylie decided to ignore that. This was an excellent time to dig a bit more deeply into what she wanted to know.

"I've heard stories of what happened in the Highlands. What you did to free your people."

"I wouldn't believe all the stories."

"In every story there's likely a kernel of truth," she replied.

"True."

They rode on for a time in silence, Kaylie growing more frustrated by Thomas' one-word answers to her questions and her inability to engage him in conversation. She glanced at him and saw that his eyes were closed, though he was perfectly erect in the saddle. She understood immediately what he was doing.

"Did you see anything?"

Thomas slowly released the Talent, opening his eyes and blinking in the bright sunlight.

"Nothing to worry about. A few traders on the river and some farmers traveling on the roads. There's nothing else around us for the moment."

He looked over at Kaylie, taking in everything about her. Every time he saw her, she was more beautiful than he had remembered. Yet the wall between them remained, and he knew it was a barrier of his own construction. Though he had forgiven her, realizing that what had happened to him was likely not her fault, he was still wary. His ability and desire to trust people had not improved with time. Moreover, with the challenges he faced in the months ahead in addition to his ultimate responsibility, he was afraid to get too close to anyone.

"You've been practicing," said Thomas. "You're stronger than before."

"How do you know?"

"I can feel the Talent in you."

Thomas' comment secretly pleased Kaylie. She had sensed an energy in Thomas, a strong power that surpassed her own, and now she had confirmed her suspicions. The fact that she, too, could sense the Talent in him made her even happier. And she was a bit awed. His apparent strength in the Talent stunned her.

"The additional lessons have helped quite a bit."

"I have no doubt about that," replied Thomas. "Your instructor is excellent though quite exacting and precise."

"Last time we spoke, you never really answered my question. How do you know Rya? How did she become your instructor in the Talent?"

Thomas smiled. At first, he thought about how to respond, then decided that there was really no reason to hold anything back.

"Rya Keldragan is my grandmother. She and my grandfather raised me."

The revelation shocked Kaylie. All she could do was stare at Thomas as she processed this unexpected knowledge. First, Keldragan was an ancient name, one that had circulated through the stories and legends of the Kingdoms for millennia. A Keldragan had been involved in almost every major event in the Kingdoms as far back as the histories were written.

Second, Keldragan was synonymous with the Sylvan Warriors, the family helping to found that warrior society. Thinking about it more deeply, she realized that based on his display while fighting the Shade, he, too, likely was a member of that legendary group.

Third, Thomas had the blood of the Kestrels and the Keldragans in his veins. Rodric was attempting to assert his authority as High King, returning the Kingdoms to the time of Ollav Fola and a single Kingdom. Yet the young man riding his horse next to hers had the strongest claim of any living monarch if he chose to take that path and seek to unite the Kingdoms. It was almost too much for her to think about at once. Needing time to take in the conclusions she had just reached, Kaylie decided to push most of that to the side for now.

"Rya is your grandmother?"

Thomas nodded, amused that Kaylie was somewhat surprised by this new information.

"She's a wonderful teacher." Kaylie took a few moments to center herself again, her mind still a jumble of disparate thoughts. "I know I still have so much to learn, but I've enjoyed every second I've spent with her."

She chose not to share that having grown up without a mother, it was the first time that she had felt such a strong female presence in her life. The guiding hand of a confident, accomplished woman had given Kaylie something she desperately desired and needed, though she didn't realize what it would mean to her at the time.

"She is," agreed Thomas.

He gathered there was more to the relationship between his grandmother and Kaylie than she wanted to reveal, and he chose not to pry.

"So, what was it like growing up with Rya?" asked Kaylie.

Thomas smiled, thinking of how best to answer that question. He gave himself a moment to gather his myriad possible responses as he remembered all that had happened in just the last decade.

"It was fascinating, challenging, fun, frustrating ..." Thomas' voice trailed off as his memories threatened to overwhelm him.

"I can see how that could be the case. My father expects me to act like a queen someday. But Rya? There's a power and presence to her, beyond that of the Talent, an inner strength that at times can be frightening, but also quite useful. I learned just as much from her with respect to the Talent as I did in terms of what will be expected of me when it's time to rule Fal Carrach."

"Yes, she's good at that," replied Thomas. "She's always trying to teach you something, even if you don't realize it at the time."

"So where did you grow up?"

"The Isle of Mist."

"I thought that island was haunted."

Kaylie knew the tales. She had spent a good bit of time wandering the docks of Ballinasloe with her friends, exploring the markets that sold strange and exotic goods from every corner of the known world. The sailors spoke of that forsaken island often, about how those who were unfortunate or stupid enough to land there usually didn't return, or if they did, they were never the same.

"It is," said Thomas, slightly amused at how his grandfather's efforts to spread rumors and innuendo about their island home had been so effective. "But just by my grandparents. All the stories are just that. If a ship lands on the island, my grandfather Rynlin takes particular pleasure in making the stories come to life."

"It must have been quite a childhood."

"It was. They found me during my escape from the Crag. I had made it to the eastern shore near one of the branches of the Southern River. I was carrying Beluil, having found him along the way."

Kaylie laughed, finding it hard to believe that the massive wolf, all black but for a strip of white across his eyes, had once been small enough for Thomas to hold in his hands.

"I had this massive sword dragging in the dirt behind me." Thomas gestured to the blade that was now strapped across his back. "And I walked into a clearing with Rynlin and Rya sitting at the far end, a small fire between us. My grandfather was the scariest person I had ever seen, even more frightening than the reivers pursuing me. Tall, thin, imposing. Piercing blue eyes that could see the truth no matter how hard you tried to hide it. I would have bolted, but I was too tired."

"How did they know where to find you?"

"Because of this."

Thomas reached beneath his shirt and showed Kaylie his silver necklace, the horn of a unicorn spiraling to a sharp point carved into the gleaming metal. A necklace that matched Rya's and was a marker of a Sylvan Warrior, just as she had surmised.

"It had belonged to my mother. My grandfather Talyn gave it to me before he helped me escape the Crag, and Rynlin and Rya tracked me with it."

"So, it's a beacon?"

"In part, yes. When I wear the necklace, they know where I am."

"They can keep track of you," teased Kaylie.

"Well, you have met my grandmother," answered Thomas. "When I was younger, yes, it was a bit irritating. Although when I reached a certain age Rynlin and Rya gave me a good bit of freedom, allowing me to wander the island or the eastern coast of the Highlands with Beluil. But you probably already guessed that since that's how we met that first time in the Burren."

Kaylie did remember that incredible day. In fact, she would

never forget it. She had wanted an adventure and had gotten more than she had bargained for. Sneaking off to a hidden pool in the Burren, against her father's wishes, had almost cost her and her friends their lives. If not for Thomas and Beluil, who had appeared seemingly out of nowhere to kill two Ogren, she and her friends would be dead. Nevertheless, though the excursion had been a mistake, she had learned several valuable lessons that day.

"Now with everything that's going on, it doesn't bother me. It's good to know that they're there if I need them."

"I imagine it is. I get the sense that Rya has a bit of a temper."

"That would be an understatement," laughed Thomas. "And you, Kaylie Carlomin. What was it like growing up in the Rock of Ballinasloe?"

Kaylie smiled, her face warming and not because of the afternoon sun. She enjoyed how her name rolled off of Thomas' tongue.

"Confining."

"How so?"

"You're the Lord of the Highlands, yet you can go and do whatever you want. I, on the other hand, have had to act like a princess ever since I was a child. You cannot imagine how many boring dances, balls or social affairs I have had to attend, simply to play the part of my father's daughter. My mother died when I was young, so I understand my father being somewhat overprotective. It just became tiresome after awhile."

"It sounds like you didn't have any fun at all."

"I did," Kaylie corrected quickly, realizing that she had sounded a bit ungrateful. With a life of privilege, her plight was certainly better than most. "My father spent as much time with me as he could. And then after meeting you that second time with the Fearhounds, that's when he allowed me to begin learning the blade. I guess he realized that trying to use a dagger against a Fearhound was a losing proposition."

"That it is," confirmed Thomas. "I'm glad I could help. So how good are you with that blade?"

"There's only one way to find out," she replied with a grin, the challenge clear in her voice.

33

FRUSTRATING EXPERIENCE

"This will be a fair contest," said Kael. "Just as we would have if we were on the training ground at the Rock. Three points for the win."

The two combatants nodded their understanding, brandishing the wooden swords Fal Carrach's Swordmaster had provided to them to prevent any major injuries.

The rest of the day had gone by uneventfully. Using the Talent, Thomas knew that there was no one around them for several leagues other than traders, farmers or villagers, something that the scouts confirmed. All seemed normal with no touch of evil on the land. That, for some, made for a slow journey. When word spread among the Highlanders and soldiers of Fal Carrach that there would be a friendly duel, they finally had something to get excited about that would break the monotony of their travel.

After establishing their camp for the night, the patrols tasked, and dinner started, several of the soldiers helped Kael clear a space near where they tethered the horses so that Thomas and Kaylie could engage in their combat. The Princess of Fal Carrach had been insistent about going forward with the challenge, wanting to test her rapidly improving skills against Thomas. Gregory had talked with Kael about the wisdom of allowing the session. Kael had found some spare practice swords in his travel bag – what was a Swordmaster if not prepared – and he had convinced Gregory to allow the duel to proceed under his strict training rules. Whatever the result, though he was fairly certain that he knew what the outcome would be, it would be a valuable lesson for Kaylie.

"Remember, no strikes to the head. And what I say goes. If one of you isn't listening when I tell you to withdraw, I'll join the combat myself and whip the both of you."

The soldiers who had stationed themselves around the hastily created training circle laughed at that, as did Kaylie. Thomas stood there quietly, legs slightly apart, wooden sword pointed to the ground and held comfortably in his hand. Kael concluded that Thomas had decided that he could likely beat Fal Carrach's Swordmaster in a duel, and the Swordmaster admitted much the same to himself, though he would never confess that to anyone.

"Good luck to both of you then. Begin!"

Kaylie started circling Thomas slowly, wooden blade held at the ready. She had seen Thomas fight several times before, so as soon as she had issued her challenge, she had begun to worry about not thinking things through, her nerves coming to the forefront. She hoped that she wouldn't regret her impetuousness. But then the butterflies that flitted around in her stomach burned away as her irritation started to grow. Thomas just stood there, motionless, not moving a muscle, not even bothering to track her movements with his eyes. It was close to insulting. Wait. He had closed his eyes! Her irritation quickly turned to anger. She had used her anger to her advantage when training against the boys she had grown up with in the Rock at Ballinasloe, besting Maddan, Rohn and the others. She had even beaten Eric, who was twice her size and as strong as an ox. She sought to use her pique now as she had done then.

Screaming in fury, she lunged toward Thomas' back, sword arm outstretched. She immediately found herself on her hands and knees, wooden sword knocked from her hand, murmurs from the soldiers around them grating on her nerves.

"Point to the Lord of the Highlands," said Kael, keeping a straight face and appreciating how Thomas had used Kaylie's ire against her.

Thomas had deftly dodged Kaylie's thrust, appearing to have eyes in the back of his head. With her overextended, he had flicked the blade from her grasp with an upward swipe. As she stumbled past and fell to the grass, he had lightly touched his wooden blade to the small of her back.

Kaylie pushed herself to her feet, her face red with embarrassment as she picked up her practice sword. He had toyed with her! Her anger increased even more when she examined her opponent once again. His posture hadn't changed. Thomas simply stood there, expressionless. She lunged forward again, but Thomas easily deflected the blow, having turned himself sideways, sword at the ready.

He stayed on his toes, maintaining his balance, as he defended against several of Kaylie's attacks. She started to recognize a pattern as the seconds dragged into minutes. Every time she lunged or swung her wooden blade in attack, as soon as Thomas defended against the blow, he stepped closer to her, pushing her back. For every step forward, she took two steps back. Was he trying to get inside her guard?

"Point to the Lord of the Highlands. Return to your places."

Kaylie stared at Kael in bewilderment, not understanding his decision. Kael nodded to her feet. Looking down she realized Thomas had forced her out of the circle. Shaking her head in frustration, she stalked back to her place, blade at the ready.

"Begin!" yelled the Swordmaster.

This time Kaylie waited, standing her ground, studying Thomas. She thought she caught a quick glimmer of a smile from him, but she couldn't pursue the thought as she raised her blade just in time to deflect the blow that Thomas had directed at her ribs. The speed of his strike amazed her. But she didn't have time to dwell on it. She backpedaled, getting her blade up just in time again as he swung toward her chest, then again as he came in low at her knees.

Trying to keep track of his attacks became mind-numbing. She relied on her instincts. Not having the time to think, she willed her body to move in response to his unceasing lunges, swings and slashes. His blade was a blur. Half-a-dozen times she barely got her wooden blade where it needed to be in order to meet his attack. And then it was over. Thomas' blade slipped past her defenses, grazing her thighs.

"Point to the Highland Lord. Winner."

The men surrounding Kaylie and Thomas let out a whoop, cheering raucously. The last few minutes had been mesmerizing, many gaining a new respect for the Princess of Fal Carrach as she defended against an attacker faster than any of them had ever seen. Yet Kaylie didn't perceive it that way, her rising fury clouding her perspective.

"A good contest, Princess." Thomas extended his hand, a smile on his face. "Well fought."

Kaylie took his outstretched hand. Then she thrust the wooden sword point first into the ground and stalked away, muttering a string of curses under her breath.

34

UNEXPECTED LESSON

For the next several days, Kaylie kept to herself, avoiding Thomas whenever possible. Thomas was obviously better with a sword, but she couldn't help but wonder if Thomas had wanted to embarrass her, seeking some type of revenge, her mind once more stuck on what had occurred in Tinnakilly. Though the soldiers who had witnessed the contest nodded to her with a newfound respect, admitting to themselves that they could not have done as well as she did during the combat, she misinterpreted their looks and words of admiration. Her perspective didn't change until Oso rode next to her as a cold breeze pushed at their backs and the dark smudge of the Highland peaks became visible far off on the horizon.

"You shouldn't be angry, Princess," the large Marcher said, his gaze always moving in an arc as they rode through the last stretch of grassland before reaching the shore of the Inland Sea.

"I'm not angry," replied Kaylie testily, still not wanting to talk and preferring the irritation that continued to course through her.

"Yes, you are. Anara, a Highland girl I met in the Black

Hole, gets like this sometimes. I usually avoid her until she calms down, especially when I'm the apparent cause of her annoyance. But I've never seen anyone be able to hold on to their anger for so long as you. It puts Anara to shame."

Kaylie took a deep breath, finding it hard not to smile at Oso's insinuation. Though physically imposing and a deadly fighter, she had come to learn that Oso had a gentle heart. He wouldn't have chosen to ride with her unless he had cause to do so. Rather than continue to stew, she instead decided to engage with the big Highlander. She didn't want to be perceived as someone skilled at holding a grudge.

"What's the Black Hole?"

"It was Killeran's fort in the Highlands. He used it as a base for his reivers. The Highlanders he enslaved as miners were forced to stay there in metal cages when not working. He kept his warlocks there as well when they weren't sent off in search of more miners."

"You were enslaved?"

Kaylie was shocked, never having heard of what really had happened in the Highlands while Killeran served as regent.

"For a short time only. Thomas saw to that." Oso smiled at the memory. "Killeran and his warlocks attacked my village. I was charged with getting the women and children to safety, and I did for the most part. But when the reivers and warlocks caught up to us, they captured me and a dozen others who couldn't make it to the higher passes in time."

"That's how you first met Thomas?"

"Yes. He came for us that first night after we were taken. Killeran couldn't reach the Black Hole that evening, so he was forced to make camp. Thomas freed me and the other High- landers, but we were found out. We made sure the other High- landers escaped, but Thomas and I didn't. Thomas could have. He could have killed Killeran and gotten away as he had his blade to that fool's neck, but if he did one of Killeran's sergeants would have cut my throat. Thomas surrendered instead, trading his freedom for my life."

Kaylie took a moment to think about that. She had thought initially that Thomas had approached their duel in a mean-spirited way, but perhaps that wasn't the case. If Thomas was angry or upset, you knew it. He didn't appear to have the patience for the schemes and machinations that were a common part of a Kingdom's court. He was who he was and didn't feel the need to hide anything, which was very unlike most of the people who inhabited the world Kaylie was used to.

"You said it was Killeran's fort. It's not there anymore?"

"No," laughed Oso. "Killeran brought us there, but we escaped within a few months. When we did, we freed the enslaved Highlanders and Thomas burned the Black Hole to the ground. You might have noticed Killeran's animosity during the Council of the Kingdoms?"

"It was hard to miss."

"It was justified," smirked Oso. "Thomas seems to have made it his mission in life to make that bastard's very existence as miserable as possible."

They lapsed into a comfortable silence as they passed through the last of the flowing grasslands. Kaylie thought on what the big Marcher had said, Oso apparently content to ride by her side, a comforting and calming presence.

"Can I speak plainly, Princess?"

Kaylie nodded her assent, a touch of worry settling in her stomach.

"Thomas is different. That's probably the easiest way to put it. No offense, but your anger and pouting ..."

"I'm not pouting," Kaylie declared indignantly in her own defense.

Oso just stared at her, maintaining his silence and waiting her out, his experience with Anara coming in handy. Kaylie relented.

"Fine. You may be right, if only a little bit."

"As I was saying, Thomas was raised by his grandparents. He's always been an independent type, always surviving because of his wits. As a result, he is very direct. He doesn't like games. He goes right to the heart of the matter. I can tell he likes you, Princess, but he probably doesn't understand what's going on right now. His grandparents taught him many things. For example, the fastest way to kill a Shade or an Ogren, as you've seen. But he has very little experience with women or with all the doings of the court."

Oso's words deflated her entirely. She had been acting poorly. She had known it from the start but gotten comfortable in her vexation and melancholy. Kaylie closed her eyes for a moment, now irritated with herself. She had been acting as would Corelia, daughter of the High King, playing a specific role in order to gain an advantage. That thought embarrassed her more than she cared to admit.

"You seem to think that he toyed with you in the training circle. He didn't. I've sparred with him many times, and he's defeated me just as fast if not faster. Do you know how he learned to use a blade? A bow? Pretty much any weapon you can employ on the battlefield?"

"No, he hasn't told me much since we began riding together."

"That stands to reason. After Tinnakilly ..."

"You know about Tinnakilly?" asked Kaylie, mortified. "I swear, I didn't have any idea what ..."

"Please, Princess. You don't need to try to convince me of anything. Yes, Thomas told me, at least roughly, what happened. He doesn't blame you. But he's cautious."

"I know. It's like he's built a wall around himself, and no matter what I try I can't get past his defenses."

"Why would you expect it to be easy? If you haven't noticed, Thomas can be incredibly stubborn. All you can do is keep trying. I'm not suggesting that you're guaranteed success for your efforts. It's hard to gain his trust. But if it matters to you, keep trying. Put your own obstinance to work for you rather than against you."

"Thank you, Oso. I'll remember that." She felt better for the first time in days, her anger flowing out of her and leaving her with a lighter spirit. The big Highlander was right. "You never finished explaining how Thomas became so skilled in weapons."

"His grandfather had him fight ghosts."

"What?"

"You know of Thomas' ability in the Talent?"

"Yes," answered Kaylie, keeping her own increasing skill in the natural magic of the world to herself.

"Well, his grandfather, Rynlin, and his grandmother, Rya, have the same ability. Thomas told me that Rynlin -- and just let me say that without even speaking a word Thomas' grandfather can be scarier than the Shadow Lord himself at times -- used the Talent to awaken the spirits of great warriors, such as Antonin, First Spear of the Carthanians, or Fergus Steelheart, Captain of the Golden Blades. Thomas sparred with them daily, receiving the finest weapons training in all the Kingdoms."

"You can't be serious."

How could this even be possible? Kaylie knew that Antonin and Fergus were heroes from another age, from even before the time of Ollav Fola, the first High King of the Kingdoms, if the stories were to be believed.

"I'm completely serious. Rynlin even showed me how he did it once, because I didn't believe him. That was a mistake."

"Frightening?"

"In part, but rather more enlightening."

Oso would never forget the beating he received from the spirit of Alicia, Hunter of the North. Alicia had barely come up to his chest, and her thin frame belied her strength and skill. He had fought her in the training circle using a quarterstaff. By the time it was over, and it didn't last long thankfully, his body was covered in angry, blue bruises and welts, Alicia demonstrating an ability with that weapon that was almost ethereal. It was an embarrassment he would never live down since Thomas and several Marchers had the opportunity to watch. Of course, after Alicia had defeated him, and much to Oso's annoyance, none of the other Marchers had deigned to step into the training circle and challenge the famed hunter themselves. Cowards every one of them. Or maybe they had been smart enough to know they didn't stand a chance either.

"The point I'm trying to make is that Thomas has received training that no one else has. You've seen him. He fights like a demon. When you sparred with him, the first two rounds he used your anger against you. In the last round, once you controlled your temper and allowed your instinct to take over, you did well, probably better than any of us could have. You believed that the Marchers and soldiers who watched thought you failed, right?"

Kaylie nodded reluctantly.

"You're mistaken. That's not the case. They were impressed. Very impressed. Don't let your anger cloud reality."

Kaylie sat on her horse somewhat chagrined, the cold wind buffeting her, pushing her to the east. She had misinterpreted the entire event, and as a result had made the lives of everyone around her miserable for days.

"Oso, thank you for explaining this all to me. I do appreciate it."

"You're welcome, Princess." Oso gave his horse a slight nudge in the ribs so he could pick up his pace. "Just remember, if you believe Thomas is worth it, it's worth the effort."

35

TEASING CONVERSATION

Kaylie spent much of the rest of the day thinking about what Oso had said. That night, she found Thomas sitting on a knoll that allowed him to look beyond their small camp and catch the first glimpse of the blue water of the Inland Sea just a league off to the east.

"Good evening, Kaylie."

The Princess of Fal Carrach stopped in her tracks, halfway up the hillock. Thomas hadn't bothered to turn around, still gazing at the shimmering water, the last rays of the sun imbuing it with an orange hue.

"How did you know it was me?"

"Where's the fun if I give away all of my secrets?"

"You know, Thomas, you can be extremely difficult at times."

Kaylie reached the top of the tor, spreading out her riding dress as she sat down next to Thomas on the thick grass.

"So I've been told. Many, many times."

"I wanted to apologize. I've acted badly since our contest." Kaylie shifted in her seat, somewhat nervous. "I'm sorry for that."

"There's no need. But thank you." Thomas finally turned toward her, smiling. "You did quite well, you know. I've faced few opponents faster than you. Even that Shade a few days ago."

"Oso explained it to me earlier today. He told me how you received your training."

"Yes, it was a unique approach. But then again, my grandfather is a unique individual."

Thomas turned back toward the Inland Sea, watching as the last rays of light touched the water before the sun dipped below the western horizon.

"Why so fascinated with the water?" asked Kaylie.

"It reminds me of growing up on the Isle of Mist. I haven't been back for a while. I used to spend a lot of time on the beach, looking across to the Highlands, wondering when I should go back."

"Why did you go back?"

"You must do what you must do," replied Thomas cryptically.

"I'm sorry?"

"It's something Rya says quite often. 'You must do what you must do.' It stuck with me. Before I escaped the Crag, my grandfather Talyn gave me that charge. To reclaim the Highlands. But Rya and Rynlin convinced me to wait, knowing that if I tried too soon, I'd die. When I joined the Sylvan Warriors, I was finally able to travel the Highlands on my own. That's when I met Oso and confirmed with my own eyes what was happening there."

"Was it difficult, knowing you had this responsibility following you around?"

Kaylie could relate. She felt the burden of one day ruling Fal Carrach, oftentimes dreaming about what it would be like if she had complete control of her life rather than having a large portion of it already decided.

"Extremely. To be honest, it wasn't until I returned to the Highlands and saw for myself the depredations of the reivers that I knew I had to do as my grandfather had required. Growing up in the Crag, the Highlanders treated me as an outsider. Most people feared my mother because of her skill in the Talent. And when I started to exhibit some of the same abilities, well, you can imagine what happened."

"It must have been lonely."

"Sometimes. Talyn tried to help when he could, but he was busy. He did allow me to wander the forest surrounding the Crag, which was a welcome break." Thomas turned toward Kaylie, his gaze knowing. "But I'm sure you've experienced something similar, haven't you?"

"Yes." Kaylie grew up surrounded by children her own age, but there were times when even with people always around her, she felt isolated and alone. "I always wondered if my friends were my friends because of who I was or who I would become."

"A valid concern," said Thomas. "Particularly after meeting some of your friends in the Burren."

"Yes, that was an eye-opening experience."

Kaylie laughed, remembering how foolish she had been to think that picnicking in the Burren was a good idea. The two Ogren that appeared had dissuaded her of that notion immediately. If not for Thomas and Beluil, she and her friends likely wouldn't have survived.

"I learned a lot that day, not only about myself, but it also confirmed that some of my so-called friends, such as Maddan Dinnegan, were all talk and no action."

"Better to learn that sooner rather than later."

"Agreed."

Norin Dinnegan, Maddan's father, was the richest man in Fal Carrach and perhaps all the Kingdoms, or at least had been. Though both Norin and Maddan had insinuated many times that Maddan was the perfect match for Kaylie, her father always hesitated, putting them off every time they attempted to pursue the matter. Kaylie never understood why until that day in the Burren. Her father had seen something that she had missed, beyond Maddan's obvious immaturity and conceit. And that failing was made plain when Kaylie stumbled onto Norin Dinnegan's plot to kill her father and claim Fal Carrach for his own.

She and Thomas settled into a comfortable silence, the grey dusk turning to dark. For a time, she looked up at the clear evening sky, watching as the night's stars slowly took the stage. Kaylie noticed that Thomas had closed his eyes, his attention elsewhere.

"What do you see?" she asked.

"Why don't you tell me what you see, Princess."

She recalled the time in the glade, before Thomas had been betrayed at Tinnakilly, when he had taught her how to use the Talent for the first time. She wanted to work with him again, though felt that it would presume too much. But now he was giving her that opportunity.

Remembering her lessons with Rya, Kaylie reached for the Talent, reveling in the energy that filled her. Gradually she extended her senses to the north, stretching her perception for leagues, imagining she was a hawk winging her way to the Clanwar Desert, then swinging to the west into Kenmare before turning south for Eamhain Mhacha. Finally, she looped back to the east before settling on the Inland Sea.

"Nothing to worry about," she said, releasing the Talent, a huge smile on her face. "But there was something in the Inland Sea, close to the western shore. Several large fins cutting through the water."

"Great Sharks," muttered Thomas, not surprised.

The Shadow Lord was flexing his muscles, Thomas thought. The massive beasts normally didn't make their way through Stormy Bay then up into the Inland Sea, preferring the waters along the coast. Or perhaps the Great Sharks being there had a more direct cause. Oso had killed the dark creature that resembled a Nightstalker, one that Thomas had never come across before nor wanted to see again, just a few days before, so the Shadow Lord probably had sensed Thomas' location when his friend had killed that demon. Perhaps his nemesis hoped that Thomas would take a boat across the Inland Sea and his Great Sharks could attack during the journey.

"Really!" said Kaylie with some excitement. "Sailors coming into Ballinasloe tell tales of Great Sharks. Many said that they actually attacked the ships. But the Great Sharks rarely came close to the port."

"They prefer deeper water," said Thomas.

Often fifty feet or more in length, the terrifyingly large sharks could easily swallow a man whole or destroy a small skiff. Though the beasts would track the larger merchant vessels knowing that these ships were too large to be prey, from time to time they would attack smaller craft with some success.

"You've seen them before?"

"Many times. I spent a lot of time on the beach at the Isle of Mist, at a place aptly named Shark Cove. You could swim out about a hundred feet, then the sea floor dropped precipitously. You didn't go beyond that point, because that's where the Great Sharks waited. At certain times during the year, sea lions would use the beach to raise their pups. Most of the time, the sea lions escaped the Great Sharks, but sometimes not. The Great Sharks stayed below the sea lions, then would swim up toward them, often breaching the water's surface with a sea lion between its jaws. It was a tremendous, scary sight."

"I can only imagine," said Kaylie. "Seems like a lesson to be learned there."

"You're right about that," replied Thomas with a straight face. "Don't go swimming when Great Sharks are about."

Kaylie looked at him for a moment, then broke out into a laugh. Thomas laughed as well, his green eyes sparkling brightly with mischief.

"Are you teasing me, Thomas?"

"Yes, Kaylie. I am."

Kaylie blushed slightly, glad that the darkness hid her reaction from Thomas. They sat there quietly for some time, watching as more stars appeared in the sky, simply enjoying the quiet of the early evening and each other's company.

36

A SYMBOL

The next morning, the Highlanders and Fal Carrachians made their final preparations to go their own ways, the Marchers to the north around the Inland Sea and then into the western Highlands, the Fal Carrachians to the south to make for Ballinasloe. The hustle and bustle of breaking camp consumed much of the early morning, but as the soldiers for both sides mounted their horses, Thomas pulled Gregory aside, drawing their horses away from the others.

"I wanted to give you this. To serve as a symbol of peace between Fal Carrach and the Highlands, which has lasted for almost one thousand years. And also because you and Kaylie need a little help from time to time."

With a grin, Thomas handed Gregory an intricately carved horn, which spiraled much like a unicorn's horn.

Gregory chuckled at the quip, somewhat vexed but acknowledging the truth in Thomas' words. Looking more closely at the horn, the King of Fal Carrach ran his hands along the carved metal, then his breath caught in his throat. He drew his horse closer to Thomas' steed.

"This is a Horn of the Sylvana," Gregory exclaimed.

"Yes, it is."

"The only way you could have gotten one of these is ..." Gregory studied Thomas with a keen eye, noting the young man's serious expression and the complete lack of guile. "But that would mean you're one of the ..."

Gregory struggled to finish his thoughts, so Thomas pulled his necklace from beneath his shirt so that the King of Fal Carrach could see the silver amulet twisted in the shape of a unicorn's horn.

"They were only a myth for so long, and then you come along, and everything changes," said Gregory.

"The Lost Kestrel was a myth as well, Gregory, yet a myth stands before you in flesh and blood. Do with the horn what you will. But know that a ruler of one of the Kingdoms has not had in his or her possession a Horn of the Sylvana since the High King tried to make the Sylvan Warriors his own centuries ago."

"Thomas, why?" asked Gregory. "I appreciate this gift, and I understand its value. But why now?"

Before the traitorous High King destroyed the Sylvana's faith in the Kingdoms, every ruler in the Kingdoms had a Horn of the Sylvana to call for aid when attacked by the dark creatures of the Shadow Lord. Gregory knew the lore. If you blew the Horn three times, the Sylvana would come. With an unmatched vengeance and wrath.

Through the ages, many had sworn that they could put words to the three blasts from the Horn, for the Sylvan Warriors always answered with three blasts of their own before appearing as if out of nowhere, swords drawn, spears and battle axes poised, lightning bolts and fire clearing a path: *We hear. We come. We conquer.*

"Times are changing," replied Thomas. "You can see it as well as I can. Dark creatures travel unimpeded across the Northern Steppes and plague the Highlands, some trickling into other Kingdoms. We spend more time and effort now killing Shades and Ogren than we do the remnants of Killeran's Army of the Black Sword. Look out on the Inland Sea as the fins of the Great Sharks cut through the waves. When was the last time that happened?"

Gregory couldn't recall, but he knew the stories. And the chill in the air, carried on the breeze with ever greater frequency, as if a bitter cold were about to settle across the land, reminded him of the stories that had been passed down to him by his forebearers, of a time when the survival of the Kingdoms hung in the balance.

"If you are faced with a dire need, we will be there," said Thomas. "Fal Carrach is bound once again not only to the Highlands, but also to the Sylvana."

Thomas smiled, shook Gregory's hand, then turned his horse to the north. Giving Kaylie a quick wave, his Marchers followed after, intent on reaching the lower Highlands as soon as possible.

Gregory studied the Horn in his possession, marveling at the intricacy of its workmanship. Surprises. That boy was full of surprises. He placed the Horn in his saddlebag before urging his horse to the front of the column as he and his men began the final part of their journey back to Fal Carrach. Thomas was right. The world was changing, and not for the better. He feared that he would have cause to use the Horn sooner rather than later.

37

UNWANTED REMINDER

High King Rodric Tessaril, soon to be ruler of all the Kingdoms, or so he dreamed despite the unexpected and unwanted happenings at the Council of the Kingdoms, sat on his throne staring off into space. The torches flickered in response to a cold wind that forced its way into the room through an open window, setting the shadows in the large chamber dancing. Well past midnight, Rodric couldn't sleep again. Several months had passed since Thomas Kestrel had been confirmed as Lord of the Highlands in this very room, and every time he thought about it, Rodric got a headache and his insides twisted into knots. Hence his decision to alight on his symbol of power and brood, as he'd done many of the nights since that terrible day.

"You don't have time to sit and think, if you even have the capacity to think. Your master's plans are in disarray. He has commanded that you correct the mistakes that have been made."

The whispered hiss jolted Rodric from his macabre musings. He placed his hands on the armrests of the throne, ready to push off and bolt for the hidden door behind him, until he saw the shadow in front of him coalesce into a man, dressed all in black, his sharp-featured face nothing but angles. Lord Chertney, who had a particular knack for appearing unannounced.

"All the preparations are completed," answered Rodric. "We move by the end of the week."

"I hope so, Rodric, for your sake," said Chertney. His master had said that the High King's usefulness was coming to an end. Remembering the pain the Shadow Lord had inflicted upon him for his own recent failure, Chertney could only imagine what that might mean for the High King if the Shadow Lord did, indeed, withdraw his support. "Is it wise to trust in Killeran to accomplish the goal we've set for him? He's yet to achieve any of his objectives."

"It should be a simple matter," replied Rodric wearily. "It's his own Kingdom after all. What could he possibly do to harm our plans?"

"You tell me, Rodric, king of only Armagh. If you and Killeran had succeeded in implementing our master's original plan, you'd have the Highlands by now. In fact, you would have had the Highlands ten years ago."

Rodric's face turned a bright red at the slight, but he controlled his temper. Previously, he had thought that he and Chertney were equals. He now realized that he had been mistaken, maintaining a foolish and arrogant assumption. The gifts their master had given to Chertney not only scared him, but also filled him with a jealousy that he found difficult to control.

"Killeran will do as he's told," said Rodric, hoping that he spoke the truth.

"That better prove to be the case." Chertney chuckled, the sound more like steel scraping against stone. "The Shadow Lord is not pleased. This new Highland Lord must be elimi-nated. The Marchers have driven almost all of his dark creatures from the Highlands. That cannot continue. The Shadow Lord must have the Highlands."

"He will, Lord Chertney. He will. I promise you. You know that if I attack the Highlands outright, Fal Carrach, Benewyn and several other Kingdoms will oppose me. I'm not strong enough yet to take them on openly, so a less direct approach is needed still."

"I understand your dilemma, Rodric. But remember, it's your dilemma. Our master has only so much patience, and time is running out. He grows tired of the failures and the excuses. Our master's plans move quickly. He must have the Highlands."

38

MARAUDERS

"All has been done as you've ordered, Lord Killeran," said a burly, stout reiver. "All of the villagers have been accounted for except for a couple shepherds. It won't be long before we have them as well."

"Good," replied Killeran. "We can't have any loose ends. That would not be good for either of us."

"Yes, Lord Killeran." The reiver captain saluted, then ran off to make sure his men had found the missing boys. He had understood the veiled threat in Killeran's comment all too well.

Killeran walked through the remains of the Dunmoorian village, located just a few leagues from the Highlands near the northernmost shore of the Inland Sea, surveying the handiwork of the reivers he still led. Most of the cottages had burned to their foundations, though several still smoldered, the flames not yet having caught and their inhabitants still inside screaming to be freed. Screaming for mercy, but their cries and pleas fell on deaf ears. A few bodies lay on the ground, but Killeran told his men to leave them there. It would serve as more convincing evidence. Despite the smoke, the fires, the destruction, much to his relief Killeran's immaculate armor retained its shine and his snow-white cloak remained pristine.

His men would be done soon, rooting out the last of the survivors, then they could move on to the next village, this one even closer to the Highlands. Two of his sergeants shot Highland arrows so that they punched into the trees, while several of his soldiers dressed a few of the dead men in Highland garb. Perhaps not the strongest claim against the Highlands if examined more closely, but it was enough. It would give them what they required.

Rodric needed an excuse to attack the Highlands, and Killeran was certain that this would do the trick, giving the High King the story that he needed to invade unimpeded and without the danger of bringing other Kingdoms into the dispute. The new Highland Lord had proven to be nothing more than an outlaw, sending his bands of marauding Marchers out into an adjacent, peaceful Kingdom to kill and pillage. Gregory and some of the other rulers would protest, but that's likely all they would do. They would worry too much about their own borders, not wanting to get drawn into a conflict with Armagh. Gregory, in particular, would remain wary of Loris of Dunmoor, who would seek any excuse to bring his soldiers across the border into Fal Carrach, a Kingdom he had lusted after since he first ascended his throne. So once the narrative was complete, the other pieces would fall into place.

Killeran laughed softly as he wandered through the village, ignoring the screams of the Dunmoorian peasants, his own people, trapped in their burning homes. He had worried that the new Highland Lord had eliminated his one chance for wealth when he was expelled from the Highlands along with his reivers. But he now viewed that as only a temporary setback. He would be back in the Highlands quite soon by his reckoning, and this time with a much larger force behind him. And then, then he would finally receive what he so justly deserved.

39

MORE TO LEARN

Kaylie walked into her chambers tired and sweaty. She placed her sheathed sword next to her bed, then dropped the daggers she'd worn at her belt onto the floor. The Princess of Fal Carrach had just completed her morning training session with Kael Bellilil, the focus today on knife-work, how to defend and how to attack when fighting in close quarters. Fal Carrach's Swordmaster had kept her at it for hours, not letting her go until she perfected the technique, he taught her to the point where he had drained all the energy from her. In fact, this had become her morning routine in the weeks since returning to Ballinasloe and the Rock, extended sessions in the training circle. Although she had not enjoyed her bout with Thomas on the way back from Eamhain Mhacha, she had learned quite a bit, and she wanted to learn even more. But now all she wanted, no, needed, was a bath and nap.

"You look like you've been dragged across the training yard," said a commanding voice off to the side.

Kaylie turned quickly, reaching for the Talent, knowing that she could take hold of the natural magic of the world faster than she could reach down for her discarded sword or daggers.

"Well done, girl," the voice said, obviously pleased. "Much faster than the last time we were together."

"Where have you been, Rya?" Kaylie asked with some exasperation, releasing her hold on the Talent. She was excited that her tutor in the Talent had returned but she was a little irritated as well. "It's been more than a month since I've seen you."

"Things to do, girl," replied the diminutive woman, her sharp blue eyes shining brightly.

Kaylie stood there waiting for more, then realized that Rya had said what she was going say. She shook her head in resignation. It was like talking with Thomas. He only said what needed to be said, and no more. Which brought a key question to mind.

"Why didn't you tell me Thomas was your grandson? And you never told me he was alive after what happened in Tinnakilly. You let me believe he was dead."

Rya snorted at Kaylie's angry outburst. "So many questions, so little time. I didn't tell you that Thomas was my grandson because you didn't need to know. It wasn't relevant to our training together."

"But why didn't you tell me he was alive?" Kaylie repeated. "You didn't need to make me suffer."

"I did tell you," said Rya, rising from the chair she had been sitting in by the balcony. "You just weren't paying attention. I told you his body was never found. That should have been enough."

Kaylie stared at the forceful woman somewhat perplexed, not knowing what to say. Having this conversation with Rya felt like she was knocking her head against a brick wall.

"That doesn't make sense. You could have simply said ..."

Rya stepped up to Kaylie, wrinkling her nose. "You need a bath, girl. But that will have to wait. If you're done trying to argue over this nonsense, I came here to continue your instruction. Time is moving faster than I expected. I need to make certain you're ready."

"Ready for what?" asked Kaylie, her confusion obvious.

"You'll know when the time is right," replied Rya cryptically. "Now if you're not able to shift your focus, we can do this another time."

Kaylie bit back an angry retort. Arguing with this woman was like trying to convince a bull to move from the center of the street. It wasn't worth the effort. The bull was going to go where the bull wanted to go. She took a deep breath, trying to release some of her growing irritation.

"What did you have in mind?" Kaylie asked.

"That's the spirit," said Rya. "You had mentioned that when you first met Thomas, he taught you how to search."

"Yes, he did."

"Have you tried to do it since?"

"A few times. Just a few weeks ago I did it again with Thomas by the Inland Sea. We were ..."

Rya's keen look cut off the flow of Kaylie's words. "We can discuss the details of your relationship with my grandson another time. Can we focus on the task at hand?"

"Of course," replied Kaylie sheepishly, her cheeks coloring slightly.

"Good. Now, how far can you search?"

"From Ballinasloe to the borders of Dunmoor and Benewyn. Maybe just a bit beyond. That's about it." Kaylie's frustration at her failure to expand the radius of her search was plain on her face. No matter what she tried, she'd hit a wall in this particular application of the Talent.

"We're going to change that this morning," said Rya. "Take hold of the Talent."

Kaylie did so, enjoying the feel of the natural magic of the world as it settled within her.

"Take in a bit more than that, girl," instructed Rya. "We're going well beyond Fal Carrach today."

Kaylie quickly complied, excited by the prospect of what was going to happen next.

"Good. Well done, girl. Do you remember how Thomas showed you how to extend your senses?"

Kaylie nodded.

"Do that now," instructed Rya.

Kaylie closed her eyes, seeking to focus her thoughts. In an instant, she felt as if she were floating above herself, looking down as she stood in the center of the room, eyes closed, hands held slightly raised to the side. Rya had come to stand next to her, close enough to whisper in her ear.

"Well done, girl," said Rya. "Well done, indeed. Now take in more of the Talent and gradually extend your senses."

Kaylie pulled in more of the Talent as Rya instructed and then began pushing out her senses in all directions. Droplets of sweat popped out on her forehead, her energy draining quickly as she grew tired trying to manage so much of the Talent at one time.

"There's the problem, girl," said Rya. "Focus your search. Trying to search in all directions at once won't get you anywhere. Concentrate on the west, toward the Burren and then the Inland Sea. Take it a step at a time."

Kaylie responded to the whispered command, centering herself once more, then expanding her search again, but this time only in the direction Rya had specified. In seconds she was soaring above Ballinasloe, heading toward the west, the trees of the Burren quickly approaching.

"Well done, girl. Keep going. Let's see what you can do."

Kaylie sensed the pride in Rya's whispered voice, the woman pleased by her success. Taking in more of the Talent, she sped across the forest then out over the Grasslands, the shimmering water of the Inland Sea beckoning. She exulted in the freedom she felt, reveling in the knowledge that she could see so much of the Kingdoms whenever she desired. She already had searched farther than she had the last time that she had been with Thomas. As she approached the glistening blue of the Inland Sea, Rya gave her a new instruction.

"Take us to the north, girl. Take us into the Highlands."

Kaylie smiled to herself. Rya must have known that's where she wanted to go next. She turned her focus toward the peaks of the Highlands, which she could see rising into the sky just beyond the northern shore of the Inland Sea. In less than a minute she had entered the lower Highlands. The beautiful, rugged countryside, the craggy mountaintops separated by deep, evergreen forests, streaked by below her.

"That's it, girl. Now a slightly different task. Locate the Crag."

Kaylie slowed her progress. She knew the Crag was somewhere to the north, maybe to the east as well. But how did she get there? She had never visited the Crag before. In fact, she had only been to the very southern edge of the Highlands as a young girl, and that was the extent of her experience in the Kingdom to the north of Fal Carrach. Simply searching the Highlands for the fortress would be a waste of time and energy, and obviously Rya was judging how she would solve the problem. So, what to do?

An idea came to her. Whether it was a good idea or not she didn't know. But at least it was an idea. She thought of Thomas, knowing that he had returned to the Highlands and guessing that he was in the vicinity of the Crag. Much to her delight, she could feel him, faintly, to the northeast. Excited by her discovery, she began searching in that direction. The minutes passed quickly as she flew between the mountain peaks, enjoying the crispness of the view, marveling as the bright sunshine played off the snow-covered spires. As the leagues passed beneath her, her sense of Thomas became stronger. She was getting closer.

Finally, she broke through the rocky peaks into a lush valley of green that stretched between the mountains for more than a league. A dark mass appeared in the very center. Skimming over the treetops, Kaylie smiled victoriously knowing that Thomas was just in front of her as an enormous rock came into focus that rose hundreds of feet into the air and dominated the valley. As she approached, the stone coalesced into the Crag, the stronghold of the Highlanders. She took in the eight towers that formed the Crag's perimeter, the tops of some no more than piles of stone. One tower, though, standing on the eastern side closest to the sea, rose higher than the rest and caught her attention. A large kestrel perched on the top of the tower, its sharp eyes scanning the terrain in all directions. And in the sky around it almost a dozen kestrels circled the fortress and surrounding forest, the large raptors twisting and turning in response to the strong gusts of mountain air that blew into the valley.

Kaylie halted her progress, settling over the Crag.

"Wonderfully done, girl," said Rya, more than satisfied with her student's ingenuity in solving the problem placed before her. "Now let's head back to Ballinasloe."

Kaylie acknowledged Rya's request with a slight nod, but remained where she was for a time, gazing down on the Crag. She began to circle the Highland fortress slowly, watching the many Highlanders below as they repaired the massive citadel. Various work crews were filling the huge holes in the outer curtain while others rebuilt the towers that had collapsed. Yet still she drifted over the Crag until finally she found what she was looking for.

Thomas was by the northeastern side of the keep, working with a group of Highlanders as they moved large blocks of black stone in place to replace those that had been blown apart by the warlocks when they attacked the Crag a decade before.

She watched him for a moment, not knowing why she did so, other than desiring a quick glimpse.

"Are we done mooning, girl?" asked Rya sharply.

Kaylie pulled back from the Crag, though not before she thought she saw Thomas peer up into the sky. She guessed that he had sensed someone observing, much as she did that night on the knoll. Thomas had mentioned that knowing the person might help them identify who was searching, but was there more to it than that? Did the closeness between the individuals have something to do with it? Those were questions for another day. Reluctantly, Kaylie turned to the southeast, quickly finding her way through the mountain peaks to the Sea of Mist and then following the coast down to Ballinasloe.

Opening her eyes, Kaylie released the Talent. If she had thought she was tired after training with Kael, that was nothing compared to how she felt now. She was drenched in sweat and every muscle in her body trembled.

"You did well," said Rya. "Though you may have overdone it just a bit. How did you know to focus on something, or rather someone, you were familiar with to find the Crag?"

"It just made sense," replied Kaylie wearily, dropping into a chair before her legs gave out.

Rya nodded, glad that the girl was thinking. "Now you know the trick. If you know someone or you've been somewhere, you can return to them or that place easily. It's been ingrained in your memory, so you can find it again without any trouble. If you've never been somewhere, or don't know the person, it's harder. All you can do is move in the general direction of what you're looking for and hope that you locate it."

"So if I wanted to return to the Crag ..."

"You should be able to get there without any difficulty."

"Good to know," said Kaylie.

Rya smiled at the girl, understanding the purpose of her question and approving of what she would likely do next. But there was still something else that Rya could teach Kaylie that might aid her in that task.

"You look exhausted," said Rya, walking toward the balcony. "Rest, eat, definitely bathe. I will return tomorrow at the same time for your next lesson."

Kaylie smiled broadly, happy that Rya would be back the next day, enjoying her company despite her often pointed comments.

"What will we be working on tomorrow?"

Rya didn't bother to turn around, heading out into the fresh air of the late morning.

"Tomorrow, girl, I will teach you how to shape change."

40

NEW STRATEGY

Thomas stood at the base of the battlements of the south wall of the Crag. He was dressed in breeches and boots, having discarded his shirt as the warm sun alleviated the chill of the day. A pickaxe in hand, he had spent the last several hours chipping away at one of the jagged holes the warlocks had blown into the wall that fated day a decade ago, which had allowed the Ogren and the reivers to take the Crag. Despite the cold temperature, the sun felt good beating down upon him. Teams of Highlanders worked all around the Crag, engaged in the same task of removing the rubble and rebuilding the Highland fortress.

Some cleared the debris and carved at the holes in the walls so that the masons could fill the gaps more easily. Others reconstructed the towers and strengthened the walls of the Crag. Still others concentrated on the defenses that ran not only across the wall, but also extended to the land surrounding the Crag, while adding a few tricks and surprises to make the lives of any would-be attackers all the more difficult.

Thomas had no doubt that those invaders would come. Rodric still desperately wanted the Highlands, thus the need to rebuild the Crag as quickly as possible. But Thomas wasn't tied to the citadel. He understood its perceived importance and value as the capital of the Highlands and seat of the Highland Lord, but he didn't believe a structure could represent the strength and resilience of his people. The Highlanders were linked to their land in a way that other Kingdoms couldn't even begin to understand, and though the Crag proved useful at times, it was not essential to maintaining the strength of the Kingdom. It was, however, a target that could and likely would pull at the High King.

The beauty of the Highland peaks hid a harshness and danger that had molded the Highlanders into the most fearsome warriors in all the Kingdoms. It was that connection to the Highlands that made them into what they had become, so the real tie wasn't to one place in the Highlands, but rather to the Highlands in its entirety. Thomas recognized the need for the Crag, at least in the minds of some, but he viewed the strength of the Marchers as emanating from the entire Highlands, not just from a single manmade structure within his mountainous homeland.

Thomas pondered that thought as well as a dark worry about what the next few months might hold for him and his people as he cut out pieces of jagged, loose stone. The Highlanders had regained control of their Kingdom at the expense of Rodric and his reivers, but Thomas was anxious about whether he and his Marchers could defend it against a stronger, concerted attack. He was certain that the High King and his army would do whatever was necessary to justify an invasion by Armagh and its allies. It was simply a matter of time. His biggest worry? The Marchers could not defeat the High King on their own. Though fearsome warriors, they were too few compared to the many soldiers Armagh could call upon. If it devolved into a battle of attrition, eventually the

Armaghians would win no matter how well or how hard the Marchers fought.

That also meant that those Kingdoms that might support the Highlands, besides Fal Carrach and Benewyn, as he had already received assurances from Gregory and Sarelle that they would stand with him, would not risk a confrontation with the High King unless Thomas could offer some proof of Rodric's treachery. How to obtain that proof was the puzzle Thomas struggled with for most of the morning and into the early afternoon. As late afternoon approached, he stopped shaping the stone of the broken wall, setting the pickaxe onto the ground. Sweaty hair matted to his head, Thomas removed his heavy work gloves and turned his attention to the robed figures he had sensed making their way to the Crag. They had emerged finally from the forest surrounding the fortress following a path that led directly to where he was working, many of the Marchers stopping their own work to stare at the intimidating group as they passed.

"You're making good progress," said a beautiful woman, petite, but with a fierce gaze. She walked up to Thomas and hugged him strongly, not put off by his dirty and sweaty appearance.

"We're doing what we can," replied Thomas, enjoying his grandmother Rya's embrace.

"When do you expect to have this done?" asked Rynlin.

His grandfather, tall and thin, looked down on Thomas with a gleam of pride in his eyes. His roguish smile gave him a dastardly appearance that he relished.

"Hopefully within the month," said Thomas, surveying the remainder of the group.

Two Sylvan Warriors stood with his grandfather. The first, Tiro Lessaro, was short and portly, his frizzy gray hair standing up in all directions. He had taken Thomas through the challenges to become a Sylvan Warrior. The second, Maden Grenis, always had a half-smile on his face, as if everything he saw and came upon in the world in some way amused him.

"That's all well and good," said Tiro, having no patience for family reunions and wanting to get down to business immediately. "But the fate of one Kingdom is of little consequence compared to the fate of all."

"Speak for yourself," said Thomas, his face hardening with anger. "The Highlands is my responsibility, whether Sylvan Warrior or Highland Lord, and I'll do all I can to protect my people."

"Be that as it may," countered Tiro, adopting the superior tone he was known for, and which rankled all who had to bear it, "you are the one. You know that don't you? You are the one who will have to contest the Shadow Lord. You are the one who must fight him if he is to be defeated."

"I know," answered Thomas simply.

Thomas' response with no visible emotion, with no sense of urgency, infuriated Tiro, his face turning a dark shade of purple.

"You know? Then what are you going to do about it? What plans do you have? Rebuilding this citadel won't help very much, unless you plan on inviting the Shadow Lord and his Dark Horde to come here to fight."

"I am doing what I can," said Thomas, Tiro having a hard time holding the young Sylvan Warrior's intense gaze.

"You are doing what you can," repeated Tiro, his scorn almost tangible. "You are doing what you can! That isn't good enough. You must do more!"

Rynlin stepped forward, about to intercede for his grandson, but Rya lay a gentle hand on his arm, shaking her head to communicate that he shouldn't involve himself. Maden simply watched the battle of wills with what appeared to be wry levity, although his intense eyes suggested otherwise.

"Do you not understand what we're talking about?"

exclaimed Tiro, the little man working himself up into a lather. "Do you have any concept of what's at stake? Nothing else compares to this threat. The outcome of this one event affects the lives of everyone and everything in the Kingdoms, not just the Highlands, and you're doing what you can? You're doing what you can?"

"That's enough, Tiro," said Rynlin in a deadly calm voice, losing patience with the Sylvan Warrior's tirade. But Tiro had reached such a point of apoplexy that he simply ignored Rynlin's warning.

"Holding back the Shadow Lord has been the task of the Sylvana for the last thousand years. And for the last thousand years, ever since the Great War, we've been waiting for the one who can challenge him. Now we finally have him, yet he's doing what he can. You must do more!"

Thomas stared at Tiro stonily, his anger escalating. He took advantage of the incensed Sylvan Warrior needing to take a breath before he could continue his diatribe.

"I know who I am, and I know what I must do," began Thomas quietly, his voice slowly rising, becoming stronger. "I am a member of the Sylvana, and I am Lord of the Highlands. I am supposed to fight the Shadow Lord. I am likely supposed to die at the hands of the Shadow Lord. I am very aware of those facts."

Thomas stepped forward so that he was no more than a hand away from Tiro, the stout Sylvan Warrior beginning to realize that he may have gone too far with his harangue.

"I've had to escape the Shadow Lord's assassins for the last ten years. So be it. I did not ask for any of this. All I ever wanted was a family, a mother and a father. It wasn't meant to be, though I'm thankful for what my grandparents have given me."

There was a sadness now in Thomas' voice, and tears in Rya's eyes.

"I did not ask for any of this, but I accept what must be

done, and I will do the best that I can. As you can see, I have several responsibilities that I must juggle. Now, my responsibility is protecting my people so that they can protect themselves. I have not forgotten the Shadow Lord. I will never forget the Shadow Lord. He's with me every waking moment, and often when I dream. I can feel him every second of the day. No matter what I do I cannot escape the Shadow Lord. I know what's to come, and I know the anticipated result. I will do the best that I can. But I can do nothing about it this very minute."

Thomas swept his arm toward the Crag and its surroundings to take in the reconstruction of the Highland keep.

"But I can do something about this. Do not doubt that I will be there when the time comes. Do not doubt that I will do what must be done to defend the Kingdoms, but I do not have to do it yet." Thomas' eyes blazed like green fire as he bit off the last few words.

Rynlin stood there smiling, struggling to maintain his silence. He was very proud of how Thomas had responded to Tiro's antagonism. He didn't think he could have done better himself.

Tiro stood there in stunned silence, never having expected such a retort from a barely risen Sylvan Warrior, Lord of the Highlands or not. Before he could attempt another verbal onslaught, Maden spoke up.

"That brings us to the more important question," said the tall Sylvan Warrior with a sardonic grin. "We are preparing for what we expect to be another attack from the Shadow Lord. Can we hold him this time as we've done in the past?"

Tiro immediately piped up. "We always have, and we will once ..."

"In the past, yes, we have held," interrupted Maden, his smile replaced by a frown, concern etched clearly in the lines of his weathered face. "But we are much fewer now with no guarantee that the Kingdoms are prepared for the coming invasion.

By all indications, the Shadow Lord will have a tremendous host, larger than ever before. The war parties coming across the Northern Steppes testify to that."

"He wouldn't send those bands of dark creatures as a test if he didn't have plenty of Ogren and Shades in reserve," stated Rynlin, concurring with Maden's assessment.

"Agreed." Maden looked sharply at Tiro. "The information we've gotten from those Sylvan Warriors scouting the Charnel Mountains confirms it. The Shadow Lord is building his strength, and we might not be able to hold him at the Breaker."

The tall Sylvan Warrior fell silent, the others as well. They knew the truth of his words.

"That's why we need a different strategy," Thomas said quietly.

All eyes turned to Thomas in curiosity, except for Tiro.

"You became Lord of the Highlands, boy, and that is a great feat, but don't let it go to your head. We have been fighting the Shadow Lord a lot longer than you."

The stout Sylvan Warrior would have said more, but Rya interrupted him. "Let him speak, Tiro."

Maden and Rynlin nodded their heads in agreement, wanting to hear what the youngest Sylvan Warrior had to say. Tiro peered from one Sylvan Warrior to the next, then grumbled his acquiescence.

"The Shadow Lord fears us," said Thomas, beginning to walk slowly up and down in front of the hole in the Crag's wall. Much like his grandfather, he always thought better while on the move. "One thousand years ago, when he last attacked, the Sylvana stopped him. Not the Kingdoms, but the Sylvana. If the Sylvana had not defeated him, his dark creatures would have broken through and who knows what would have happened. Why do you think he is trying to kill as many of us as he can before his Dark Horde marches?"

"What are you talking about?" demanded Tiro. He was

about to say more but the unexpected glare Maden gave him forced him back to silence.

"You know exactly what I mean," said Thomas. "The Shadow Lord is sending out his dark creatures and assassins, attempting to eliminate as many Sylvan Warriors as possible before he attacks. Three Sylvana have been killed in the last year. As Maden noted, there aren't as many of us left as there were the last time the Dark Horde descended from the Charnel Mountains. Why kill three of us and try to eliminate several others? Because he fears us. He remembers how we defeated him the last time he attacked, so he is trying to improve his chances for victory."

Thomas waited a moment to let what he had just said sink in. "Always in the past, the Shadow Lord has attacked. Always. And the Sylvana have defended the Kingdoms. In fact, we're doing it now. Several Sylvan Warriors are helping my Marchers in the northern Highlands, seeking to prevent the encroachment of the Ogren raiding parties coming across the Northern Steppes. But this time we need a different strategy. This time we cannot afford to wait. This time we need to attack."

Tiro stared at Thomas in shock; Maden and Rya smiled, liking the suggestion. Rynlin, never having the capacity for patience, positively loved it. His bloodthirsty expression suggested that he was ready to head for Blackstone that very moment.

"We have always waited to defend the Kingdoms. We do not have the numbers we used to, nor the support. I doubt many of the Western Kingdoms will send troops to fight at the Breaker. So we don't have the luxury of relying on that stone barrier. No matter how strong it might be, we won't have the fighters needed to hold it. We should attack and beat the Shadow Lord at his own game."

"What do you have in mind, Thomas?" Maden liked where Thomas was headed, always thinking to do the unexpected.

"I can guarantee that the Marchers will be at the Breaker, as will the soldiers of Fal Carrach and Benewyn. I expect Kenmare will join us."

"The Desert Clans as well," said Rynlin.

"And the Desert Clans. They will be there to meet the Shadow Lord's Dark Horde as they have in the past, but we won't be. We will move north along the coast, avoid the Horde, and attack Blackstone once the Shadow Lord's host has begun its march south across the Northern Steppes."

"Attack Blackstone!" sputtered Tiro. "No one has ever conquered Blackstone! It's simply not possible. This is nothing but a hare-brained idea."

"The only reason Blackstone has never fallen is because it hasn't been attacked since the Great War," said Thomas in a quiet, compelling voice. "The Shadow Lord's attention will be focused on the Breaker. He will be distracted, worried. Waiting to see when the Sylvana will get to the Breaker to help the Kingdoms. Instead, while the Kingdoms occupy his Dark Horde, we will appear on his doorstep and attack him directly. To be honest, Ogren, Shades, Fearhounds, all the other dark creatures are of little consequence. The only thing that matters is that we defeat the Shadow Lord, and that I get into Blackstone to fight him."

Thomas wasn't quite sure how he or, in fact, the Sylvana could actually enter Blackstone, knowing that the Shadow Lord had surrounded that dead metropolis with an impenetrable Dark Magic that prevented all but his creatures and servants from crossing the boundary of what had become his city. But he decided not to focus on that small issue at the moment. He could work out that small part of the plan later.

The Sylvan Warriors stared at him for a moment. Then Maden broke out into a huge smile.

"Thomas, I like the way you think. I believe I can speak for everyone when I say that your plan just might work."

Rynlin looked at Thomas an instant longer with his piercing eyes, then said quietly, "You never mentioned how you were going to break into Blackstone and get past all of the Shadow Lord's protective seals."

Thomas grinned at his grandfather. "I can't figure everything out all at once. I was hoping that you might be able to help me with that."

"I should have figured as much," said Rynlin with a resigned chuckle, though his mind already had turned toward this new challenge, several possible avenues for researching the problem coming to mind. "I'll see what I can do."

Thomas nodded his appreciation. "By the way, my thanks to you and the others for working with Nestor and Beluil and helping to protect the Highlands. Nestor says that you seem to be enjoying yourself."

"What's not to like about eliminating dark creatures," said Rynlin with a wicked grin. "That big black beast of yours is a menace, Thomas. Almost as crafty as you, but much larger teeth."

"Beluil has a mean streak," admitted Thomas. "I'm glad he's putting it to good use."

Thomas patted his grandfather on his back, then hugged his grandmother. She held onto him longer than expected.

"Stay safe, Thomas," she told him.

"As safe as can be," he replied.

His response seemed to satisfy her, although he could tell that she was still worried, despite her best efforts to hide it.

"Kaylie wishes you well," said Rya, before turning away. "She's just as stubborn as you, by the way. With the Talent she's never satisfied until she does as I've asked perfectly. And even then, she finds areas for improvement."

"Sounds like a difficult pupil," he said.

"Yes," Rya replied, giving him a sly look over her shoulder. "But often that makes the experience all the more worthwhile. Reminds me of someone, in fact. Keep that in mind, Thomas."

Thomas watched his grandfather, grandmother, and the two Sylvan Warriors walk down the path and disappear among the evergreens. He stood there for several minutes, his grandmother's words playing through his mind. There was always a deeper meaning in what Rya had to say, sometimes you just had to dig for it. His mind fixed on the dark-haired girl who had entranced him when he had first seen her in the Burren, Thomas walked back through the hole in the Crag's wall to check on the progress of the Highlanders repairing the outer curtain. The sun was beginning to set, and he wanted to make sure the transition to the night work parties went smoothly.

The Sylvan Warriors walked away from the Crag and threaded their way through the trees, heading for the glade at which they had first arrived after making use of their shapeshifting abilities with the Talent.

"The boy has fire in him," said Tiro.

"And rock," said Maden, who sang a short poem. "Beware the one made of fire and rock. Always standing, free and strong, ready to burn."

"I would hate to fight against him," continued Maden. "He would be a formidable opponent."

"Yes, yes," murmured Tiro.

Rynlin waited in silence, knowing that there was more to this conversation. It just hadn't been revealed yet. They were almost to the glade when Maden got to the heart of the matter.

"Can he do it?"

They had reached the clearing, the small group stopping. The approaching evening wrapped the small dell in shadow. Tiro wore an anxious expression, almost fearful. Rynlin studied the mountain peaks that surrounded them for a time, forming his words, but it was Rya who stepped into the conversation.

"Yes, I think he can. Nothing is ever certain, but I have no doubt that he will fight the Shadow Lord to his last breath. That's all we have a right to ask of him. It's more than most anyone else would do."

"You have raised him well," said Maden.

"No," responded Rynlin. "He has raised himself. Rya and I have only helped him out from time to time along the way."

Maden laughed at that, but he understood what Rynlin was implying.

Before Rynlin shifted into his hawk form to wing his way back to the Isle of Mist with his wife, he pondered the dilemma that confounded him. The dilemma that this new, ambitious, and potentially suicidal plan hinged upon. How could he help Thomas survive the Shadow Lord's Dark Magic and enter Blackstone when no one knew the location of the Key?

41

EMPTY PROMISES

"Think of it, King Gregory. A free rein in the east and Loris of Dunmoor no longer a threat. It would give Fal Carrach a dominance on the eastern coast that no other Kingdom would dare to challenge."

The quiet, hissing voice of Lord Chertney reminded Gregory of a snake. He sat composed on his throne, his daughter standing behind him, his soldiers ringing the chamber. Gregory kept a wary eye on Chertney, giving some credence to the rumors that this tall, shadowy, wraith-like figure had gained some unique powers through his subservience to the Shadow Lord. The King of Fal Carrach wanted to remind Chertney that he wasn't like several of the other monarchs who had acquiesced to Rodric's demands or offers -- it often was hard to tell the difference between the two -- either out of fear or greed.

Kaylie stood to the side, watching her father's exchange with Rodric's emissary. Neither had forgotten the role that Chertney likely had played in using Kaylie to capture Thomas Kestrel during the Eastern Festival. But they didn't have proof, only a strong suspicion, so they weren't in a position to take action, no matter how much they might desire to do so. As the conversation continued, her blood began to boil as her anger burned hotter within her. She had no doubt that Rodric had sent Chertney to Fal Carrach knowing it would reopen a still raw wound. She suspected that he thought that such an action served as a reminder of the power he exercised as King of Armagh and High King. Yet all it did was incense her. Chertney being sent to Fal Carrach as an envoy was a slap in the face.

"It would cost you very little, King Gregory," continued Chertney in a sibilant rasp. "Simply a promise not to become involved if a conflict should erupt between Armagh and the Highlands."

It was all coming to pass as Gregory had expected. Rodric had failed to take the Highlands after the new Highland Lord had sent his regent, Lord Killeran, packing. Nevertheless, Rodric still wanted the Highlands. Whether for himself or for his hidden master, he couldn't say. Therefore, to create some perception of legitimacy, several Dunmoorian villages had been attacked, supposedly by the Marchers, thereby giving Rodric the poor excuse, but excuse nonetheless, that he needed to invade the Highlands.

Many of the Kingdoms didn't care or didn't want to get involved, recognizing the baselessness of the claims behind the ploy but still unwilling to stand against a vengeful High King and the Armaghian army, which dwarfed any other fighting force in the Kingdoms. Moreover, these other rulers realized that if Rodric remained focused on the Highlands, the High King couldn't bother them at the same time. Gregory viewed such reasoning as short-sighted. Rodric wanted all the Kingdoms. Anyone who didn't see that was blind or a fool. Allowing the High King to focus on one Kingdom at a time rather than dealing with organized resistance on the part of the other Kingdoms only simplified his task.

For Rodric the Highlands was only the beginning. Yes, the

Marchers would cut at the edges of the Armaghian army, but in time the sheer size of that host would win out. And then Rodric would turn his attention to the next Kingdom that he wanted, his allies staying out of the way and allowing him to move forward as he wished. As time passed, he would become too strong to oppose. It wasn't politics. It was simple strategy.

Once Rodric disposed of the Kingdoms opposing him, he would turn his attention to his allies. Gregory didn't know if those supposed partner Kingdoms simply didn't understand the expanse of Rodric's greed or they chose to ignore it because that was the easiest thing to do at the moment. Perhaps they didn't care, thinking that they could pick up any scraps Rodric left for them by riding on his coattails.

"Enough, Chertney." Gregory rose from his throne and walked down the steps to stand in front of Rodric's emissary, his eyes burning brightly with anger. "No more promises of riches or land or power. I refuse Rodric's offer. Fal Carrach is an independent Kingdom and will remain so."

"Is that a wise decision?" asked Chertney, a slight smile turning his thin lips. He had not expected Gregory to accede to Rodric's request. The King of Fal Carrach was too proud. Still, the offer needed to be made, if only so that he could move on to the next step in his mission, the part he had been looking forward to since arriving in Ballinasloe that morning. "Armagh has the largest army in all the Kingdoms. I would hate to think what could happen if that army turned its attention on you."

"Armagh may have the largest army, but not the best army, Chertney. You may leave now. Go back to your master and tell him I'm not interested in his bargains."

Chertney stared at Gregory for a long moment, thinking about which master to which Gregory referred. He realized that the fear he had expected and craved didn't exist within the King of Fal Carrach, unlike some of the other monarchs he had visited at Rodric's behest. As he had expected from the start, there was another way, an easier way, to achieve his goal. Taking hold of his Dark Magic, he focused his attention on the King of Fal Carrach, almost invisible wisps of black mist beginning to form around Gregory's head.

Kaylie watched with satisfaction as her father rejected Rodric's offer, her anger at Chertney threatening to explode. Proof or no, she felt the need to do something. To show Rodric's emissary that she would never again be swayed in such a way. That she was not someone to be trifled with. But she knew that she couldn't. She shouldn't, no matter how much she might want to remind Chertney that accounts had not yet been settled between them.

A strange, unexpected touch on her senses brought Kaylie back to what was going on around her. Something was out of place in the throne room. It seemed like she could even smell the faint taint of corruption, similar to a compost pile slowly rotting. Thinking back to her lessons with Rya, it took her a few seconds to realize what it could be. Dark Magic! She noticed that Chertney stared intently at her father, whose normally sharp gaze was beginning to turn glassy, small, barely visible tendrils of black circling around her father's head. Kaylie responded based entirely on instinct, grasping hold of the Talent and sending a spinning web of white light toward her father, the strands of white energy dropping down over the King of Fal Carrach and consuming the wispy threads of black. Satisfied that she had succeeded in stopping Chertney's attempt at compulsion, she decided that she did, indeed, need to make a point. Kaylie fashioned a small ball of white energy, then threw it down at Chertney's feet. The blast left a scorch mark on the stone right between her father and Chertney, the sound reverberating like thunder throughout the chamber.

As if struck a physical blow, Chertney staggered back in shock, losing control of his Dark Magic.

"You dare to try to compel me!" roared Gregory.

The soldiers lining the walls had drawn their swords, several holding their blades just inches from Chertney's chest and back. Gregory struggled to control his temper. His first instinct was to allow his soldiers to use Chertney as a pincushion and be done with the bastard. But the easy way was not always the best way.

Nodding his thanks to his daughter, he approached Chertney, his balled fists reflecting his scarcely controlled rage. "You may leave now, Chertney. You have one day to cross the border. And know that from this day forward you are not welcome in Fal Carrach. The penalty for ignoring this sanction is death."

Chertney glared at Gregory with palpable hatred, considering his limited options as the circle of steel grew tighter, then fixed his gaze on the Princess of Fal Carrach. He had never thought that the girl could exercise such power, and he had not expected such strength from someone so new to the Talent. He considered escalating the situation, employing his Dark Magic more directly, then glanced back to the dais. He could sense the power that the girl held within her grasp. She was a formidable opponent, and she clearly had the skill to shield her ability from those who might be able to sense it, so he assumed that she was receiving instruction in its use. Much to his chagrin, he realized that she could defend against anything he tried, at least for a time. At least long enough for one of the soldiers standing near him to drive a sword into his body, and his Dark Magic would not protect against a steel blade through his heart. Not wanting to take a dangerous risk, he gave Gregory a final malevolent sneer, then turned away and stalked from the room. Several soldiers followed after, intent on escorting Chertney from Ballinasloe.

"Very impressive, Kaylie," said Gregory, staring down at the black mark that marred the floor. "If you hadn't been here, who knows what would have happened."

Kaylie smiled, pleased by her father's praise. "Maybe we can get that mark out of the stone, father," she suggested. "It certainly stands out."

"No, we'll leave it as is," her father replied quickly. "People will ask questions. It will give me an opportunity to explain what happened. It will make them think twice about trying to get the better of Fal Carrach knowing that you're here."

Kaylie's smile broadened, pleased by her father's comment. "I'm glad he tried something," she said, her blood still up. "He deserves more than I gave him, but at least it's a start."

"I have a feeling that he will receive his just desserts in time. As the Highlanders would say, I get the impression that there is a long list of people seeking to repay their debts to that dark-hearted scoundrel."

"Father, why not declare your support for the Highlands? Why not support Thomas over the High King?" asked Kaylie, turning her mind to the problems of state.

"I am, Kaylie. Just not openly."

"What do you mean?"

"If I declared for the Highlands, I would have to worry about not only Rodric's army, but also Dunmoor's. We could take on one army, but it would be a long, drawn-out affair, and there is no guarantee that the other Kingdoms would come to help. Other than Sarelle of Benewyn and Rendael of Kenmare, the other Kingdoms listen to Rodric either out of greed or fear."

"What about the Highlanders?"

"The Highlanders would help us in an instant. But remember, they're Rodric's first target. Everyone knows Rodric's claim that the Marchers are destroying villages in Dunmoor is a sham, but that doesn't matter. Rodric just wants to create an excuse for his actions. Keep in mind as well that the Marchers don't have a large army. They've never had a large army. They can't afford to waste their fighters. Besides, if we declared against Rodric and were forced to engage either him or Loris, the Marchers couldn't come to our aid. They'll be too busy defending their homeland."

"So you seek to delay and keep Rodric off balance. And by not getting directly drawn into the conflict, you can ..."

"Aid the Highlands indirectly. Correct."

"Then what are we doing for the Highlands?"

"I've closed the border between the Highlands and Fal Carrach, forcing Rodric to stage his men in Dunmoor and take them through to the west of the Burren. As a result, he can only bring his army across the Inland Sea, which requires ships, and that means the need for more resources and more money. It will slow him down and give Thomas more time to prepare."

"It might also provide the Marchers with some tempting targets," offered Kaylie.

"Very true. Having to land men and supplies on the northern shore of the Inland Sea makes them more vulnerable, particularly if I'm remembering accurately the poor quality and the narrowness of the trails in that part of the Highlands. From what I've heard, in just the last few days it's been great sport for the Marchers. In addition, we're keeping Loris busy on our border. We've turned the tables somewhat, sending our own raiding parties across the Gullet to create havoc at those sites where Loris is gathering his troops and Rodric has staged his army for the trip across the Inland Sea. Kael is leading those soldiers, and they're focused on destroying supplies and barges, which should help. Thomas only has so many fighters, so by doing this, he can concentrate his Marchers in one part of the Highlands without having to worry too much about his flanks. Thomas had suggested the approach and I readily agreed."

"Wait. What?" Kaylie asked in surprise. "You've talked with him?"

"Of course I have. We spoke just a few nights ago."

"He was here!" she exclaimed incredulously.

"Yes, he snuck in somehow in the middle of the night.

Scared me half to death when he appeared in my chambers. This is what we decided. I can't declare for him openly, and he doesn't want me to. Not yet anyway. He has some scheme in mind. My guess is that he wants to pull as much of the Armaghian army as he can deeper into the Highlands before he strikes."

"That's a good plan," she agreed, but her mind was already elsewhere. Perhaps it was time to continue her practice in the Talent.

42

QUICK VISIT

Darkness had consumed the Crag, the stars shining brightly on a clear, cold night. After working to rebuild the citadel all day, Thomas finally had time to grab a bowl of dinner from the campfire and wander to the edge of the forest. He understood the importance of the Crag to his people, as it served as a powerful symbol for them and the Highlands. Moreover, the reconstruction effort was another way to energize the Highlanders, as it was a critical part of the larger struggle to restore their Kingdom and maintain their newly found freedom.

But Thomas could remain within its walls for only so long, finding the cut stone too constricting. The memories of what had occurred here too much. That's why he took every opportunity to step away and into the trees surrounding the Crag, much as he did when he was a child. The quiet and solitude helped him gain some much-needed peace and time to think. Thomas had wandered over to one of his favorite places, a large rock at the very edge of the plateau on which the Crag rose. With the Crag at his back, it gave him an excellent view of half the valley and the mountains beyond. He dug hungrily into his stew, then stopped, catching movement in the sky above him. With the darkness, it could be a bat, but the shadow that had disturbed the falling night was much too large for that.

"Good evening, Princess."

Thomas went back to his bowl, scraping the last of the stew into his mouth with his last crust of bread.

A bright flash of white light disturbed the dark of the night. Then the Princess of Fal Carrach stepped out from between the trees and settled herself next to Thomas on the large rock.

"Why should I even be surprised that you knew it was me?"

Thomas smiled, though it was difficult to see in the gloom. "I could sense you," explained Thomas.

Kaylie assumed it was because of her use of the Talent, but Thomas wasn't so sure. He thought that there might be more to it than that. As if a connection were forming between him and Kaylie. But he didn't have the time, and reluctantly he admitted to himself the courage, to explore that theory just yet.

"So how is your training in the Talent going? Clearly you've mastered the ability to shape change."

"As well as can be expected, I guess. When Rya isn't available, I try to improve on all the lessons your grandmother has taught me. That's actually why I came here. I was hoping to find Rya, but I can tell she's gone."

"Yes, she and some others left about an hour ago." Thomas glanced over at Kaylie, noting how she looked off in the distance rather than at him. He suspected that searching for Rya wasn't the primary reason she had chosen to visit with him.

"I could sense them while I flew here." She had felt the Talent surging through them. Strong, everyone. Though none as strong as Thomas. "Who were they?"

"Sylvan Warriors." Normally Thomas was quite reticent in revealing what he was feeling, preferring to keep it inside. But now, for some reason, he experienced an urge to share. "Tiro and Maden were here, along with my grandfather, Rynlin. Tiro felt the need to remind me of my greater responsibilities."

"Greater responsibilities?"

"Yes, as a Sylvan Warrior I have some burdens that he believes should take precedence over my duties as Lord of the Highlands. We have yet to reach a meeting of the minds." Thomas' frustration was evident, his green eyes flashing brightly in the dark of the night.

Kaylie sat there for a time, thinking of what it must be like to have competing demands made of you. She had told herself that making use of the Talent to change her shape into that of a hawk and visit the Highlands was simply a part of her training. A small part of her unwillingly acknowledged it was a jealous reaction to Thomas speaking with her father in the Rock and not taking the time to visit with her.

Initially, she wanted to take Thomas to task for that oversight, but that desire had dissolved as quickly as it had sprung up. Childish, she knew, and not worthy of her. It seemed that Thomas was burdened continually with more and more to worry about, making the duties she faced as Princess of Fal Carrach pale in comparison.

"How do you balance it all?" she asked. "I have a hard enough time dealing with what my father gives me to do, then the training with Rya, Kael, and the myriad other tasks that are required of the Princess of Fal Carrach." She said the last with a trace of irritation.

Thomas smiled, looking into Kaylie's eyes. He was caught for a moment, his mind wandering in a direction that he found quite pleasing before he brought himself back to the topic at hand.

"I guess it's just a matter of perspective. I don't worry about something until I have to. Works for me, but it irritates Tiro to no end."

"Well, you can be quite aggravating, you know," Kaylie said lightly, a mischievous gleam in her eyes.

Thomas laughed, the tension he had felt building as he recalled his conversation with the Sylvan Warriors instead dissipating. "So I've been told. Many times."

Kaylie laughed as well, then looked up at the stars. They remained on the large rock in companionable silence, content simply to spend time with one another. As she sat there, she realized that for the first time since the incident in Tinnakilly, she had connected with Thomas. The distrust or circumspection wasn't there as it had been in the past, replaced by an openness that reminded her of when she had first met him. She smiled but didn't allow herself to get too excited. She hoped that openness would continue.

43

HOMEWARD BOUND

The massive kestrel glided over the Inland Sea from west to east. Its sharp eyes picked out the camps along the western coast and the troop carriers, which resembled over-sized barges, docked there, taking on supplies and men for the journey across the water. After several hours of flying, the endless blue finally gave way to towering peaks off in the distance. As it approached the mountains, the kestrel turned its attention to the northern shore, which butted up against the lower Highlands. The soldiers wearing the same colors as those on the other side of the Inland Sea had started building a handful of piers that jutted out from the shore to make it easier for the troop carriers to unload, while also cutting back the densely forested coast to create space for the soldiers' camps.

It was exactly as Thomas had seen when he used the Talent, but he had wanted to view it with his own eyes, or rather through his own eyes having assumed the shape of a raptor. Thomas circled lazily above the slowly forming encampment a couple more times before turning to the east and winging his way among the Highland peaks.

He had been flying for most of the day, tracking the

progress of Rodric's Armaghian army as it prepared to invade the Highlands, yet the entire time he had never been alone. Kestrels, the symbol of the Highlands, tended to be solitary creatures. But as soon as Thomas had used the Talent to change his shape and taken to the skies five raptors had joined him. Four flew the points of the compass always keeping him in the center, the fifth never strayed far from his side. It felt like an honor guard, as if the large kestrels wanted to ensure his safety.

Whether his perception was real or not, he couldn't say. He recognized the fifth raptor, having met this bird time and time again. He could tell by its eyes. There was a recognition there, as had been the case several times before. It gave him comfort, as if this kestrel knew him intimately and had been with him since the day he was born. Moreover, the kestrel filled him with a necessary confidence, for he and his Marchers were about to face the greatest challenge yet to his short rule.

With all that had been going on in the Highlands as the Marchers prepared for war, Thomas relished the opportunity to get away from the constant decisions, the always occurring negotiations, the inevitable crises that had to be addressed, if only for the better part of the day. He enjoyed soaring among the mountains of his homeland. He brightened even more as he and his escort flew past the final peaks in the east and out across the short channel to the Isle of Mist, his home for ten years before returning to his birthplace to claim his place as Highland Lord. He hadn't returned to where his grandparents had raised him since becoming Lord of the Highlands, so he looked forward to the opportunity as he and his raptor guard descended in lazy circles into a clearing in the middle of the island.

"You could have told us you were coming," said Rya, chestnut hair streaming down her back, her eyes sharp and intelligent.

Thomas used the Talent to take his human form, watching

as several of the raptors settled into the trees around them, though two remained aloft, gliding through the sky on the strong air currents coming off the Sea of Mist.

"It seems you've picked up several protectors," stated Rynlin, his features sharp, dark beard speckled with grey. Those who didn't know him would describe his appearance as ominous or dangerous, which was exactly what he wanted.

"I'm sorry, grandmother. I didn't know I had to ask before I could come home."

"Don't be smart, Thomas," the beautiful woman chided. "We rarely get to see you with all that's happening."

Rya stepped forward and hugged her grandson to her tightly. It had been months since she and Rynlin had visited him at the Crag with Tiro and Maden, though she had been keeping track of his exploits.

Rynlin stepped forward and gave his grandson an affectionate slap on the back.

"Come on. Let's go to the house. We have a stew over the fire and I'm hungry."

Rynlin led the way on the narrow trail, dodging the massive heart trees that rose around them. Very few heart trees remained in the Kingdoms, except for those that still clung to the remoter parts of the Highlands and the Isle of Mist. The trees grew several hundred feet into the air, the trunks often a hundred feet or more in width at the base, their roots gnarled and twisting across the forest floor and deep into the earth. With Rynlin's height he had to pay particular attention to where he stepped, ducking beneath several roots that resembled wooden arches that spanned the trail they walked upon.

They were almost home when Thomas tripped, falling flat on his face. Most would have assumed that he had stumbled on a root, but Thomas knew better.

"Beluil, I haven't seen you for months and that's how you

greet me, swiping one of your paws across my boot like when we were younger?"

Thomas pushed himself up and dusted himself off, addressing his comments to the large wolf that sat on his haunches in the middle of the trail, an innocent expression on his face. The beast's eyes twinkled with mischief. Sitting still, in the growing darkness his black fur allowed him to fade into the night, only the patch of white fur across his eyes giving any hint of where Beluil was situated.

"How did Beluil get here?"

"Your grandfather brought him across in that skiff you used to sail as a boy. He wanted to see you. Apparently, he knew you were on the way. We didn't see any harm in doing so. Your Marcher, Nestor, working with your grandfather and Beluil's wolfpacks, has all but eliminated the Ogren raiding parties seeking to enter the Highlands from the north, at least for the time being. And it seems their success has given the Shadow Lord reason to pause. The Sylvan Warriors scouting in the Charnel Mountains report that much of the dark creature activity has died down for now."

"Yes, they have been extremely effective," agreed Thomas, turning toward Beluil. "I missed you as well."

With that the deadly, pony-sized wolf launched himself in the air to land on Thomas' chest, taking him down onto the trail again, slathering his face with licks.

"All right, all right," said Thomas with a laugh, trying to keep the wolf slobber out of his eyes and mouth. He wrestled with Beluil in the dirt for a few minutes before giving his friend a hug across his neck. "Let's go home. I'm famished."

44

REQUEST FOR HELP

They had settled in front of the fire before dinner, Beluil stretching out his full frame on the floor so that Thomas could run his fingers lazily through the wolf's thick black fur. Being back in the home he had grown up in, the hollowed out trunk of a heart tree, it felt as if nothing had changed as he sat there contentedly. But he knew that was a false perception. Everything had changed.

Rynlin stood by the fire, adding carrots, onions, and some root vegetables to the stew he was preparing for that evening's dinner. Thomas noticed that Rynlin was quieter than usual, either intent on his task or deep in thought, though he couldn't determine which it might be.

"I understand that Kaylie visited you at the Crag," began Rya, sitting on a stool in front of her grandson.

"Yes, she said that she was looking for you."

"Did she?" replied Rya. "That's interesting. I'd already visited with her earlier that morning."

Thomas stared at his grandmother, eyes tight. She had done this to him when he was younger. She wanted something. Rather than ask her question directly, she liked to dance around the edges first and see what other tidbits of information she could peel away from him first.

"What are you suggesting?" he asked warily.

"Nothing, nothing at all. I just find it interesting that Kaylie decided to put all that effort into visiting you at the Crag. Perhaps there was more to her going to see you than she revealed."

"Maybe she just wanted more practice in the Talent," suggested Thomas, uneasy about the direction the conversation was taking.

"Maybe," agreed Rya. "But perhaps there was more to it than that. Perhaps she just wanted to see you. I understand you made quite an impression in Eamhain Mhacha and then on the journey back to the east."

"Where did you hear that?" asked Thomas, growing more and more uncomfortable.

Rya ignored Thomas' question. "You know Kaylie is quite an impressive young lady. Smart. Talented. Beautiful. Don't you agree, Rynlin?"

"You can leave me out of this," grumbled Thomas' grandfather as he sliced an onion and dropped the pieces into the pot.

"Why are you telling me this?" asked Thomas, the heat rising in his face.

"You know but you don't want to admit it," said Rya, her voice filled with a certainty that made Thomas fidget.

"Admit what?" demanded Thomas, his cheeks redder than a campfire. After all this time and everything he had been through, his grandmother could still make him feel uneasy with little effort.

"Your interest in Kaylie," replied Rya. "It's quite obvious."

"Maybe to you," said Thomas. "At the moment my focus is on other matters that are a bit more important than my interest in the Princess of Fal Carrach."

"Ha!" exclaimed Rya, her eyes shining brightly. "So, you are interested."

"That was a mistake, Thomas," interjected Rynlin. "You fell right into your grandmother's trap."

"Could we move on to a more relevant topic?" pleaded Thomas. "I need your help."

"For now," said Rya, a wicked smile on her face. "But don't think that this conversation is over."

"We thought you might," said Rynlin, who had taken out his pipe. Although he no longer smoked, holding it between his lips gave him some comfort.

"You've been tracking the dark creatures?"

"We have," said Rya, her voice laced with worry. "They're becoming more brazen. As we mentioned earlier, although the flow across the Northern Steppes has slowed for the moment, we expect the number of Ogren war parties slipping out of the Charnel Mountains to increase. We've seen signs of them massing closer to Blackstone before making their way to the flatlands."

"It's to be expected," said Rynlin. "The time is coming. We just don't know when exactly."

Thomas nodded at Rynlin, acknowledging the truth of his words. The Shadow Lord was building his strength, biding his time in the Charnel Mountains, and seeking the right moment to return. He had last been defeated during the Great War, but he had not been destroyed. Then the Kingdoms were stronger and more united and the Sylvana were more powerful, if only because of their greater number those centuries past. What would happen this time if only a few Kingdoms and the remaining Sylvan Warriors answered the call to fight the Dark Horde at the Breaker? Could they prevent the Shadow Lord and his servants from flooding the Kingdoms? All important questions with no good answers.

Thomas' grandparents thought that the Shadow Lord would

reveal himself soon, tiring of the need for proxies such as Rodric and Killeran. The two Sylvan Warriors had seen the signs, and they were worried. Very worried. Circumstances had changed a great deal since the last time the Shadow Lord had sought the Kingdoms for his own during the Great War. The ranks of the Sylvan Warriors had dwindled since then, even more so in just the last few years thanks to the Shadow Lord's assassins. The fact that the Kingdoms were weaker didn't help. Several had turned inward, focused on internal challenges, such as the threat of rebellion, or, in the cases of a few, warring factions for the crown. Much of this unrest was driven by Rodric, who deftly used the instability to his advantage. Only the eastern Kingdoms could be counted on to stand at the Breaker when the time came. And when the Shadow Lord attacked, try as the eastern Kingdoms might, they would not be strong enough on their own to hold back the Shadow Lord and keep the Dark Horde from wreaking its havoc on the Kingdoms. Something that had been touched upon just a few months before when Rynlin and Rya, along with Tiro and Maden, had visited Thomas at the Crag.

As a result, more and more of the Sylvan Warriors were placing their faith in Thomas, hoping that he could overcome the weaknesses that plagued them in their fight against the Shadow Lord. Tiro had said as much while berating Thomas. The prophecies had spoken of the Defender of the Light, arising at the Kingdoms' time of greatest need to oppose the Lord of the Shadow. As if Rynlin could read this thoughts, Thomas' grandfather began reciting what sounded like poetry, but offered an uncertain clue as to the future.

WHEN A CHILD of life and death
   Stands on high
   Drawn by faith

He shall hold the key to victory in his hand.

*S*WORDS OF FIRE *echo in the burned rock*
  Balancing the future on their blades.

*L*IGHT DANCES *with dark*
  Green fire burns in the night
  Hopes and dreams follow the wind
  To fall in black or white.

THOMAS REMEMBERED VIVIDLY that he had been in this very room the first time that Rynlin had offered his argument as to why he believed Thomas was the Defender of the Light, the one fated to fight the Shadow Lord. His grandfather had begun with the first line: *When a child of life and death.* Rynlin had explained, "When you were born, you had green eyes, which throughout the Kingdoms is recognized as a symbol for life. And any birth obviously symbolizes life. On a sadder note, your mother, Marya, died during your birth."

"That could apply to many people," Thomas had remembered protesting.

"Yes, it could," Rynlin had said. "But I don't think it does. Look at the next line: *Stands on high.* It's a very vague reference. However, it could be speaking about two critical parts of your life. When one becomes Lord of the Highlands, it has traditionally been known as standing on high. And, when you join the Sylvana, you will be standing on high as well. In fact, you will be standing on the tallest peak in all the Kingdoms. I think the double reference to the Highlands and the Sylvana serves as added confirmation."

Of course, that portion of the prophecy had come to pass. Thomas' thoughts returned to that night so long ago.

"What about the rest of the prophecy? What else applies to me?" Thomas had asked.

"All of it, I think. We just won't know for sure until each event takes place. But I believe the last six lines refer to your battle with the Shadow Lord."

Rynlin had explained. "Let me repeat the lines of the prophecy that I think apply to you, and I'll give you my reasoning. Admittedly, the prophecies are all very obscure, and we really won't know if you are, in fact, the Defender of the Light until some later point in time. But, if you are fated to meet the Shadow Lord in combat, then it will happen. There will be no way you can avoid it. That's why I'm telling you this now. I want you to be prepared for that possibility. But I must repeat. I think it's more than just a possibility.

"Also, keep in mind that the prophecies have never been wrong, and though there are several different ones that vary in certain places, they are never very far off when it comes to the important events. For example, all the prophecies were correct as to when the Shadow Lord would appear in the world, and that we would defeat him at certain points in time. Now, this is the intriguing point.

"Before, the result of what would happen was always predetermined, meaning that the Great War was fated to occur, and it was expected that we would successfully push the Shadow Lord and his Dark Horde back into the Charnel Mountains. Of course, we didn't know this for certain until the Great War ended, and we went back to look at the prophecies. Then we were able to decipher what had largely been unintelligible to us before.

"At that time, we looked ahead and saw that a battle between the Defender of the Light and the Lord of the Shadow would take place sometime in the near future. Of course, when you're dealing with the prophecies the near future could be a hundred years, two hundred years or more. Anyway, the interesting thing ..."

"Frightening thing," Rya had interjected.

"Yes, that's probably the better word. The frightening thing is that that's where the prophecies end. That's as far as the Seers of Alfeos went in their forecasts — to the actual battle between the Defender of the Light and the Lord of the Shadow."

"What do you mean? They stopped seeing the future?" Thomas had asked. He had understood everything up to that point, but he still wasn't sure how he had fit into it.

"I mean that the prophecies end during the battle. The seers foretold nothing more beyond that point. They just stopped, and no one can explain why. Listen to the last six lines that I believe are relevant:

SWORDS OF FIRE *echo in the burned rock*
    Balancing the future on their blades.

LIGHT DANCES *with dark*
    Green fire burns in the night
    Hopes and dreams follow the wind
    To fall in black or white.

"SWORDS OF FIRE *echo in the burned rock.* That's a clear reference to the last battle, a point that is no longer debated by those who have studied the prophecies, some for hundreds of years longer than I. The battle will take place, and most likely somewhere in Shadow's Reach, or rather Blackstone, as it's known today."

"So, the Defender of the Light has to fight the Lord of the Shadow on his ground."

"Exactly, Thomas. Certainly not an auspicious beginning for the contest. Another reference, *Balancing the future on their blades*, gives us a hint as to what comes next, or rather what won't come next. The prophecies end with those six lines. Why? Because this battle will determine what will happen next. That's what the last line confirms: *To fall in black or white*. In the past, throughout the millennia since the Shadow Lord came to be, the victor of the battles between good and evil was always foretold. We have always been able to hold back the Dark Horde. To shackle the Lord of the Shadow. But not this time. The result will not be known until the battle is fought. There is nothing telling us what to expect."

"This battle will determine the future?"

"Yes, it will."

"And if the Defender of the Light loses?" Thomas had had a feeling that he already knew the answer, and he recalled how his stomach had soured as the realization had struck him.

"Then the Kingdoms have no future at all. The Shadow Lord and his Dark Horde will reign supreme, and humanity will face the possibility of servitude or extinction."

It had almost been too much for Thomas to take in at that time. He had guessed at this possibility, or perhaps even already knew it. He just didn't want to admit it to himself, not yearning to take on this additional potentially suffocating burden just yet. His grandfather's argument was logical. Logical enough for Thomas to believe it and to accept it. A part of him wanted to deny it, hoping desperately that Rynlin was wrong. The first attack by a Nightstalker as soon as he left the Isle of Mist for the first time so many years ago and the ones to follow suggested otherwise, however, and he knew that his wish was simply that — a wish. A path had been set before him, and no matter how he might try to change it, to find a new direction, he understood that such effort would be for naught. The course that had been given to him led in only one direction. Still, a small part of him wanted to resist that conclusion. But he knew in his heart that he couldn't as the memory of that conversation continued to play through his mind.

"And you think I'm the Defender of the Light? Just because a few lines seem to apply to me?"

"Yes, we do." Rya had nodded her agreement. "You are a child of life and death. You are expected to stand on high, at least once, when you return to the Highlands. And it also seems that you may become a member of the Sylvana. If you succeed, at the time you join the Sylvana, you will be standing in the Circle on a rocky promontory that sits atop the highest peak in the Highlands. The highest peak, in fact, in all the Kingdoms, even taller than those in the Charnel Mountains. When you are raised to Sylvan Warrior, much like when you become Lord of the Highlands, it is called standing on high. Another line seems to apply to you as well — *Green fire burns in the night.* You know, as well as I, what your eyes look like when you're angry, and especially during the night."

"I think green fire is a very appropriate description," Rynlin had agreed.

"That may be," Thomas had said. "But your argument is still quite flimsy."

Why? Why did they have to do this to him? Didn't he have enough to worry about as it was? He recalled the fear that had surged within him then, threatening to incapacitate him, a fear that still surfaced when he dreamed.

"I know," Rynlin had replied, "but I still think I'm right."

Thomas had stared at his grandfather for several long minutes after his explanation. Rynlin had watched him with a quiet intensity. He had never known his grandfather to be wrong, and he didn't think he would reach these conclusions without a great deal of thought. Thomas still wasn't sure if he believed it all himself. Nevertheless, as his grandfather had said, it was better to be prepared for the future, rather than be surprised by it.

"When will I know if I'm the Defender of the Light?" he had asked.

His grandparents had said that he would simply know, and they had been right, as always. When he had become a Sylvan Warrior, he had known. Though he didn't want to admit it then, he knew in his heart that he was the one destined to fight an evil that had never been defeated. A frightening thought, indeed, as Rya had clarified, but he needed to focus on more pressing matters at the moment, so he forced his attention back to the present, and away from an old conversation that had stayed with him over the years.

"Rodric will be bringing his army into the Highlands across the Inland Sea. In fact, he's already begun ferrying his troops. Fal Carrach stands with us but can't do so openly. Gregory needs to concentrate on Dunmoor. My Marchers can take on Rodric and his army, but we can't also deal with the dark creatures that we expect will be entering the northern Highlands more and more frequently. I need Nestor and his Marchers with me."

"And you would like more help from the Sylvan Warriors in the northern Highlands?"

"Yes. If my Marchers and I can engage Rodric, without having to worry about what might be coming at us from behind, I think we can stop the High King."

"You realize that to do this I would need more than just the handful of Sylvan Warriors helping us now," said Rynlin. "You're asking for more than what some of the Sylvan Warriors may be willing to give. Traditionally we have stood ready to fight the Shadow Lord when his armies march from Blackstone. You've already unsettled Tiro and several others by suggesting that the Sylvana ignore the Breaker and instead attack the Shadow Lord directly. I believe that Maden and a few others favor the shift in strategy, but I can't speak for all. If they choose to help, they will do so on their own."

"I know the history and traditions, Rynlin. You and Rya made sure of that. Nevertheless, times are changing. And I recall the resistance Tiro presented the last time we spoke at the Crag. But the Shadow Lord is playing a different game now. He has Rodric in his hand and he's using his dark creatures to soften the Highlands. If the Sylvan Warriors wait as they have in the past, it will be too late. They need to get into the fight now. If they're willing, ask them to focus on the raiding parties. If they do that, my Marchers can manage Rodric and his host."

"We don't disagree with you, Thomas," said Rya. "But please understand that it will be difficult to change the opinions of some of your brother and sister Sylvan Warriors. They have done things the same way for centuries. Many are set in their ways. Even a small change can be difficult."

"I know. All I'm asking is that you try."

"In addition to Maden, I know some who would be more than willing to help," said Rynlin. "I'll start with them. Tiro and some of the others won't like it, but the signs are clear. You're right, Thomas. We need to adjust our approach if we're to have any chance against the Shadow Lord. I'll see what I can do."

"Thank you," said Thomas, knowing that his grandparents would help, but not knowing if they could convince the other Sylvan Warriors. "One final request?"

"What might that be?" asked Rya.

"The Key, as we discussed briefly at the Crag," Thomas replied simply. "Let's not forget the line: *He shall hold the key to victory in his hand*. If any of this is to work, if we're to have any chance of getting into Blackstone, I need that Key, whatever it might be."

"I've reached out to others who might know more than I

about the Key," said Rynlin. "So far, I've learned nothing that we didn't know or suspect already."

"And we still don't have any confirmation about what we're looking for," added Rya. "An actual key or something else."

"But we'll keep trying," said Rynlin.

"Thank you," said Thomas, sighing, not surprised that progress had been difficult. "Any help you and the other Sylvan Warriors can provide, I'd appreciate. I know that it's important, absolutely critical, in fact, that we find the Key. But Rodric needs to take precedence right now."

Thomas settled back into his chair, staring into the fire, stroking Beluil's soft fur. He could feel the time growing short. The Shadow Lord was gaining strength, and his own trepidation was increasing. He feared that the Kingdoms wouldn't be ready. In fact, he was certain that most would not be prepared when the time came to fight the Dark Horde. He feared that despite his best efforts he would lose the Highlands to Rodric once more, ensuring the final destruction of his homeland. And, most of all, he feared that he didn't have the strength or courage required for the most important task of all – challenging the Lord of the Shadow.

45

THE KEY

Rya placed a bowl of hot vegetable stew in front of Rynlin, who sat quietly at the small table in their home. Thomas had left to take Beluil back to the Highlands in his childhood skiff, needing his friend to continue his good work in the northern Highlands. The smoke from the cook fire disappeared ingeniously up through the flue built into their tree, dissipating along the way so that anyone looking for a sign of human habitation in the forest would never see it.

Heart trees dominated the Isle of Mist, so when Rynlin and Rya first came to the island, they chose to take advantage of that fact. Rynlin crafted their home from the inside of a heart tree, creating a comfortable space, except for one mistake. A doorway built for the petite Rya rather than him, which meant that more often than not he banged his head on the frame. But it was a minor inconvenience, one that he could live with. As Rya liked to say, it helped to keep him humble.

The heart trees were the oldest in the world, most of them gone because of the demand for their wood. The legends said that you could hear the power of nature coursing through them, their roots reaching to the very center of the earth to support their massive height. The legends also said that when the last heart tree died, the world would die as well.

As Rynlin played with his stew rather than eat it, his mind focused on the challenge Thomas had placed before him, one that he had been thinking about since his visit to the Crag some months before. He knew that Tiro and some of the other more obstinate Sylvan Warriors would resist his entreaties at first, but they would come around. He was certain of that. Thomas would get the help that he needed in the northern Highlands. No, the larger, more immediate concern continued to plague him. A problem that he had mulled for longer than he cared to remember, yet he still had not found an answer that satisfied him. How could Thomas enter Blackstone, the city of the Shadow Lord, without being detected? The Shadow Lord had set wards and traps constructed of Dark Magic that would ensnare any who entered who had not pledged themselves to his service. The results would be gruesome and deadly. No matter how strong he or Thomas or any of the Sylvana were in the Talent, they could not break through all those magical protections without being discovered and likely destroyed. That was the crux of the matter. Thomas had to enter Blackstone safely to have any chance of success. To have an opportunity to challenge the Shadow Lord. The prophecy required it. Of course, if the prophecy demanded it ...

Perhaps that was it, mused Rynlin, snapping out of his reveries. The Key.

"Rya, do you think the prophecy offers a more literal answer?"

"You need to be more specific," prompted Rya.

"From earlier this evening when we spoke with Thomas. He wanted to bring the fight to the Shadow Lord, attack not defend."

"You seemed quite pleased with that as you did when he first mentioned it at the Crag."

"I was. He reminded me of myself."

"It's good to see your arrogance remains even as you've aged," said Rya with a smirk.

"Yes, well, be that as it may, Thomas is right. Defending at the Breaker as we've done in the past won't work. The Shadow Lord's Dark Horde will be too many and we'll be too few, even if the armies of the Highlands, Fal Carrach, Benewyn and the Desert Clans join us. It would simply be a matter of time before the Dark Horde broke through, and Thomas would have little chance to do what he must do."

Rynlin then recited the prophecy, one that he had studied for centuries, one that still held mysteries yet to be confirmed. One that felt more like a curse than a path to future knowledge.

When a child of life and death,
 Stands on high,
 Drawn by faith,
 He shall hold the key to victory in his hand.

Swords of fire echo in the burned rock
 Balancing the future on their blades.

Light dances with dark,
 Green fire burns in the night,
 Hopes and dreams follow the wind,
 To fall in black or white.

"As you said earlier, *Swords of fire echo in the burned rock* suggests Blackstone, doesn't it?" asked Rya. "It almost seems that Thomas is supposed to be there to challenge the Shadow

Lord. That despite all that the Lord of the Shadow might do to stop him, the prophecies seem to suggest that he will make it to that place at the appropriate time."

"It does. As Thomas suggested, could the line before be the answer: *He shall hold the key to victory in his hand*? I had always assumed that line was more metaphorical than literal. But could it be as simple as that? Thomas will hold the Key? An actual Key? Have I spent all this time looking for a solution that may have been there from the very start?"

"Have you seen any reference to this in your scrolls and books?"

"I'll go back through them after dinner, but I don't recall anything."

"If you don't have any information on this Key, where else could we find what we need?"

"I haven't been there for almost a century, but Tiro confirmed that there was a library that he believed was quite complete when it came to ancient texts and artifacts and the mysteries surrounding the prophecies."

"You want to go there? Despite the obvious danger?"

"Why not?" responded Rynlin, an evil grin splitting his face. "It might give us a chance to help Thomas in some other ways as well."

46

THE SEARCH BEGINS

Two massive hawks settled onto the darkened southern tower of the Eamhain Mhacha fortress, the sun having set several hours before. In a brief flash of white light the hawks disappeared from the windowsill, replaced by two people dressed in blacks and greys to better slide through the shadows, one rather tall, the other petite.

They stood silently in the room at the top of the tower for several minutes, allowing their senses to expand and their eyes to adjust to the darkness. They didn't move until they could pick out the shapes of the thousands of books and scrolls that littered the library of Eamhain Mhacha. Clearly, based on the fine layer of dust that covered everything, no one had visited the library, which descended several floors into the tower, for quite some time. Decades at the least.

"You know where you're going?" asked Rynlin, who gazed around the library, trying to plan an appropriate line of attack for the books and scrolls in front of him, some neatly shelved and organized, others resting haphazardly in piles on the floor or the long wooden tables that ran the diameter of the circular room.

Rodric and the bulk of his guard had left the capital of Armagh for their invasion of the Highlands, so neither Rya nor Rynlin worried about being disturbed. Their quick search with the Talent confirmed that no one was about in the tower. But Rynlin and Rya still wanted to be careful. Therefore, they had given themselves until one hour before dawn to complete their respective tasks.

"Yes," replied Rya, as she opened the door to the library quietly, thankful that the rusty hinges didn't squeak so loudly that the sound would draw someone's attention, and slipped into the hallway, the darkness complete as the torches lining the walls remained dark and cold in their sconces.

As Rynlin closed the door behind his wife, he conjured a small ball of white light that hovered just above his head, illuminating his way for a few feet in all directions. Satisfied that no one looking up at the tower from below would see the glow of his magical torch, he walked between two shelves stacked to the ceiling with books to begin his search.

47

———

BOUNTY FOUND

Rya slipped back into the library with the sun just about to touch the horizon and later than Rynlin had expected. But the extra time she had given him had proven fruitful.

"Any luck?" asked Rya as she closed the door behind her.

"Yes, I think I have what we need, or at least a good path to follow."

"It'll have to do for now. We need to leave. I sensed dark creatures in the caves below the keep, possibly a Dragas or two."

"Then it's time for us to go. Did you find what you were looking for?"

Rynlin and Rya knew that Rodric was meticulous. Though he adhered to a treaty only so long as it benefited him, never fearful of the consequences of breaking it, they had hoped that his obsessiveness with capturing everything in writing would work to their advantage. Therefore, Rya's decision to search Rodric's private office behind his throne room to see if she could locate anything that might prove useful in the future.

She had worked for hours to find all his hidden caches and

secret safes, and then opened each one carefully without being detected or setting off any nasty surprises, as all were protected by a Dark Magic placed there by one of Rodric's allies. She had found more than she had hoped for. The documents laid out in stark detail several of the secret alliances and agreements that Rodric had put in place with his future goals in mind.

"I found more than I expected. Rodric has been busy. And some of our guesses are now fact."

"We'll deal with it later," said Rynlin. "Time to go."

Taking hold of the Talent, the two Sylvan Warriors changed back into hawks and launched themselves from the windowsill. They began winging their way to the east and toward the rising sun, hoping that their work during the night would prove useful to their grandson and the Highlands.

48

THE GAME BEGINS

Arriving at the clearing he had selected, one that was more of a ledge that reached out from the peak and gave him an excellent view of the southern Highlands and the Inland Sea that abutted the peaks, Thomas patted Acero on the neck in thanks as he dropped down from the unicorn's back. The black unicorn compared in size to an overlarge draft horse, though he was built for both speed and stamina, his twisting black horn that extended almost eight feet in length adding to his formidable appearance.

Acero had arrived on his own several weeks before, finding Thomas near the Crag. Overjoyed to see his friend, Thomas had touched the unicorn's horn, images flowing through Thomas' mind and showing the massive steed what had happened since he had become the Lord of the Highlands.

Shortly thereafter, Beluil appeared, tackling Thomas in his preferred way of greeting. After rolling around in the dirt for a time, much to the amusement and shock of the watching Marchers, Thomas gave Beluil a hug, pleased to have his childhood friend with him again. After Thomas returned with Beluil to the Highlands from the Isle of Mist several weeks before, the huge wolf had continued his efforts at keeping the mountains clear of dark creatures, using the brief respite from Ogren raiding parties to bring together all his packs and sweep through the Highlands from north to south in search of any dark creatures that may have escaped their attention.

Taking one glance at the massive wolf, whose shoulder came up to his own, Oso suggested, "With a friend like that, there's no need to worry about Rodric's army at all. He can probably go through it all on his own."

The howls of Beluil's pack, actually several dozen packs all brought together as one, only strengthened Oso's opinion. Thomas thanked his friend for the efforts of the wolves. He asked that Beluil and his packs scour the mountains once more as they returned to where the Highlands met the Northern Steppes in order to continue to assist Rynlin and the Sylvan Warriors in their efforts to protect against encroachment from the dark creatures that had once again begun making their way out of the Charnel Mountains. Though the flow of the Shadow Lord's servants had slowed to a trickle for a time, the number of Ogren and Shades seeking to cross the Northern Steppes had started to increase once more. Thomas assumed that the escalation in activity in the north was designed to distract from what was about to occur in the southern Highlands. Beluil happily obliged Thomas, he and his packs moving quickly through the Highlands to connect once again with the Sylvan Warriors.

Walking to the edge of the clearing, a thousand-foot drop just a step away, Thomas used the Talent as Rynlin had shown him when he was first training as a warrior. In just seconds, two hazy forms took shape at his sides, then solidified as Thomas pulled in more of the natural magic of the world and applied it to his task. Antonin, First Spear of the Carthanians, and Fergus Steelheart, Captain of the Golden Blades, now stood next to him.

To teach Thomas how to defend himself, Rynlin had recalled the great heroes of the past from the spirit world so that he could learn from the very best no matter the fighting discipline. After mastering how to use the Talent for this purpose, Thomas had continued his training on his own, calling forth the warriors of legend to improve his skills whenever time allowed. But he also took advantage of the knowledge these legendary fighters could share with him regarding strategy and tactics, having already employed their advice in various skirmishes and battles.

"That's quite a host," said Fergus, looking down at the steadily increasing Armaghian army, a dozen or so troop transports rocking in the waves and waiting to dock, others having disembarked their soldiers to a makeshift camp on the northern shore of the Inland Sea and preparing for the journey back to Dunmoor in order to pick up the next wave of soldiers.

A tall man, Fergus had led the Golden Blades, a famed troop of mercenaries who never failed to complete a task given to them by whichever employer they were working for at the time. Fergus had only one rule. He would never work for someone who had sworn allegiance to the Shadow Lord. His long, golden moustache covered much of his face from his lip down, curling up at the ends to give the bushy hair the appearance of an ox's horn.

"Agreed," said Antonin, standing next to Thomas in a loincloth and holding a spear that reached above the tall warrior's head.

The First Spear of the Carthanians towered over both Thomas and Fergus. He had never lost a duel, defeating more than a thousand men in single combats that could end only one way. After such long service to his king, and fearing that his heart had turned to stone because of the number of challengers he had dispatched, Antonin had left his ancient kingdom in an attempt to regain his humanity. Thomas had never had the courage to ask whether Antonin had succeeded in achieving his goal.

"What's your strategy?" asked Fergus, watching the soldiers scurrying around the beach.

"They're too many to fight at once," answered Thomas. "Even if I gathered all the Marchers in the Highlands, they would outnumber us ten to one. I don't mind those odds, but I don't trust Rodric and his ally, and I can't take that risk."

"Agreed," said Antonin.

"Try not to talk so much," said Fergus with a grin, enjoying the opportunity to irritate his spirit companion. Antonin looked down on Fergus as if he were no more than a bug to be stepped on, but the mercenary captain ignored him. "Then what do you do, Thomas?"

"Rodric feels safe with that many soldiers, but it's also a weakness. He won't be able to bring his full force through any one pass into the Highlands without creating a bottleneck that would make his host easy pickings, assuming, of course, that his goal is to reach the Crag. He'll need to divide his army."

"Agreed," said Antonin.

Thomas bit his lip, holding back a smile as Fergus fought the urge to offer another smart remark, knowing Antonin's legendary short temper, and not wanting to bear the brunt of it even if they were only spirits.

"That's when we'll attack," said Thomas. "I'll form the Marchers into autonomous raiding parties. I'll have them strike each of Rodric's columns separately. Rodric and the distinct columns of his army can go where they want. We'll follow, track, and winnow the Armaghians down, kill as many as we can through quick attacks, then melt back into the wilderness. We'll see if we can lead the High King where we want him to go."

"I like it," said Fergus, nodding his head in approval. "After the first few attacks, the soldiers' fears will begin to multiply.

They'll jump at their own shadows. That fear will play on their minds, wear them down faster as a fighting force."

"Agreed," said Antonin.

Fergus shook his head in exasperation, Thomas barely able to hold back a laugh.

49

___

PLANS REVEALED

"You didn't have to make such a dramatic entrance," said Gregory, his daughter Kaylie sitting beside him on one of the couches in his private office.

Rynlin and Rya sat across from them on another couch, their haggard appearance testifying to the challenges of their journey.

After reviewing the documents Rya had stolen from Rodric, they knew what they had to do with the opportunity presented to them. Making use of the Talent and their shapeshifting abilities, Rynlin and Rya visited the Desert Clans, Benewyn and Kenmare, all traditional allies of the Highlands. They left their final stop for Fal Carrach.

"My apologies, Gregory. My husband has always preferred a little drama whenever possible."

"Think of it as a training exercise, Gregory," said Rynlin. "The guards we startled upon appearing on your battlements will be all the more vigilant now."

"Of that I have no doubt," agreed Gregory. "And if I may, Lady Keldragan, thank you for taking the time to teach Kaylie how to make use of her newfound skill. I never knew she had such an ability, but it certainly has proven useful."

"It's a pleasure," said Rya. "She's not as headstrong as our grandson, so teaching Kaylie is a much simpler task. Besides, she's a quick learner, which makes working with her all the more enjoyable."

"That I've discovered," said Gregory. "She's been taking great pleasure in offering me little surprises whenever she can, just to gauge my reaction."

"Well, I just wanted to ..." Kaylie began, but she stopped her attempted explanation when she saw Rya's hard glare.

"I'm sure Kaylie will find better uses for her Talent, am I right, girl?"

"Yes, Rya. I certainly will." Kaylie looked as if she had been caught with her hand in the cookie jar.

Gregory struggled not to laugh, never having seen his daughter so thoroughly disciplined with nary a harsh word and no more than an intense frown. He'd have to talk with Rya about how he might be able to do that himself, but first he needed to attend to business. He held out the documents he had just read, all bearing the well-known signature of the High King.

"You've shown these to Rendael and Sarelle?" The King of Fal Carrach's expression had transformed into a dark cloud.

"We have, Gregory. And to Chuma and the other Desert Clan chiefs."

Gregory was not surprised to see Rodric's signed order for the assassination of Talyn Kestrel, an act that sent a scorching anger through him. But what did surprise him was with whom he had made the agreement. To say nothing of all the other agreements he had concocted with Loris of Dunmoor, Norin Dinnegan and several others. Taken together, the documents essentially set out his plans for taking control of the Kingdoms.

"I had assumed that the past was becoming the present,"

said Gregory. "Your grandson, when he helped us against the Fearhounds, suggested as much. And I've seen it with my own eyes, as my men have come up against Ogren and other dark creatures in recent months during their patrols."

"It's just the beginning, Gregory," said Rya, with some sadness in her voice. "As you can see, the Shadow Lord has a willing ally. If he gets a foothold beyond the Breaker, all will be lost."

"The other Kingdoms?" asked Kaylie. "How have they responded?"

His daughter's question pleased Gregory. She would rule well when the time came.

"They understand the threat they face," said Rynlin. "The Desert Clans will create problems on Dunmoor's northern border, forcing Loris to keep a guard and hopefully prevent his moving his army in support of Rodric's."

"Sarelle will have the bulk of her forces moving up through the Gullet within the week," said Rya. "Rendael's are already on the move."

Gregory nodded his approval. "That's good to hear. Your grandson saved my daughter's life, my life, the lives of my men. Fal Carrach remains an ally of the Highlands. We will stand with the Highland Lord."

50

NO EXCUSES

High King Rodric Tessaril arrived at General Chengiz's base of operations in the southern Highlands in a venomous mood, which only became more toxic when he saw the Armaghian soldiers drawn up before him, their armor shining brightly in the midday sun and putting to shame the soldiers in Rodric's escort. The High King's personal guard, their armor dented and scratched and showing the signs of rust and hard use, cloaks torn or missing altogether, several wearing blood-stained bandages, and with half as many men as started out from the northern shore of the Inland Sea, only served to stoke the Armaghian King's anger.

Before Chengiz, a reserved man with the habits and formalities of his long service to Armagh deeply ingrained, could direct Rodric to his tent, the anger boiling just beneath the surface of the High King's volatile temper burst forth.

"They fight like cowards!" shouted Rodric. "As soon as we entered the Highlands, arrows rained down on us. Then one surprise attack after another. We'd wake up in the morning and find a squad murdered during the night. Yet not once would those Highland cowards stand against us. Not once would they fight a fair combat! Cowardly dogs!"

Chengiz listened to the tirade with no expression betraying his true feelings. He could have replied that from a military perspective, knowing that his forces overmatched the Highlanders in terms of numbers but not in fighting ability, he would have adopted the same strategy as that of his opponent. But wisely he chose not to speak, knowing the potential result. Instead he stood there calmly, allowing the High King to tire himself out, much as he did when his children threw tantrums as toddlers.

"I've lost half my men, and we barely made it here at all!" Rodric screamed as he stormed into Chengiz's command tent. The High King began pacing, a nervous energy infusing him, his mind spinning furiously. "But something is not right. Those cowards are trying to play with us. It's almost as if the Marchers let us through, like they want us to be here. Why haven't you defeated them yet, Chengiz? They are so few compared to our much larger host."

"That is part of the problem, my king," said Chengiz, having absorbed the verbal onslaught and hoping that Rodric's thoughts and emotions had settled so that he could explain his own strategy. "Compared to our forces, the Marchers are fewer in number. They can't take us on directly and hope to win, so they're trying to pick when and where they fight. If they can slice off a piece here, a piece there, without getting drawn into a pitched battle, it's to their advantage. Because of the rugged terrain and limited options for traveling through the countryside, we have few other good choices, and it plays to the Marchers' strengths. We simply need to absorb the losses as we can and continue with our agreed-upon strategy."

"It's a waste of time," grumbled Rodric. "We need to drive toward the Crag and take that damn fortress. Then we can finish the Marchers once and for all."

Chengiz chose not to correct his king. He understood Rodric's fixation with the symbol of Highland power, but in his opinion the Crag, still being rebuilt, was of little consequence as a military target. Conquering the Highlands had little to do with capturing a citadel or broad swathes of the Kingdom's territory, as had been made plain during Killeran's regency and the occupation by the Army of the Black Sword. Rather, it had everything to do with defeating the Marchers themselves. For the Marchers were the Highlands. If the Marchers were no longer a viable fighting force, the Kingdom would fall. Yet as Chengiz thought on it, the whisper in the back of his mind suggested that try as he might, he would not defeat the Marchers with the army he led, or the king he served.

"I don't care how many men are killed!" shouted the High King. "We can replace them. We will take the Crag, no matter the cost."

"Marching a large army through the Highlands, in this particular terrain surrounded by gullies, peaks and trenches, does nothing more than put a huge target on our back," argued Chengiz, locking away his mounting frustration. He then tried to explain in a reasonable tone the challenges faced by the Armaghian host. "With such a sizable force our movement is limited. And if we break the army into smaller pieces, as we did to get the men and supplies here because of the few passable trails, the Marchers can decide who to attack first, destroy them, then move on to the next target. That's the dilemma we face now. Time and the terrain work against us and favor the Marchers."

"I will have no excuses, General Chengiz." Rodric stared at him with a gaze that hinted at an encroaching madness. "Do whatever you need to do. Just get the men ready to march by morning. We head for the Crag at first light."

51

LOOSE THE MARCHERS

The sun began to rise behind Thomas, Oso and Coban as they watched from a hidden spot on a finger of rock that jutted out from a craggy summit and overlooked the Armaghian army's base of operations. They studied the soldiers as they formed into their ranks, the advance guard already beginning to march out on the only trail that wound its way around the snow-capped mountains toward the Crag. It was a tight path and treacherous as it snaked along the fringe of several towering peaks, thousand-foot or more drops a constant danger for any not wary of the verge. No more than four or five men abreast could travel along the trail safely, to say nothing of the problems it would create for the Armaghians' wagons and supplies.

"Will you look at that," said Oso with a soft chuckle. "I've never seen a peacock ride a horse before."

Rodric had emerged from his tent and was now using a step stool to climb onto his horse. His immaculately scrubbed armor shined brightly in the sunlight, and his plumed helmet seemed to rise forever into the sky.

"He makes quite a target," mused Coban. "If only we were a bit closer."

"We'll have our chance," said Thomas. "Are the Marchers ready?"

"Yes, Thomas. Squads of ten as you ordered. They know what to do."

"Good. Oso, you're in command. If Rodric thought his journey to this point in the Highlands was punishing, it's time to demonstrate just how much more difficult his trek to the Crag will be."

"With pleasure."

Thomas turned away from the scene, scrabbling back from the lip of the rock until he was out of sight before standing up. Oso and Coban mimicked his actions.

"Let loose the Marchers. Let them show the High King the error of his ways."

52

CAT AND MOUSE

General Chengiz, First Lord of Armagh, stood silently in his tent, trying to show no emotion as he received the report from the young soldier who struggled against pain and fatigue to remain on his feet before him. Tall and ramrod straight with a flowing mustache that dipped several inches below his chin, Chengiz had the bearing of a man born to be a soldier, and in fact he was. A male member of the Chengiz family had served in the Armaghian army for an unbroken period of more than three hundred years.

Chengiz valued duty and honor above all else. Therefore, he would listen to this soldier without losing his temper, already guessing at what he was about to learn. With his uniform torn and blood still seeping from wounds to his head and arm, the young man sought to do his duty by reporting to his commanding officer before seeking medical attention. Chengiz respected that.

"I was lucky to escape, General Chengiz," the soldier said in a labored breath, having run through the craggy landscape of the Highlands for the last few hours.

Chengiz had established a forward base deeper among the

mountain peaks, where he could gather his soldiers and make ready for the next step now that he had no choice but to break his army into distinct wings in order to reach the Crag. The initial trail that the Armaghian army had taken east had become more and more treacherous for an army to march upon. The narrow track tightened as the incline increased, what had once been a path for five soldiers across narrowing to space for no more than two or three, until finally it had come to an end at a crossroads. From there three different tracks meandered through the mountains and eventually converged once again near the Crag, though these new routes appeared to be no more than game trails. Chengiz hoped to use this base, situated several leagues from the valley that surrounded the Crag, to prepare for the assault that would allow him to take the Highland capital as his king commanded, despite his several attempts at changing the High King's mind.

"You were selected to escape."

The soldier stopped short in his recounting, confused. "What do you mean, General?"

"You were the only man to escape the attack, correct?"

"Yes, General."

"It wasn't luck. The Marchers did a very thorough job from what you've said, not only killing your compatriots but also destroying all the wagons and supplies. Obviously, if they wanted to kill you, they would have. The Marchers are the best fighters in the Kingdoms. The only way to defeat them is through the application of overwhelming force or sorcery. And with this new Highland Lord, the sorcery upon which our illustrious king has relied upon in the past apparently is useless." Chengiz said the last as if it left a bad taste in his mouth. Clearly, he did not approve of all of the decisions his monarch had made or the tools he had employed.

"They let me escape?"

"Yes, they did. Because the Marchers wanted me to know

what had happened, and you were their messenger. So you weren't lucky to escape, you were lucky to live."

The soldier had been through a lot during the last day, and his exhaustion had fogged his mind. But understanding slowly dawned. He grinned sadly at the thought.

"I'll take it."

"As would I," said Chengiz. "You've done well, soldier. Now off to the physick for your wounds."

"Yes, General. Thank you, General."

After the soldier left, Chengiz slumped in his chair, shaking his head in irritation. He had known from the start that invading the Highlands and attacking the Marchers would be a difficult challenge. Based on the results of the last few weeks, it appeared to be madness and the recipe for disaster. In fact, he had argued against it. Chengiz had seen through the flimsy excuse offered for the invasion, not believing for a second the outrageous claims made by Lord Killeran regarding the Marchers burning homesteads and villages. Of course, the Dunmoorian Lord had conveniently made himself scarce as the Armaghian host slogged its way deeper into the Highland wilderness. But Chengiz had no choice in the matter, having to do his duty once the High King issued his orders.

Chengiz had been surprised when the Marchers had not attacked immediately upon his entering the Highlands with his first column of men to set up this forward camp. But now he understood why. The Marchers had wanted to give the Armaghians a goal, one that they could likely achieve. All they had to do was march from the camp at the Inland Sea a couple dozen leagues into the Highlands. From there they would be in a position to strike at the Crag. And Rodric had fallen for it. Chengiz felt as if he were being led around by the nose, and he hated it.

The Marchers knew that the Armaghians had more men, but because of the limitations of the Highland trails and passes,

Chengiz had to break his larger force into smaller groups. That requirement had played right into the hands of the Marchers, who excelled at striking and then fading back into the Highland wild before the Armaghians could respond. What worried him was that from what the soldier who had just left had explained, the Marchers were growing more confident, and as a result bolder. Their hit and run attacks had proven extraordinarily effective to the point where the supplies he had here at this forward camp were precipitously low and continued to dwindle by the day as barely a trickle of what his army needed to survive made it from the Armaghian depot on the shore of the Inland Sea.

But the Marchers had changed their strategy in the last few days. They had hit the supply column and then hit again and again, until not a single Armaghian soldier survived, except for the one who had made his way here. The Armaghians had lost the horses and oxen dragging the supply wagons, and he assumed the Marchers now benefited from the supplies and transport that he and his men so desperately needed.

Three other columns had left the camp at the Inland Sea the same day as the one that had just been destroyed. They should have been here by now. But he had not heard a word. How could he? None of the scouts he had sent out to find the supply parties had returned yet, and he did not expect them to. Chengiz, ever the realist, had assumed the worst.

Rodric's quest to take the Highlands for his own, and demanding that Chengiz capture the Crag first, was making the strategic situation much easier and simpler for the Marchers, who didn't seem to care about the Crag. The Highland Lord had split his forces smartly, allowing them to work independently in their specific areas of responsibility. The way to the Crag had been left open, and that old fortress beckoned like a death wish. The Marchers didn't have to worry about the quality of the trails, the lack of supplies or ridiculously inappropriate orders from a king who didn't understand the reality of their situation. No, they only had to fight, and for their homes and families no less.

Yet when Chengiz got to the Crag, what happened next? Would he be in a position to extend his reach in the Highlands, making use of his superior numbers? Or would he be the one in a cage, tied to a capital the Marchers didn't care about in a place where his opponent could do to his rapidly diminishing forces whatever he wanted?

In this game of cat and mouse, Rodric had thought that the Marchers would be the mice, slinking off into their protected valleys and high peaks to hide. But Rodric didn't understand the Marchers as Chengiz did. With his superior numbers, he could certainly play the role of the cat. But no matter the number of Marchers, in their homeland they would always play the role of the mountain lion. As a soldier he appreciated the simplicity and effectiveness of the strategy. He also detested the fact that he now bore the brunt of its success.

Chengiz raised his head when he heard a commotion outside his tent. He pounded his fists against the arms of his chair in frustration. He had no doubt about what the messenger who likely had just survived a similar experience as the soldier who had just left had to report.

53

FAIR FIGHT

The Shade was proving more difficult to kill than Rynlin had expected. When he and Catal Huyuk had sprung their trap at the very edge of the northern Highlands eliminating the Ogren had been a fairly simple task, but the Shade had slithered free. The creature reminded Rynlin of a poisonous snake, its movements sinuous, its touch with that corrupted black blade deadly. The Sylvan Warrior circled the dark creature, the milky white eyes tracking his movements. He could have used the Talent to destroy the dark creature, but he chose to use a blade instead. He wanted to conserve his strength and not give away his location to any practitioner of Dark Magic, knowing that there were more Ogren raiding parties heading across the Northern Steppes and that he and the other Sylvan Warriors needed to intercept them before they reached the higher passes in the Highlands.

"Would you finish this already," a deep voice rumbled behind him. "We need to get moving."

Rynlin ignored the tremor of irritation that began to grow within him, instead channeling his annoyance into a renewed focus on his bladework. The tall Sylvan Warrior lunged forward, leaving his left side open. The Shade saw the mistake, twisting down below the attempted strike and seeking to stab his sword into Rynlin's exposed chest. But Rynlin wasn't there, using his feint to gain the little bit of space he needed to cut down with his sword, which stabbed into the back of the Shade's neck. The dark creature collapsed, its black blood staining the hard scrabble of the gully.

Rynlin took a moment to wipe the Shade's blood that was running down his sword onto the creature's black cloak before turning his attention to his companion.

"You could have helped."

"It didn't seem necessary. Besides, it appeared that you wanted the practice. Or I should say that it appeared that clearly you needed the practice."

Rynlin chuckled. His partner rarely attempted a joke. "Where are Tiro and Maden?"

"They've already moved to the south," replied Catal Huyuk, a mountain of a man dressed in leathers. He knelt in the grass, using a cloth pulled from one of the dead Ogren to wipe the blood from the blade of his axe before it pitted the steel.

Rynlin walked over to the large Sylvan Warrior, surveying the carnage around them. A column of Ogren led by the Shade had tried to sneak through a narrow defile. The two Sylvan Warriors hid among the rocks above as the dark creatures made their way along the constricting path. With the Talent, Rynlin had nudged several large boulders out of place, causing a rockslide and forcing tons of stone and shale onto the narrow trail and its unsuspecting occupants.

Only a few of the Ogren had survived. Much to their misfortune, Catal Huyuk waited for them as they pulled themselves out of the rubble, the massive Sylvan Warrior quickly dispatching them.

Definitely not a fair fight, thought Rynlin. Of course, those were the best kind.

"Let's see if we can catch up to them. I'd hate to miss another opportunity to tweak the nose of the Shadow Lord."

54

INSPIRED IDEA

"I liked what you did with the logs. Truly an inspired idea."

"Dammit, Thomas, you have to stop doing that," Oso spluttered, having almost dropped his bowl of stew on the ground as he slipped off the back of the fallen tree trunk that served as his seat.

The Marchers sitting in the small clearing and enjoying their evening meal watched in amusement as their Highland Lord stepped out of the shadows behind their leader and made his way to the pot bubbling over the fire. They had come to expect these visits, no longer bothering to wonder how Thomas had escaped the notice of the sentries.

Thomas helped himself to a small bowl of stew, speaking a few words to each of the Marchers and congratulating the men and women on their success before sitting down next to Oso, who had regained his place on the timber after a bit of a struggle.

Oso harrumphed his displeasure at being surprised, but his anger quickly dissipated.

"I'm just glad it worked. They could dodge the rocks, but the logs were another matter."

As the column of Armaghian soldiers had almost reached the top of the trail that would have taken them to a plateau between two cloud-hidden peaks, Oso and his Marchers had loosed a small avalanche of rock and scrabble, which had eliminated a good number of Rodric's men. But the rocks were too few to take them all. The logs that followed had completed the job.

The Marchers then had cut down with their arrows the few Armaghian soldiers who had survived the initial ambush, only stepping out of the cover provided by their hiding places among the trees to finish off the soldiers who had been mortally wounded. Invader or no, they had no desire to see someone suffer needlessly.

"It was a smart thing to do," said Thomas. "Well done."

Oso smiled at the compliment. "And the others?"

"All successful," said Thomas. "Renn, Seneca and Coban all completed their assignments with not a single Marcher injured."

"All the better."

"Indeed. But this won't last. Chengiz is a real soldier, not one playacting like Rodric. He will change his strategy if Rodric allows it."

"Then what do we do?" asked Oso.

"We change our strategy before he does," said Thomas with a grin.

55

CHANGING THE GAME

The hidden Highland glade had become the Marcher command post. Thomas had gathered his chiefs, and with them had come their tired but pleased fighters. For the last several weeks, the Armaghians had marched inexorably toward the Crag. They started as one force, but as the trail tapered and became more difficult to traverse, General Chengiz had broken his army into a handful of smaller groups and given them different routes to follow.

The Marchers didn't care what tactics Chengiz employed. Following Thomas' instructions, Oso, Renn, Seneca, Coban and Nestor had responded in kind, dividing their forces into independent squads and charging them with attacking the Armaghians as frequently and ferociously as possible. The Marchers had done so, releasing the pent-up fury that had bubbled within them for the last decade. Often each assault lasted no more than a few minutes, but in that brief time the Marchers caused devastating damage, eliminating soldiers and destroying supplies in various parts of the long, often disjointed and disconnected columns, and then slipping back into the forest with nary a loss.

With their men and women resting, the chiefs sat with Thomas under a large tree, its exposed roots providing excellent seats, and partook of the evening meal. Though they welcomed the quiet and calm of night falling in the Highlands, their thoughts were on the tasks still to be done.

"We can't stop them," said Renn, between mouthfuls of the stew that had been hastily prepared. "We've hurt them badly and can continue to do so, but there are too many. Eventually they will reach the Crag."

"True," said Seneca. "But it's been a fun and enjoyable last few weeks."

"That it has," agreed Renn, the gangly Marcher's eyes shining brightly as a result of the Marchers' many successes against the encroaching Armaghians. "But we still must deal with the cards we've been dealt."

"Our efforts haven't been in vain," said Oso. "Every Armaghian soldier killed or wounded now reduces the number we'll face in the future."

"Yes, we have been effective, even more so than I expected. But the concern is legitimate," said Coban. "We can continue to whittle away at Rodric's army, but that won't drive them from the Highlands. Our homes and families will still be in danger."

"We need a new strategy," said Nestor. "Once Rodric and his army reach the Crag, what we're doing now won't work."

The oldest and most experienced of the chiefs, Nestor said little, but when he did all who heard listened. All eyes turned to Thomas, who sat there comfortably finishing his stew. He was as tired as his chiefs, having participated in as many of the attacks as he could. The resulting whispers of his skill with the weapons of war as well as what he could accomplish when applying the Talent, though he tended to reserve his unique skill in the natural magic of the world as much as possible for dark creatures, had taken on a life of their own.

"Nestor's right," agreed Thomas, setting down his bowl and

standing to stretch his tired legs. He stood there for a moment, taking in the expanse of the Highlands revealed at one end of the glade, the many snow-covered peaks just barely visible in the dying light dominating his view. "We leave just after midnight. Only Oso stays with his Marchers to harass Rodric and Chengiz, to make them think that nothing has changed. The rest of us will gather once more at the Crag. It's time to end the Armaghian threat once and for all."

56

FEARSOME ALLIES

The diminutive woman, thick chestnut hair whipping behind her in response to the gusts of wind cascading between the mountain peaks, surveyed the harsh terrain that sloped away beneath her. The loose rock and uneven ground would serve her purpose quite well. Quite well indeed.

A large black wolf, a streak of white fur across his eyes, peered at Rya, who stood next to him. Her head only came to his shoulders as he sat on his haunches. Beluil gave her a nudge, careful not to knock her over, and she absently began scratching the fur behind his right ear.

"Are you ready, Beluil?"

The large wolf growled softly in response.

"Then time to get started," she said.

For a time all had been quiet, the bands of dark creatures seeking to enter the Highlands having been reduced to no more than one or two raiding parties a week. But no longer. The number of incursions had increased substantially, coinciding with the Armaghian invasion from the south.

Grasping hold of the Talent, Rya Keldragan focused her attention on the two Shades leading a large troop of Ogren through one of the many narrow passes that ran from the Northern Steppes into the lower Highlands. Two bolts of white hot energy shot from her palms, blasting through the chests of the two servants of the Shadow Lord. The dark creatures remained standing for just a second, not comprehending their fate, before collapsing to the rough ground, smoking holes visible in their chests and backs.

The Ogren had no time to register what had happened to the Shades as the hundreds of shapes hidden among the surrounding trees sprinted toward them, responding to Beluil's howl, which bounced off the rocky walls of the pass.

The Ogrens' once orderly march immediately descended into chaos as the Highland wolves attacked, their powerful jaws snapping at heels and hamstrings as they sought to take down the giant beasts and then use their larger numbers to their advantage. The Ogrens' initial roars of anger quickly turned to screams of terror as the wolves made fast work of their prey. After just a few minutes had passed, silence descended once more in the lower Highlands. Then a large black wolf raised his snout to the sky and released a howl that was soon imitated by all the wolves that had just destroyed the Ogren raiding party, the haunting sound traveling the wind as it twisted and turned among the Highland peaks.

57
____

SCHEMES

O so stood at the very edge of the tree line, looking down the steep slope through which a small trail, barely wide enough for one wagon, switchbacked up the steep incline from the shore of the Inland Sea into the southern Highlands. The camp at the base of the slope was a hive of activity as more soldiers poured off the cargo vessels and barges that docked at the pier jutting out over the water, followed by all their necessary supplies. Where the camp met the first, gentle hills of the lower Highlands, soldiers formed into companies to make the trek in and among the peaks, their goal the Crag, citadel of the Highland Lord.

It was quite an undertaking, thought Oso, and one that he would take great joy in disrupting. He had led his troop of Marchers around the Armaghian army that had already marched into the Highlands, given the task by Thomas of destroying Rodric's supply base and as many troop carriers as possible. If successful, Oso and his Marchers would cut off the High King from Armagh, leaving him with little in the way of supplies and few reinforcements.

"Are they coming?" asked Oso, his eyes never leaving what was going on by the shore.

Aric had walked up on silent feet, having positioned the Marchers under Oso's command as ordered.

"They are."

Oso confirmed that the Armaghian troops were beginning to make their way up the roughly cut trail, wagons full of supplies interspersed between each company of soldiers. The trail twisted and turned toward where Oso and his fighters waited. The rough terrain, garnished with loose rocks, some taller than a man, complicated the climb for the Armaghians. The soldiers at the front of the long column that curled its way up the trail already were struggling as the gentle slope abruptly became a precipitous ascent. As a result, many of the soldiers were forced to aid the wagons, bending their backs to push them up the tortuous path, and in the process taking their attention away from the surrounding countryside.

"Is everything ready?"

"Yes," said Aric, stepping up to get a better look at the happenings below them. "We just completed the task you gave us."

"Good. I hope it works."

Oso wasn't concerned about fighting the soldiers of Armagh. He knew his Marchers were more than a match. But it always came down to numbers. The Armaghians outnumbered his Marchers by what he estimated to be a ten to one advantage. If what he had planned didn't work, they'd face a challenge they might not be able to escape.

58

UNEXPECTED HELP

With night falling, Thomas stood in front of the hole in the outer wall that he'd been working on at the Crag just a few weeks before. The huge gap, large enough for several Ogren to walk through standing abreast, finally was ready for repair. But when the Armaghian army had entered the Highlands, he and his Marchers had left the work of restoring the Crag unfinished for the more important task of defending their homeland.

The Lord of the Highlands watched his Marchers continue to trickle onto the plain in front of the Crag. He was proud of his fighters. What they had accomplished in a few short weeks. The sacrifices they had made. But he knew and acknowledged the truth. Even if all his Marchers arrived in time to face the Armaghian army, Rodric would still have a decided advantage in the number of soldiers he could bring to bear, likely as many as five to one despite the Marchers' best efforts to improve the odds through their constant, devastating, lightning attacks. Despite the carnage the Marchers had wrought as the Armaghians slowly made their way toward the Crag, the High King's host continued to press forward. Moreover, with Rodric's tendency to throw his men into a battle no matter the costs that advantage in available troops could prove fatal to the Marchers.

Thomas didn't want to waste his fighters and he couldn't afford to. In a pitched battle, no matter how well the men and women under his command fought, the Highlanders would probably lose. And as time passed that battle drew inexorably closer. Oso and his Marchers had arrived that afternoon, having destroyed Rodric's supply camp on the northern shore of the Inland Sea and harassed Rodric's columns as they wound their way through the Highlands toward the Crag. The Armaghian host was just a day and a half away at most, the large Highlander had reported.

As the last of the Marchers settled in for the night, Thomas began to ponder what to do while staring into the small fire he had built. His back turned, Thomas didn't notice the slowly moving dark shadow that meshed with the blackness just beyond the light of the flames. The shadow stalked closer and closer, absolutely silent, coming up behind an unaware Highland Lord. As the shadow coalesced the closer it came to the flames, its massive size became clear.

Just as the shadow launched itself into the air, Thomas turned to face it, but the huge shape was too quick and bore him to the ground. The beast's massive paws landed on his chest, and as Thomas looked up, a large tongue dragged across his face.

"I know this is fun for you, but the slobber can get a little old," said Thomas, hugging the massive wolf to his chest. "You've been away for too long, you shaggy beast." Beluil continued to lick his friend's face.

They had grown up together, Thomas finding Beluil during his escape from the Crag, and had been inseparable ever since, though it had proven hard to be together with Thomas' increasing responsibilities as Lord of the Highlands. They tussled on the ground for a few more minutes in greeting before Thomas walked back to his place by the fire, Beluil lying down in front of him, covering his feet much as he'd done when they lived on the Isle of Mist with Thomas' grandparents.

"How's the weather, Rynlin? Good winds coming off the northern Highlands?"

Rynlin walked out of the darkness surrounding Thomas' small campfire appearing somewhat miffed.

"I should have known I couldn't sneak up on you, even with Beluil trying to distract you, but it was fun trying."

Knowing time was tight, rather than asking after his grandson, Rynlin provided a report on how the Sylvana had bottled up the dark creatures trying to enter the northern Highlands. The threat that Thomas had feared the most – being caught between Rodric's host and a swarm of dark creatures – had been contained, at least for a time. Thomas then explained where things stood with the Marchers and the approaching Armaghian army.

"We continue to carve away at them," finished Thomas. "But Rodric has too many soldiers. If we continue with this strategy, the likelihood of a pitched battle becomes more certain. We can't afford to take that risk."

"Perhaps I can offer you some unexpected help that I think you could put to good use."

As Rynlin explained how Rya was taking care of the final arrangements, Thomas' smile grew bigger. He needed to gather his chiefs and adjust their strategy. Thanks to his grandparents the Marchers had a chance. But there was much to discuss and do before first light.

59

ARRAYED FOR BATTLE

Rodric, still resembling a peacock in his sparkling armor, feathered helmet and arrogant demeanor, sat on his horse on the edge of the forest. He looked out upon the plateau, watching his army exit from between the trees and form ranks at the very beginning of the open ground, the Crag still no more than a speck far in the distance.

General Chengiz sat on his horse next to his king, surprised, and somewhat worried, that they'd gotten this far without meeting greater resistance from the Marchers. He was even more astonished when a scout galloped up with unexpected news.

"The Marchers are arrayed for battle beneath the Crag in the next valley, my king."

Rodric smiled wickedly. Finally, after years of waiting and the recent weeks of escalating frustration, his long-sought victory was close at hand.

"And they're being led by whom?"

"The Highland Lord."

"How many?" asked Chengiz.

"An estimated ten thousand, General," replied the scout. "No more than a fifth of our force."

That was good news, thought Chengiz. Then again, the Armaghians would have enjoyed a numerical superiority of nine or ten to one if not for the Marchers' masterful tactics of the past fortnight. Yes, the Armaghians finally approached their primary objective as set by Rodric, but it had come at a terrible cost. A cost that didn't seem to faze the High King.

Rodric's smile turned into a manic laugh. After so long, his greatest desire, to crush the Marchers and eliminate the boy who had haunted him for the better part of a decade, was within his reach.

"General Chengiz, battle formation, double time march. I want to engage before we lose the light."

"My king, is that wise? The Marchers have been a tricky, unconventional enemy ever since we entered the Highlands. If I could have just a few more hours for my scouts to complete their work and ensure that there are no more surprises ..."

"General Chengiz, I have no time for your incessant caution! And I will not lose this opportunity! The Marchers have finally stopped running like the cowards they are. Their constant, biting attacks have done nothing to stop us, and now they have no choice but to face us in battle. They have nowhere to go. They know our victory is inevitable. We will crush them, once and for all!"

"Yes, my king," General Chengiz replied, unable to hide the doubt that crept into his voice.

Chengiz knew that attempting to change Rodric's mind at that very moment could be suicidal. He cursed his own weakness. He and his family had served Armagh faithfully for several hundred years, but not for the first time he wondered at Rodric's fitness to rule his homeland. Was such a thought treason? Pushing that worrisome notion from his mind, he turned his horse toward his staff, barking orders as they scattered to carry them out.

There would be a battle this day. Of this General Chengiz was certain. Despite the Armaghians overwhelming strength, he was less certain which of the opposing forces would emerge victorious.

60

TREMORS

Standing on a decaying balcony that looked out over the main square of Blackstone, the Shadow Lord turned his gaze from the dark, cloudy sky to what occurred down below his perch. Ogren, the Shadow Lord's primary soldiers, emerged from the ruined buildings and dark crevices that dotted this once formidable, now dead, city.

The dark creatures milled about, sometimes getting into fights, more than willing to use their corrupted weapons on each other. Many simply seemed lost, until a Shade appeared to bring some order out of the chaos. Once the Shade had formed a large enough troop, he led the Ogren away, inevitably to the south, through the Charnel Mountains, across the Northern Steppes, and then into the Highlands.

Despite the strong breeze, which whipped the burnt ash of the city into a frenzy, oftentimes hiding the activity occurring in the square from his view, the Shadow Lord stood as still as a statue, his blood-red eyes blazing. The sun broke through the clouds more frequently now, sending tremors through the city and the surrounding mountains with increasing, unsettling regularity. More often than not, the beam of sunlight targeted the large, circular stone set in the chamber behind him, which displayed a duel between him and a boy with a blazing white sword, a disk that he had crafted with Dark Magic more than a thousand years before. Just as fast as the sunlight broke through the clouds, the shadows and darkness fought back to repel it. But just a moment was all that was needed to upset the land and set it shaking.

The Shadow Lord's eyes blazed brighter. This boy had been a problem for far too long. He was smart, clever. More of a nuisance with each passing day. Somehow this new Highland Lord had succeeded so far in not only defending against the Armaghians, but also in holding back his dark creatures that sought to come at the Marchers from behind. He closed his blood-red eyes for just a moment, his anger that had become all too frequent threatening to explode once more.

The boy had been a constant plague, nevertheless his plans continued to move forward, though perhaps not as smoothly as he had expected and would have liked. Sometimes, no matter how clever you were, sheer numbers won the battle. And that's what the Shadow Lord counted on as he watched another Shade bring together a troop of Ogren and march them beneath his balcony toward the south.

If Rodric did as he was instructed, then success was guaranteed, for there were only so many Marchers, and they couldn't be everywhere in the Highlands, not with his almost endless supply of servants. Once his dark creatures gained a foothold, and Rodric captured the Crag, it would simply be a matter of time. The Highlands would fall, for the Marchers would have no way to escape the vise he had crafted.

61

POOR ODDS

"Do you think Rodric will come forward?" asked Oso, having learned that the Armaghian army resided just one valley over.

"After our constant attacks and knowing that the bulk of our fighters stand before him?" replied Coban. "Yes. He won't be able to resist our invitation. It's too sweet an opportunity to pass up."

"He'll attack within the hour is my guess," said Thomas distractedly. "He won't be able to stop himself. In my experience, he isn't one for much in the way of self-control."

After just a few minutes had passed, Thomas, Oso, and Coban watched the first ranks of Rodric's army come out of the forest and begin to form ranks and advance toward the Marchers.

"Sometimes, Thomas, I think you're a mind reader," said Coban.

"No, I just listen to things most people tend to ignore. Make sure the Marchers are prepared, Coban, and check with Renn, Seneca and Nestor along the wings to ensure they're ready to do as we agreed."

Coban hurried off, screaming orders to any Marcher he encountered as he went, even though he was certain that the men and women who stood in front of the Crag knew what to do. It was simply a habit that he couldn't break.

"Do you think it will work, Thomas?"

"I don't know. But it's the best chance we've got."

Gazing out across the valley, Rodric's army dwarfed his own. His plan had to work. Otherwise, there would be no one left to stop Rodric from taking the Highlands. And once the Highlands fell, all the other Kingdoms would topple as well. It would just be a matter of time.

62

ORDERS

"Thomas, arguing is simply a waste of time. I can fight. You know I can fight. I can help you."

Kaylie Carlomin stood before him in front of the Crag's main gates, or rather where they should have been, wearing leather armor that would allow her to make use of her natural speed with a blade, her rapier strapped across her back.

"Kaylie, you'll be in too much danger. What would your father say?"

"Argue all you want, Lord Kestrel, it won't work," said Kael Bellilil, Swordmaster of Fal Carrach. "Believe me, I've tried. It's like talking to a stone."

Kaylie gave Kael a sour look, but the grizzled veteran ignored her.

"Kaylie, you're making my life more difficult than it needs to be right now," protested Thomas. "I don't have time for this."

Kael replied with a grin before she could. "She excels at making most everyone's life difficult, Lord Kestrel."

Kael had discovered that even though the Princess of Fal Carrach knew her father's plans -- that Fal Carrach's support for the Highlands would be revealed at the right time -- she still felt the need to slip away from Ballinasloe and assist Thomas and the Marchers during their struggle against the Armaghian host. Resigned to the fact that he could never convince her to return to Fal Carrach, the Swordmaster had decided to accompany her and offer her what protection he could. Her father would not be pleased, but it was the best that he could do under the circumstances with his recalcitrant, stubborn charge.

"You needn't worry. I'll stay with her. It's smarter simply to accept the inevitable rather than lose time arguing."

Seeing that he had little choice, and with so much already to worry about, Thomas rolled his eyes in acquiescence and turned his attention to how she might be able to aid him.

"You've been practicing in the Talent?"

"Every day. And I grow stronger every day."

"I can sense that." Thomas used the Talent to speak as he'd done so many times with his Marcher chiefs and with Beluil. Kaylie heard his words, but only in her mind. "*Can you do this?*"

"*Yes,*" answered Kaylie, but rather than speaking out loud she, in turn, spoke directly in Thomas' mind.

"Good. Then stay close to me. You can send my orders and talk directly to my chiefs so I can concentrate on other things."

Thomas stalked off toward the Marcher front lines, Kaylie and Kael chasing after, a smile creasing the Princess of Fal Carrach's face, pleased that she had won that small battle with Thomas. And if she could win this one, perhaps she could win a few others down the road as well. As she saw it, this was her fight, too.

63

SOARING CONFIDENCE

Rodric Tessaril sat on his horse on the low rise that provided a panoramic view of the plateau. He smiled in pleasure, though he was growing uncomfortably warm in his sun-heated, steel-plated armor as sweat dripped down his scalp and back despite the brisk chill in the air. Surveying his army, his men still filing into position, he ignored the growing inconvenience as his confidence soared. The Armaghian host greatly surpassed the pitifully small force of Marchers that stood in ranks with the Crag at their back. He could taste the victory that was to be his. The victory he had deserved for so long. A victory to be savored. If only Lord Chertney would stop his incessant, annoying droning.

"I warn you, Rodric," said Chertney in his scratchy voice. "That boy is playing another of his games. My Ogren and Shades were to come down from the north to catch the Marchers between us. But they have not been able to break through from the Northern Steppes. I've heard tell of a Marcher force there holding the passes. But the Highlanders couldn't do it on their own with most, if not all, of their fighters here. They must be working with the blasted Sylvana. Only they, with the power they wield, could hold against our master's servants."

"Having your dark creatures certainly would simplify things," said Rodric, not biting out the words as he normally would. Of course, there was a benefit to that failure. The appearance of a troop of Ogren could complicate the situation, as Rodric couldn't foretell how Chengiz and his soldiers would react if they were to be allied unexpectedly with dark creatures. Better that his army defeated the Marchers on its own. His normal fretfulness had dissipated, and he felt strangely magnanimous at the moment, believing that his victory was all but assured. "Tell me, Killeran, have we anything to worry about? Some hidden force of Marchers to come at our rear? Some band of ancient, decrepit men and women to charge at us on unicorns?"

Killeran shifted uncomfortably under Rodric and Chertney's gazes, distracted for a moment by the sudden appearance of General Chengiz.

"No, King Rodric," said the Dunmoorian lord, his nasal twang grating on the nerves of all around him. "Scouts have scoured the countryside for leagues around. There have been no sightings whatsoever of Marchers or anyone else to impede us."

"Does our Lord Killeran speak true, my dear general?"

"He does," replied General Chengiz. "Though the scouts have not explored the terrain as far out as I would prefer."

"And you, Chertney, with your skills?" asked Rodric, ignoring Chengiz's veiled complaint. "Is there anything to worry about that I can't see with my own eyes?"

Chertney stared at Rodric for a moment, cursing for the hundredth time the circumstances that had put him in league with this fool who played at king.

"No, Rodric. Killeran is correct."

"Then I see no reason to delay our long-awaited success,"

said Rodric. "This moment has been a decade in the making. So on with it, General Chengiz. Clear the field of Marchers once and for all."

"Yes, my king," replied the Armaghian general, who was glad to leave the group and trot his horse toward his subordinates so that he could relay his orders to attack to his troops.

The High King was likely right, Chengiz thought. By all appearances it should be an easy victory. But in his recent skirmishes against the Highland Lord, boy or not, he had been a worthy adversary. Therefore, he was certain that even with the advantage in numbers that the Armaghians enjoyed, they were in for more of a struggle than any of them expected.

64

DEFENDING THE FRONT

The clash of swords and din of battle echoed in the valley into the late afternoon, to the point where the Marchers became desensitized to it, the men and women fighting fiercely in front of the Crag focused solely on what stood before them. The Armaghian host had charged three times, and each time the Marchers repulsed the attack with minimal casualties. Marchers with spears stood to the fore, archers behind, sword fighters in the gaps to prevent any possible breakthrough. But there was little for them to do at the moment, rarely having need of their blades. The archers shot with a deadly, almost inhuman, accuracy at such close range, Rodric's soldiers unable to force their way past the spears.

Oso had seen the brilliance of Thomas' decision to stand and fight in front of the Crag within minutes of the first attack on the Marcher line. The valley naturally funneled the Armaghian soldiers to the center of the Marcher line, the impassable wood pressing in on both sides and not allowing Rodric to bring his full force to bear. Therefore, the Marchers did not have to worry about attacks on their flanks and could instead concentrate on defending their position against the

Armaghian frontal assaults. Moreover, after each attack, Thomas rotated the Marchers in the center so that fresh fighters always stood ready to meet the next attack.

"I have to hand it to you," said Oso. "I had expected this to be more of a challenge."

"So far, so good," replied Thomas. "But all good things must come to an end." The two Highlanders stood just behind the Marcher spears, swords at the ready. But the opportunities to blood their blades that afternoon had been few and far between. "Besides, I'm tired of having to drag Kaylie away from the battle line."

Thomas had agreed that Kaylie could stay with him during the battle, tasking her with using the Talent to communicate with the Highland chiefs. Kael was never more than a few feet away from her. But despite the Swordmaster's best efforts, she seemed to find her way to the thick of the fighting, apparently wanting to test her skills against the Armaghians. Thomas had pulled her back several times. Yet each time, soon after she was back in the middle of the battle.

"It will be dark in an hour. Should we begin the chase?" asked Oso.

"Yes, I'll have Kaylie send the orders. As soon as night begins to fall, we break contact, and we move."

65

MOUNTING FRUSTRATION

As each hour passed, Rodric's frustration grew. He watched each assault with anticipation, expecting it to be the breakthrough he needed to crush the Highland Lord and his Marchers once and for all. But each time the Marchers threw his men back seemingly with ease. The Marchers never broke and ran. In fact, their line didn't even budge. They stood their ground and maintained their discipline despite the constant onslaught. It was as if the Marchers played with him, taunting him. As that thought settled within him, his rage intensified, threatening to get the better of him. He couldn't believe that his army with such overwhelming strength had failed to crush the few soldiers arrayed against it during any of its attacks.

"Look!" exclaimed Killeran.

The Dunmoorian lord saw the first tell-tale signs of a possible breach in the Marcher line, a slight bend beginning in the middle as the Armaghians forced the Marchers positioned there back toward the Crag.

It only took a few more seconds for the bend to expand. The Marchers fought desperately, but the number of attackers was too much for them. In just a few minutes the widening bend became a break. For the first time since the battle began, Armaghian soldiers pushed behind the Marcher defensive line. General Chengiz immediately sought to take advantage, having a sergeant signal his cavalry commander to attack down the center and widen the gap. Even with much of his infantry still in the way, it was a price that the Armaghian commander was willing to pay. They needed to crack the Marcher defense, and this could be their only chance.

Rodric's mounting fury dissolved into glee as the Marchers fell back faster and faster, until they were in full retreat, moving away from the Highland fortress along both sides of the citadel.

"Killeran, form an honor guard," commanded Rodric, his eyes shining brightly with anticipation. "We're going to claim the Crag."

66

ORDERLY RETREAT

Thomas and Oso fell back with the Marchers, who maintained an orderly withdrawal despite what appeared to be a full-scale retreat to the Armaghians. Rodric's soldiers followed carefully at a distance, unwilling to press the Marchers too hard with night falling. They remembered the toll of breaking the Marcher line and had no desire to do anything foolish against such a formidable foe. As a result, the Marchers gained some much-needed space once they crossed the valley and entered the forest behind the Crag. Once free of the Armaghians, they moved swiftly to meet at their assigned places. Thomas was pleased to see that only a few Marchers had been hurt during the retreat, and not severely at that. Coban, Renn, Seneca and Nestor reported together.

"Everything went as planned, Thomas," stated Coban, smiling with the knowledge that the first step in their plan had proven successful with minimal effect on his fighters.

"Has Rodric mounted any follow-up attacks?"

"No," replied Nestor. "He's assumed that we're routed and will need to reassemble."

"No patrols or skirmishers?" Thomas didn't want to question his luck, not having expected the withdrawal to go so smoothly, but he was still a bit surprised.

"Instead of pressing any advantage he might have, the High King is more interested in the Crag right now," interjected Seneca.

"Good. He can stare at the stone walls for as long as he wants. Let's get some distance from him and move on to the next staging ground. I'm sure Chengiz will talk sense to him eventually."

67

CLAIMING THE CRAG

Rodric relished his stroll through the yet to be rebuilt Crag, the Marchers leaving the reconstruction and restoration unfinished in order to oppose the Armaghian host. The recent battle, just hours old, was a distant memory for him. He instead thought about what he would rename the Highland fortress once he destroyed the Marchers. The High King's Seat, perhaps. That had a nice ring to it. Yes, that might be it. Much to his annoyance, Killeran interrupted his fun, reporting that the Marchers now headed west, having shifted direction once they gained the safety of the forest and looping around the Armaghian host in a wide arc.

"They have circled around the Crag, likely so that they don't get bottled up against the coast and are making for the higher passes."

"Let them go for a time," said Rodric. "The Highlands belong to me now. Finally, after so many years. I want to enjoy this, Killeran. I deserve it."

"But, my lord," protested Killeran. "The Marchers remain a sizable and dangerous force. They will threaten your rule until we eliminate them. Giving them time to escape only will make matters more difficult for us in the future."

Rodric tamped down his annoyance, pulling his mind away from his visions of glory, instead remembering all the problems the Marchers created for Killeran while he functioned as nominal regent of the Highlands for a decade following the murder of Talyn Kestrel. Although he had no doubt that the difficulties with the Highlanders during that time were magnified by Killeran's incompetence, he couldn't deny the Dunmoorian Lord's logic. The same logic that General Chengiz had impressed upon him when he first arrived in the Highlands. His fun would have to wait a bit longer.

"Fine. Get Chengiz up here. We'll follow after the Highland boy until we destroy him and the Marchers once and for all."

68

JUST AHEAD

As the days passed, dozens of skirmishes erupted as the Armaghians pursued their quarry, seeking to eliminate the Marchers as a fighting force. But the Marchers continued their rearguard action, maintaining their order and holding to their purpose. Close enough to tease Rodric's host to continue its pursuit, and thereby draw them deeper into the Highlands, yet never so close as to allow for a pitched battle. Something that the Marchers knew the Armaghians craved. Even so, with every clash, the Marchers cut away more soldiers from the Armaghian army with the men and women of the Highlands experiencing few casualties themselves.

Always staying just far enough ahead so that Rodric couldn't catch them, but near enough to keep the High King's appetite for victory whetted. A daily challenge, but one Thomas thought well worth the effort. He just hoped that his luck would hold for a bit longer as the setting of each sun brought the Marchers closer to their ultimate objective.

He walked among his Marchers now as they rested for a few minutes before beginning the next leg of their journey. He saw Kaylie sitting against a tree, eyes closed, head resting against the rough bark. Kael, ever present, sat next to his charge. The Fal Carrachian Swordmaster nodded to Thomas in approval, clearly liking the strategy in play. The respect reflected in his eyes was apparent. Thomas nodded in return.

The Princess of Fal Carrach looked exhausted, taxed by her frequent use of the Talent to communicate with Thomas' chiefs so that Thomas could conserve his strength for what was likely coming. The strong-willed princess had done everything asked of her without a word of complaint. He hadn't expected this of Kaylie. But then again, she continued to surprise him daily. He thought about going over to thank her, then decided against it, believing that just a few minutes more of sleep would benefit her.

Instead he continued to walk among his Marchers, offering greetings and encouragement. His fighters brightened when he appeared, the weariness draining from them as they had a chance to speak with their Highland Lord. Once an outsider, that was no longer the case. Thomas was a Highlander, a Marcher, and in their eyes, he could see their belief, their hope. The time of troubles was coming to an end. Once more, the Highlands would belong to them. Only one obstacle kept them from achieving that objective. The Armaghian army.

69

THE END

Rodric barely opened an eye when the flap to his tent fluttered and John Killeran stepped in, the bright sunlight thankfully disappearing quickly when the flap returned to its place. But the brief flash of light provided enough time for the Dunmoorian Lord to comprehend that Rodric had spent much of the last night drinking, several empty wine bottles strewn about the extravagant rugs that covered the long Highland grass. As Rodric began to disentangle himself from his blankets, the sounds of an army preparing for battle jarred his muddled senses.

"My lord," began Killeran in a high-pitched squeak, unable to contain his excitement. "The Highlanders have stopped running. They've formed into ranks at the edge of the plateau. They stand no more than a mile away."

"It's about time," muttered Rodric, as he searched for a missing boot to pull on, tired of the constant pursuit. His host had trailed the Highlanders for almost a week. He felt like a mouse chasing after a morsel of cheese tied to a piece of string. Just when he was about to gain the cheese, it was pulled from his grasp time after time. What had started as an exciting pursuit had devolved into an exercise in frustration. "They have no choice. They have nowhere else to go."

Rising from his bed, Rodric grasped Killeran's arm before he could fall, the wine from the previous night leaving him wobbly and feeling ill. But no matter. Today was the day. Today was the end.

Gathering his strength as he dressed, Rodric stumbled from the tent, his legs still shaky as he started across the plateau. In the distance, he caught sight of the Marchers just as Killeran described, framed by the beginnings of the Clanwar Desert far to the northwest and the last of the Highland peaks to their backs. The dark smudge of the Breaker rose prominently into the sky to the west just a few leagues distant, standing tall and defiant as the final barrier between the dark creatures in the north and the Kingdoms.

Rodric never wondered why the Marchers would stand and fight now when they still had multiple options for escape. Instead, his jumbled mind focused on one thing only. Still having a vast advantage in soldiers, if the Marchers finally had stopped running like the cowards they were and fought, Armagh would conquer the Highlands this day, and as a result he would be one step closer to achieving his larger objective.

Calling for his servants in a harsh voice, the High King returned to his tent for almost an hour to prepare himself for battle. When he emerged, he appeared as the triumphant High King that he worked so desperately to project. Wearing his battle armor, the sun reflected blindingly off the well-polished steel plates. The gigantic, feathered ornament on his helmet continued to give him an appearance that resembled that of a preening peacock looking for a mate. His diminutive size compared to his war horse only compounded the effect of a man continually struggling to earn his own respect. He ignored the fact that his servants had to place a stool in front of him in order to mount his horse.

Finally, the Armaghian army having already formed ranks, Rodric trotted his horse to the vanguard to get a better look at his opponents. As he approached the first ranks of his infantry, he noticed a small group of riders a quarter mile in front of the Marchers. A white flag flew above them. Rodric snickered, thinking that the Marchers had finally come to their senses. Perhaps the whelp had concluded that surrender was his only option, the only way to save his people. That the Armaghian host was too much for him.

Calling for Killeran, Chertney and Chengiz, he urged his horse out between the armies. He would allow the Marchers to surrender and return to their homes, so long as they acknowledged him as ruler of the Highlands and accepted indentured service in the mines. The boy, on the other hand, would die.

70

ACCOUNTABILITY

As he trotted his war horse out between the two armies, Rodric was shocked to see the Highland whelp sitting astride a unicorn, the massive animal dark as night, its horn twisting to a sharp point at least eight feet from the top of its head. Two others in the small group waiting for him rode unicorns, an older man with close-cropped dark hair and a short beard peppered with gray and a diminutive woman with flowing chestnut locks.

Perhaps Chertney had been right after all regarding the assistance the Marchers had been receiving to the north. But he found it difficult to take that thought in the most obvious direction. The sight of these mythical creatures so unnerved Rodric that he barely registered the fact that King Gregory of Fal Carrach, Chuma as a representative for the Desert Clans, and the rulers of Benewyn and Kenmare formed the rest of the party, their expressions determined and grim.

"So the Sylvana have returned to the world," Rodric spat with contempt, trying to regain control of himself and keep his rising uncertainty and fear from his voice. "And now they're so desperate that they must accept foolish brats within their ranks."

Rodric caught the eyes of all those before him, flinching at the hard glints, sensing anger and resolve.

"Why are you here?" Rodric demanded, turning his gaze to the monarchs of Fal Carrach, Benewyn and Kenmare, ignoring the Desert Chief as unworthy of his attention. He was beginning to realize that he had stepped onto more dangerous ground than he had expected. Nevertheless, he hoped that he could bluster his way out of an already tenuous situation. "This is a matter between Armagh and the Highlands. As High King I must uphold the laws of all the Kingdoms. The Marchers have burned countless villages and farms in Dunmoor, slaughtering innocents. They have much to be held accountable for, and for you to oppose me in seeking justice for these crimes puts your own Kingdoms at risk."

"You can't hold a Kingdom accountable for something it didn't do," said Sarelle, Queen of Benewyn, sitting on her white stallion while wearing a battered breastplate.

Rynlin nudged his roan-colored unicorn, named Militus for its combative nature, forward. He handed a dry parchment to Rodric, who accepted it reluctantly.

"What's this?"

"The order you signed, giving Killeran the task of murdering Talyn Kestrel and his family ten years ago."

Rodric stared at Rynlin in shock, forgetting to even deny the claim. He had hoped to control this engagement from the start, but that desire dissipated in a flash.

"Where did you get this?" he demanded angrily.

"From your office in Eamhain Mhacha, along with several other documents that demonstrate your incapacity to serve as High King and as ruler of Armagh," stated Rya.

"Is this true?" demanded Chengiz, turning his sharp gaze to the High King. He knew Rodric Tessaril was conniving and often stretched the truth, but he never suspected that he would stoop to such depths to attain his objectives. The general served Rodric as High King, but his loyalty was to Armagh. If this claim proved valid, he could not in good conscience continue his service. More immediate action would be required to protect his own honor and that of his homeland.

Rodric ignored Chengiz, his eyes flickering between calm and concern. He began to feel ill, bile rising in his throat, as he sensed that his moment of victory might be slipping from his grasp.

"You are a traitor, Rodric," said Rendael, King of Kenmare. "Surrender and your soldiers may return to Armagh unaccosted. You will be tried for regicide as well as the other crimes revealed in the documents that have been shared with us, as well as the murder of innocents that has occurred in Dunmoor at your command. For once, think of your Kingdom rather than yourself."

"You can't do this," whined Rodric. "This document proves nothing! I am the High King."

"High King or no, you have gone against a law of the Kingdoms that has been in place since the time of Ollav Fola," said Gregory, his voice as hard as the steel of his blade. "No Kingdom may strike at another Kingdom's ruler through stealth. An openly declared war is one thing, but assassination is another. Even more shameful and cowardly is to use the creatures of the Shadow Lord in your schemes, which goes beyond the pale. You are a traitor not only to Armagh, but also to all the Kingdoms."

Chertney had maintained his silence during the entire exchange, hovering at the edge of the group. Circumstances were spiraling quickly out of control, and he realized that quick action was needed. Drawing on his Dark Magic, a portal of black, swirling mist opened in front of him with a thunderous flash. A towering demon, its body covered by red scales, leaped out in front of the assembled rulers. The creature bent at the waist and flexed its knees, preparing to pounce on its quarry, its misshapen hands twisted into sharp claws that sliced through the air.

The gathered horses danced back in fear, several rearing, but the unicorns stood their ground, lowering their heads to attack. Their horns glowed a bright white, their riders having infused them with the Talent. The demon leapt into the air, having picked out Sarelle of Benewyn as its first victim. The green-eyed monarch could only watch in horror, unable to pull her sword in time, the unnatural beast too fast for her to do anything but wait for the monstrosity's sharp claws to carve through her armor and into her flesh. As the demon soared through the air, a bolt of white lightning blasted through the space just in front of Sarelle, striking the dark creature in the chest. The demon collapsed to the ground, a massive hole in its midsection, wisps of smoke rising from its burnt, slowly disintegrating carcass. Sarelle breathed a sigh of relief at her good fortune, giving Gregory a quick, knowing smile, as she realized that he had prepared himself to leap from his saddle to her defense.

Rynlin stared daggers at Chertney, who reeled under the backlash as his magical summoning disintegrated into black ash. The practitioner of Dark Magic clutched wildly at the horn of his saddle, just barely keeping himself from crashing to the ground.

"Selling yourself to the Shadow Lord was a mistake, Rodric," said Rynlin, a deadly glint in his eye, though his attention remained focused on Chertney. "You don't know what you are losing until it is too late."

"With all of you here, when you are all dead, your Kingdoms will be mine as well," Rodric giggled, trying to hide his dismay and fear at how quickly this frightening man had defeated Chertney with a forced bravado. Rodric quickly realized that victory now was his only chance of escape. If he could win this battle, he could not only put his plan into motion, but also accelerate his timetable to conquer the eastern Kingdoms. And if not, all he had worked for would be lost and his death a foregone conclusion.

Rodric decided that the decade-long effort to maintain his subterfuge was no longer worth it. If this was the hand he had been dealt, he would play it to the hilt.

"You found me out after all these years," he said with all the false confidence that he could muster. "Well, at least I no longer have to wear a mask. You're right. I had Talyn Kestrel murdered. And very soon, you will be bowing down to me. If you refuse, if you choose to remain defiant, you'll enjoy the same painful death that he did."

"The only ruler dying today will be you," said Gregory, his voice tight with a cold anger.

Rodric surveyed the Marcher army standing in formation less than a quarter mile in front of him and laughed. "I think not. By choosing to fight today you lost the battle before it even began."

Having no more to say, Rodric galloped away, Chertney and Killeran following quickly after. Chengiz was more hesitant to do so, nodding to each of the monarchs in a sign of respect before slowly turning his horse back toward the Armaghian line.

Chuma and Oso made to go after Rodric, but Thomas called them back.

"No, let him go. Rodric is mine. After we defeat his army, his head belongs to me."

71

CHANGE IN COMMAND

"My lord, I must protest," said General Chengiz, his anger visible. "I am a soldier of Armagh. I fight for Armagh. I do not fight for those willing to ignore the laws of the Kingdoms. I do not fight for a man with ties to the Shadow Lord."

Chengiz's hand rested lightly on the sword at his hip. It was a casual gesture, but Rodric knew Chengiz, knew him for the fighter that he was. He had no illusions about what the Armaghian general could and would do if he pulled that blade.

"Chengiz, you seem to be living in a fantasy world. Have you no idea of the complexities involved in serving as High King? The decisions that must be made for Armagh to prosper?"

Rodric stared at his general as if he were a simpleton, as someone unable to comprehend the challenges and demands of ruling the Kingdom. With a glance over Chengiz's shoulder, he saw the two warlocks he had summoned step silently between the flaps of the tent. Covered in black robes, they were difficult to pick out in the gloom. Their faces held no expression, though their black eyes gleamed with an unsettling fervor.

"I live in the real world, Rodric," replied Chengiz coolly, having sensed the movement behind him. "I understand the challenges, believe me. I've had to deal with you for more than a decade, haven't I? The difference, though, is that I choose to put my Kingdom first. My Kingdom, not myself! You put yourself first."

Rodric laughed softly, shaking his head in amusement. "Who knew that a man of war could be so eloquent, so principled," said the High King. "And so soft."

Rodric motioned to the two warlocks. "Take him away. Chengiz has served his purpose. His usefulness has come to an end."

The warlocks grabbed Chengiz's arms roughly before the general could pull his sword, using their Dark Magic to knock him unconscious. As the warlocks pulled the general out of the tent, his feet dragging across the carpets, Killeran and Chertney entered.

"A problem, Rodric?" asked Chertney, his voice cold and scathing. Yet his eyes spoke of something else. The Sylvan Warrior having defeated his summoning so quickly had unnerved the servant of the Shadow Lord in a way that he had never experienced before.

"No, a solution," returned the High King. "We have struggled with Chengiz leading the army. That will no longer be the case. The warlocks can have their fun with him."

"But, my lord, who will lead?" asked Killeran.

"I will, you fool! You question my abilities?" Rodric's eyes burned brightly, the signs of madness growing more distinct.

"No, my lord, it's just that ..."

"Enough, Killeran. I rule Armagh, and soon I shall rule the Highlands. This army answers to me. And now it is time to put it to use."

"Yes, my lord," answered Killeran meekly, bowing his head in subservience.

"Chertney, any sign of threats beyond the Marchers we face?"

"No, Rodric. Nothing for leagues around."

"Good. Killeran, send the command to the troops. First rank to advance and engage, the others to follow. We end this now."

72

PLAYING HER ROLE

Kaylie pushed her anger to the side, focusing on the task at hand. Standing well behind the Marcher ranks, Kael beside her, as she had done so for so many days, she used the Talent to communicate with the Highland chiefs so that Thomas could focus on other tasks, though she had extended her reach to a few other key players now that the dynamics of the battle for the Highlands had changed. For the last hour, the Armaghian host had battered hopelessly against the Marcher ranks, which had not moved an inch since the start of the battle.

She had forced the sounds of the fight from her mind, the screams of injured and dying soldiers, the clang and screech of steel on steel, the curses and oaths that flowed across the field. Yet the recent encounter with her father had stayed with her.

Yes, she had slipped away from her father's troops when they first headed toward the Highlands. Yes, she had ignored his request to stay out of danger. But why did he worry so much with Kael next to her? Besides, she could defend herself with a blade or the Talent. She'd already demonstrated that several times. She wasn't a child, after all.

Shaking her head in frustration, she sought the calm that was so critical to her effective use of the Talent. Focused once again, she relayed new instructions from Thomas to his chiefs. She was where she needed to be, where she wanted to be. That's all she cared about at the moment. She would deal with her father later. And if an opportunity to become more engaged in the fight presented itself, she'd take it.

73

FINAL MANEUVER

Despite constant, furious assaults by Rodric's troops for several hours, the Marcher line held strong. Wave after wave of Armaghian soldiers were forced back, the Marchers refusing to yield even a step. The compressed nature of the battlefield with the trees lining the sides forced the attackers into a tight space much like at the Crag, not allowing them to throw the full weight of their larger force against the outnumbered Marchers. Moreover, it kept Rodric's troops from biting at the Marcher flanks. If the Armaghians were to take the field, they would have to break the Marcher line.

Thomas fought in the middle of the Marcher defense, Gregory and Rendael with him. Every once in a while, an Armaghian soldier would get within arm's reach, but there was little to do most of the time. The Marcher shield wall, peppered with spears and archers just behind, kept the Armaghians at bay. Pikes to the front, swords to fill the gaps, archers in support. Thomas had used the same tactic many times before, and he would continue to do so until Rodric and his soldiers demonstrated that they could negate its success. With the first part of his plan working to perfection, it was now time to take the next step.

"What say you, my lords?"

"Yes, let's put an end to this," responded Gregory, chomping at the bit to become more engaged in the fighting. Rendael nodded his agreement.

Following the instructions relayed by Thomas through Kaylie, his chiefs, Renn, Seneca, Nestor, Coban and Oso, began the same maneuver they had practiced weeks before and to such great effect in front of the Crag, the maneuver that had begun the weeklong merry chase through the Highlands that had led them here. Over the next few minutes, the center of the Marcher line began to bend, the Highlanders finally yielding ground step by slow step, though it appeared that they were doing so reluctantly rather than as part of a larger strategy. That's what was intended, as Thomas hoped that as the Marcher line took the shape of an inverted wedge, the opportunity to exploit such an obvious weakness would prove irresistible to Rodric.

74

LAST ORDER

"There, Killeran, do you see it?"

Rodric was ecstatic, pointing at the backward bulge that had appeared in the Marcher defense. After only a few hours of struggle the Marchers faced catastrophe, the center of their line unable to withstand the constant attacks. Rodric had expected no less, believing that the unrelenting pressure applied by his men would crack the cowards in the end.

"I do, my lord. Your strategy is working. The Marchers can't hold for much longer."

"Chertney, now is the time. Make use of your Dark Magic and create the breakthrough we need."

For the first time in his reluctant partnership with Rodric, Chertney felt the lesser ally, though he tried to avoid admitting it, even to himself. His disastrous encounter with the Sylvan Warrior, and his resulting defeat and repercussions, continued to haunt him.

"You don't need me now, Rodric. Allow me to rest a bit more, then I can deliver the final blow if necessary."

Rodric stared at Chertney for a moment, surprised by his response, his lips curling into a sneer as understanding dawned. The High King took Chertney's reluctance as a sign of weakness, something that he could exploit later. He didn't know that the lightning-fast skirmish with the older Sylvan Warrior had weakened the dark sorcerer to such an extent that he could barely make use of the Dark Magic his master had imbued in him. It would be days before Chertney finally felt whole again, and his weakened state frightened him. He felt dangerously vulnerable. To come up against that same Sylvan Warrior or someone equally adept in the Talent now would mean his death.

"As you wish." His sneer twisting into an exultant grin, Rodric gave what he thought would be his final order before victory was his. "To the commanders, Killeran, now. Release the reserve. Push through the center and break the Marcher line."

75

TURNING TIDE

"Rodric's committed everything he has. They're pushing to fracture the center."

Kael had been the first to see the change in Armaghian tactics, as he had followed Kaylie closer to the center of the battle. No matter how many times he warned his charge, she drifted inevitably toward Thomas and the thick of the fighting. He admired her courage, but it created a level of risk that he preferred to avoid.

"So they have, Kael. What say you? Shall we send forward our surprise?"

"Most definitely, Lord Kestrel." The excitement in Kael's voice was a rare thing for the normally taciturn warrior.

Using the Talent, Thomas reached out to his grandparents. They had stayed well back from the fighting, focused on another task. *It's time. Let's give Rodric what he deserves.*

Rynlin smiled evilly as he and Rya released their hold on the Talent. As their grasp on the world's natural magic loosened, the illusion that they had maintained since the Armaghians marched onto the battlefield dissipated. The two Sylvan Warriors had used the Talent to make the surrounding forest appear as it normally would, the tall trees standing a silent watch as the battle raged before them, and not revealing the mounted soldiers of Fal Carrach, Kenmare and Benewyn, along with the colorfully robed horsemen of the Desert Clans, hidden within the forest on both sides of the battlefield and waiting expectantly to play their part in the fight. Knowing Chertney's weakened state, Rynlin and Rya had believed that their deception would go unnoticed, and they had been proven right.

In an instant, what Rodric had perceived as a possible breakthrough had turned into a trap. The soldiers of Fal Carrach, Kenmare and Benewyn charged from the flanks, immediately compressing the Armaghian host as they sought to meet in the middle of the battlefield. The fighters of the Desert Clans, curved swords held ready to strike, swept in from behind, offering Rodric and his army no hope for escape.

The tide turned in just minutes. The Armaghian army, surrounded and now facing an opponent comparable in size, fought hard, but the soldiers found themselves in an impossible situation. With the Armaghians pressured on the flanks and in their rear, the Marchers tired of their masquerade and began to press forward, tightening the noose and making an untenable situation unbearable.

Pleased at the turn of events and confident in his success, Thomas followed resolutely after his Marchers. He knew the battle was won, but he was in search of the real prize. Thomas wanted to pay his debt to the High King.

76

A LITTLE HELP

The blood-red eyes stared impassively at the swirling black mist, which reflected a bird's-eye view of the battle occurring in the Highlands. As each second passed, the Shadow Lord's irritation increased. The Marchers and their allies squeezed the Armaghians, pushing in from all sides. It was only a matter of time until his greatest source of strength in the Kingdoms was eliminated.

That arrogant fool! So sure of himself. So sure of his superior numbers. The boy had lulled him with his tactics, retreating, always retreating, teasing Rodric along, until finally he sprang his own surprise. And now the High King had run out of options and was on the brink of defeat. All because of his unimaginative stupidity!

The Shadow Lord could not allow that to happen. The High King didn't deserve his continued support. Another time he would have allowed events to play out as they should, giving Rodric the chance to meet the fate he so richly deserved. But too much was at stake. All his carefully laid plans hinged on this very moment. The Shadow Lord struggled to control his seething rage, which burned with an intensity that threatened to cloud his thinking. Slowly, ever so slowly, he clamped down on his ire, until finally his mind cleared. He considered once more what he saw unfolding before him. Perhaps, rather than defeat, this was an opportunity. The rulers of the eastern Kingdoms fought on the battlefield. If he acted now, he could push his plans forward even more quickly by eliminating many of his opponents in one fell swoop.

Tapping into the Dark Magic that flowed within him, the Shadow Lord reached into the depths of the pits of Blackstone, unlocking a cell that had remained hidden away and forgotten for almost a thousand years.

77

SWIRLING BLACK

Thomas fought like a whirlwind, driving into the Armaghians with a wedge of Marchers, Oso leading on the left with Anara right beside him, Coban on the right. Kaylie followed a few steps behind, sword bloodied as she advanced through the enemy's ranks, Kael always at her side, protecting her flanks and her back. The allied Kingdoms forced the Armaghians into a tighter and tighter circle, all avenues of escape blocked. Yet Thomas had eyes only for Rodric, who sat on his horse at the very center of his rapidly dwindling force, his expression of shock and disgust revealing that he was slowly beginning to understand the dire circumstances that he faced.

Energized by his proximity to his objective, Thomas drove forward, forcing the Armaghian soldiers in front of him back. The Marchers filled the space behind him, cutting through Rodric's troops with a vengeance. When Thomas was just a few yards away from his target, the High King finally saw him, his face turning white with fear. Chertney had drawn his sword, ready to face Thomas, while Killeran stayed behind them, likely remembering what had happened the last time he had faced the Highland Lord in combat.

Finally, after all these years, Thomas would repay the High King for all the misery and death that he had wrought on his homeland. Finally he would meet the charge given to him by his grandfather Talyn just moments before his own death. Yet at that very moment when victory seemed certain, a portal of swirling shadow opened up right in front of the High King and began to expand until the dark mist had spread in a circle wider than a small hamlet. Terrified, the Armaghian soldiers forgot themselves, scurrying away from the portal and into the ranks of their opponents, who stood their ground, swords at the ready, ignoring the terrified Armaghians but unwilling to advance against the swirling tendrils of black mist. With the retreating soldiers blocking Thomas' path, Rodric gave a quick wave of scorn, then gleefully urged his horse through the portal, followed by Chertney and Killeran.

Thomas' anger ignited into a burning rage, not understanding how the High King could escape his grasp so easily. The dolt had more lives than a cat. But Thomas realized quickly that he couldn't dwell on the fact that once again he had lost out on taking his prey. Rather, he had to focus on the present danger.

The portal wasn't closing. Instead it grew larger, until it was big enough for several Ogren to walk through at one time. If only that were to be the case, Thomas thought, sensing the evil contained within the swirling darkness. An evil more powerful and ancient than he had ever confronted before. For a brief moment, he saw two pinpricks of red appear within the swirling gloom, then just as fast the eyes disappeared. The portal of darkness continued to expand, the thin tendrils of inky mist thickening as they churned faster and faster. As the blackness spread, the soldiers from all the Kingdoms continued to step back as the massive, twisting ball of black rose above them to blot out the sun, creating an unnatural twilight that covered the battlefield.

The jet black tendrils whipped around faster than the eye could track, almost mesmerizing in their pattern. Then one strand shot out, then another, and another, the thick black strands wrapping themselves around an Armaghian soldier. In seconds, the threads of mist pulsed with a darkness blacker than the night, consuming the energy and spirit of their victims much like a Shade, and leaving behind a dried, withered husk in their wake.

Before the misty creature could strike again at the surrounding soldiers, Rynlin and Rya urged their unicorns forward, grabbing hold of the Talent and creating a dome of white, almost translucent energy that rose higher than the Breaker to contain the swirling mass. But before they could complete the task, Thomas stepped forward. Kaylie frantically tried to pull him back, but he placed himself beyond the boundary of white energy before she could grab his arm. As the barrier took shape and then solidified, Thomas stood alone in front of what resembled a jet-black hydra. More and more pitch-black tendrils formed. A dozen, and then a dozen more, lunged futilely, trying to break free from the barricade that quickly rose to contain it, but its strikes glanced off the barrier with no effect.

Realizing what their grandson had done, Rynlin and Rya expanded their dome of energy, pushing the soldiers back slowly so that Thomas would have room to maneuver. They would save their anger at his foolish action for later, assuming he lived to receive their admonishment. For now, they could do nothing but try to protect the soldiers who stood defenseless against such a deadly, malevolent opponent.

Time after time tendrils of black swung out and slammed against the dome containing it, seeking to escape, seeking the energy and spirit of the men and women surrounding it, but who were, for the moment, unreachable. Except for one.

Thomas stood before the swirling mass of darkness, the Sword of the Highlands glowing a bright white in his hands after he infused it with the Talent. Staring into the inky blackness, two red eyes, glowing feverishly, hungering for his spirit, appeared once more in the center of the ephemeral mass. For a moment, the two adversaries simply stared at one another, the sounds beyond the dome muted, something that Thomas was thankful for. He knew the next few minutes could prove to be the deadliest challenge he had ever faced, and he could do without any distractions.

A wisp of darkness instantly formed into a strand that tentatively approached, the swirling mass testing its opponent. Thomas easily dodged the strike, having seen the consequences of getting caught in the grasp of this dark evil. Another murky tentacle whipped out, faster this time. Thomas dodged again, then again, and once more.

Picking himself up off the ground after rolling under the last attack, Thomas decided that he needed a different strategy. He could not evade forever, nor could he expect his grandparents to hold the dome in place for long. He could see through the faint glimmer of the energy surrounding him the strain on their faces as they struggled to maintain control of so much of the Talent at one time.

Throwing caution to the wind, Thomas charged forward. Swinging his blazing blade with an almost unimaginable speed, he sliced through the multiplying threads of blackness that shot toward him. With each slash a shriek of anger and pain emanated from the creature before him. With every cut that sliced through a tendril of black, Thomas reduced the power of the dark creature. The duel continued for several minutes, Thomas slashing away. Yet he knew that even this strategy would prove ineffective as time passed, for with every tendril destroyed, another formed to take its place. It had become a combat of attrition that left him with no good options.

But the decision on what to do next was taken from him. The creature shot more than a dozen tentacles of darkness toward Thomas at once, who frantically sought to defend against the onslaught, dodging, swinging his blade, then dodging some more with a speed that made him appear to be no more than a blur to those watching the fight from outside the dome. Then a dozen more. And a dozen more after that. Though Thomas was able to withstand or avoid many of the attacks, he could not stop them all.

In seconds, as dozens of newly formed tentacles shot out, the swirling threads of darkness encircled him, forcing his sword against his chest. Unable to raise his blade and ward off the continuing attack, the tendrils of black mist compressed, tightening against him as if he were being crushed within the coils of a gigantic snake.

78

HIS HANDS ALONE

Kaylie watched in horror, screaming at Thomas through the dome, but unable to break through the barrier. All she could see was the swirling mass of black, spinning faster and faster where Thomas had once stood. The Highland Lord had disappeared under a crush of inky night.

Coban, Oso and several other Marchers futilely beat on the dome of energy, seeking to help him, and not realizing or not caring that the barrier served a larger purpose -- preventing the creature from consuming every soldier on the battlefield.

For Rynlin and Rya, the strain of their efforts was becoming apparent. They had pulled in so much of the Talent to contain the evil sent against them that they had reached beyond what they thought was the limit of their power. Even with the help of their unicorns, who shared their strength with them, they were dangerously close to the limits of their abilities. They desperately wanted to assist their grandson, sensing the danger, knowing what he faced and fearful that he wouldn't be able to defend himself, but recognizing as well that releasing their control of the dome would mean death for all the soldiers surrounding the almost translucent dome of white energy.

Hate it though they might, they knew that Thomas' survival was in his hands alone.

79

BACK FROM THE EDGE

Immersed in the darkness, held so tightly that he couldn't move a muscle, Thomas felt his strength ebbing away. The creature was draining his life force, slowly and relentlessly, and Thomas had no way to fight back. He felt as if he were drifting closer and closer to the edge, and once he fell over into the abyss the end would come.

Maybe that wouldn't be such a bad thing. The thought drifted through his mind. He was tired now. So tired. More tired than he had ever been. He just needed to rest. To let go.

You must do what you must do. This second thought crashed into the first, startling his senses. It was something his grandmother liked to say, a reminder of who he was and what was expected of him. And he certainly wasn't expected to go quietly into the night.

Struggling to find himself once more, to pull back from the abyss, to oppose the darkness that now rapidly emptied him of his spirit, he grabbed hold of the Talent. The evil that constricted him tightened even more, sensing what he was doing, fighting him, trying to drain the Talent he pulled from the world around him before he could put it to use, but Thomas fought back with a will.

At first Thomas could only access a trickle of his power, and then just a tiny bit more. It was barely anything compared to the strength of the creature he fought, but it was enough for him to pull himself back from the edge he had almost fallen over. Finding his feet once again, he opened himself up even more to the power of nature, feeling the Talent flow back into him, slowly at first, and then faster and faster as it breathed new life into him, energized him, returning the strength the creature had stolen from him.

As the Talent filled him to the point of bursting, a bright white light began to take shape around him, burning into the threads of darkness, destroying the black, misty tentacles that held him. Finally, free from their grasp, he took a few seconds to regain his focus, making sure that he had control of the tremendous amount of natural energy now flowing through him and encircling him in the midst of a pitch-black sea.

Confident in his next step, he stood there calmly, eyes closed, his sword fallen to his feet, his hands open at his side. He pushed slowly but inexorably with the Talent, expanding the space around him, step by step, and with each touch of the bright, flaring light, a bit more of the darkness died.

The dark creature now knew the problem it faced. This was a power it could not defend against, but it had nowhere to escape, as the dome continued to restrict its movement. Thomas took full advantage of that fact, pushing his power outward, seeking to destroy the wispy tendrils of black mist. And as he gained more traction on his enemy, he focused his attention on those glowing red eyes in the very center of the inky, swirling mass, releasing all the power that he could as he fought for his life.

80

WHITE LIGHT

Those on the outside of the dome continued to pound on it, seeking to help, yet feeling helpless as they realized that their efforts were fruitless. Tears rolled down Kaylie's cheeks as she watched in dread, the deadly blackness having covered everything inside of the dome and consumed Thomas. Several minutes passed, and all she could see was a darkness blacker than night.

Then much to her surprise a flash of light caught her attention. A single white spark glowed deep within the murk. That spark flickered for several long seconds, fighting against the inky black mist, then slowly but steadily grew. As that spark swelled into a glowing globe of white light, the blackness retreated.

The blazing white light continued to expand, and now she could see the dim shape of a man, barely able to make him out because of the brightness that almost blinded her and the others encircling the dome. The shape stood there calmly, hands at its side, as the globe of white light continued to swell, glowing brighter and brighter as it devoured more and more of the midnight black tendrils of darkness.

Soon there was more white light than black in the dome, the brilliance so strong that she could no longer look at it. And then, in a final blinding flash that sounded like a thousand thunderclaps, the pitch-black mist dissolved.

Kaylie blinked several times, clearing the spots from her eyes. The dome had disappeared as had the darkness. Thomas stood there as if nothing of importance had occurred, calmly placing his sword in the scabbard on his back.

He had won. How he had done it she didn't know, but he was alive. Kaylie's tears of sadness turned into tears of joy as they streamed down her cheeks. Running forward, she hugged Thomas tightly to her. For someone who usually knew what to do, Thomas had no idea how to handle the unexpected emotion. So, he simply hugged her back.

Running her hands over him and satisfied that Thomas was unharmed, Kaylie stepped back, her tear-rimmed eyes appraising him. Then she formed a fist and punched him hard in the arm. Thomas winced at the blow. Kaylie's swordplay had given her some added strength.

"Don't ever do that again," she told him quietly. Captured by his shining green eyes, she reached up with both hands to cup his face, pulling his lips to hers for a soft kiss, before she released him, almost pushing him away, then walked through the throng of Marchers who rushed forward to congratulate the Highland Lord.

THE END

~

Keep reading for the first four chapters of Book 8, *The Fight Against the Dark*.

BONUS MATERIAL

If you really enjoyed this story, I need you to do me a HUGE favor – please follow me on Amazon and BookBub.

And if you have a few minutes, consider writing a review.

Keep reading for the first four chapters of Book 8 of *The Sylvan Chronicles*, *The Fight Against the Dark*. Order Book 8 on Amazon or on my website www.PeterWachtBooks.com.

PETER WACHT

THE
FIGHT
AGAINST THE
DARK

THE SYLVAN CHRONICLES
8

Published in the United States by Kestrel Media Group LLC.

ISBN: 978-1-950236-14-5

eBook ISBN: 978-1-950236-15-2

Library of Congress Control Number: 9781950236145

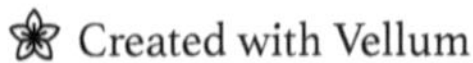 Created with Vellum

1. DREAM OR REALITY?

The tendrils of black mist snaked their way around Thomas Kestrel, whipping about as if each one had a mind of its own. The inky cords probed, testing for a weakness, twisting around one another as they sought to latch onto his body, then rearing back rapidly as the Dark Magic tried to escape the killing stroke of the Sword of the Highlands. Each time Thomas' brightly glowing blade, infused with the Talent, slashed through a strand of corrupted sorcery, the formless dark creature that towered above the Sylvan Warrior howled in pain, its tentacle dissolving as it was cut free from the beast. Yet even with the suffering that its quarry inflicted upon it, the churning mass of darkness continued its assault, a dozen new tendrils taking the place of each tentacle sliced off much like the mythical Hydra. Thomas fought with a will, his movement economical and lightning fast as he cleaved and cut through the threads of black that shot toward him time after time and gave him no chance to take a breath. But even he, his actions so quick that they seemed to blur, couldn't keep up with the speed and ferocity of the dark creature's attack.

Dozens and dozens of tendrils flailed and snapped around

him, seeking a path through the shield that he wove with his brilliantly shining steel. Sadly, despite his best efforts, he was doomed to fail, and he knew it. The Shadow Lord's servant was too much for him. First a cable of black slipped past his blade and wrapped itself around his right leg, holding him in place. He tried to cut it off, his fear growing as the cord became darker and more solid, anchoring him to the ground. Each time he slashed down with his blade more and more strands of Dark Magic got in the way, blocking his attempts and allowing that single thickening cable to maintain its tight grip. While he was distracted, another inky cord found purchase, winding its way around his waist. Before that thread could tighten its grip, Thomas cut it off. But that obstruction permitted two more black threads to curl around his left arm. He tried to slash down with his steel, but he couldn't. His sword arm wouldn't move, held tightly by another thick strand of black that had threaded its way past his defenses. He strained against the solidifying cords, desperate to free himself, but the strands only tightened their hold, constricting around him as if he were caught within the coils of a giant snake. His alarm grew. Unable to move, his rising terror threatened to engulf him.

With its prey locked in place, the billowing cloud of evil sent tendril after tendril shooting toward Thomas, curling around him tighter and tighter, compressing his sword arm against his chest and encircling his body. The seething mass of sable tentacles then began to pulse a deep black. Thomas continued to struggle against the threads that were as strong as steel, but as the cords darkened in color, he began to weaken, his strength slowly ebbing away. He imagined that what he experienced now was similar to having his life drained from him by a Shade's kiss. That thought only served to increase his panic all the more. Unable to break free, his head held tightly in place, Thomas could only stare into the two pinpricks of blood red that burned brightly in the center of the swirling mass of black. As the darkness closed around him, his body growing heavy, his thoughts drifting away, his vision blurring, all he could focus on were those points of red blazing in the encroaching shadows as his consciousness faded away ...

Thomas didn't know how long he floated through this world of inky black, but slowly, ever so slowly, a new image began to form in front of him. As his senses and memories returned to him, he recalled being in the Highlands, fighting on a plain of long grass that stretched off into the distance, imposing, snow-capped peaks surrounding him. But no more. That had all disappeared. Somehow, he had traveled to a place where the bright sunlight of the day had been replaced by a thick, grey gloom. Thankful that he could move once again, he turned around slowly. He could make out very little in the murk, seeing nothing but a wispy grey except for the two blood-red eyes that still burned brightly in front of him. He should have felt shock, surprise, terror, but he didn't. Rather, he felt whole, as if he were exactly where he was supposed to be. As Thomas' bright green eyes adjusted to the darkness, he picked out more of the cowled figure standing in front of him, still black robes hanging in the air, not even rippling at the touch of the wind.

The seconds stretched into minutes as Thomas studied the figure before him, the silence deafening, the stillness arresting. A faint disturbance in the air was the only sign that gave away the fact that something had changed. Thomas raised his sword above his head, not realizing that he still held it in his hand. His brightly shining steel caught the black sword before it cleaved him in two. Not done, his shrouded adversary flipped his blade around in a backhanded swing that targeted Thomas' midsection, but again he countered, sword sliding down to push the strike away from his body. And so it went for the next few minutes, the light-eating sword of black slicing through the gloom while Thomas danced around his attacker, deflecting each lunge, cut and slash. Each time the two swords met, sparks illuminated the blackness with a flash as the Talent and Dark Magic repelled one another. Thomas wanted to attack, to seek the advantage, to change the trajectory of the duel somehow, but it was all that he could do to defend himself, the black steel weaving around him often no more than a whisker away from slicing into his flesh.

Then just as abruptly as the cowled figure's attack began, it came to an end. The shadowy figure glided backward, the black steel disappearing. Thomas took a few steps back as well, sword still held warily in front of him, not convinced that the fight was truly over. For some strange reason, he suspected that it actually had just started.

"You fight well, boy," rasped the robed man who faded in and out of the gloom, the only constant his blood-red eyes. "But not well enough."

"Well enough to hold you off." Thomas said the words with a confidence that he didn't feel. Although he had defended himself from each of his opponent's attacks, it had been more of a struggle than he had anticipated. His adversary filled him with a fear that almost paralyzed him, slowing his ability to react.

"Believe that if you want, boy. But you know the truth."

Thomas stared into those blood-red eyes, doubt seeping into him as the two orbs burned brightly, flaring in the murk. The shadowy figure was right, though he didn't want to admit it to himself. The duel had felt more like a test rather than a fight.

"What do you want?" Thomas was pleased that his voice was steady, strong, and didn't reveal what he was actually experiencing as his emotions roiled within him.

"Isn't it obvious?" asked the cowled figure. "I want you."

"Why?"

"Don't play the fool, boy. It doesn't become you. You know why."

Thomas' eyes hardened, the rebuke angering him. His hand flexed on the hilt of his sword. For just a moment, he considered lunging for his opponent, his brightly glowing blade pulsing in response to his emotions. But he tamped down the impulse, knowing that it would lead to little good.

"I'll never serve you."

"We'll see, boy," replied the cowled figure, the quiet sibilance of his voice reminding Thomas of a bloodsnake. "We'll see very soon." The blood-red eyes sparked, giving the dark gloom a red haze. "Be ready, boy. I'm coming for you."

"Not if I come for you first."

Then in a blink of the eye the figure was gone, and darkness settled over Thomas once again.

The squawk of a kestrel flying high above the Marcher encampment broke through the fog that surrounded Thomas, waking him. He shook his head, trying to clear the cobwebs from his mind. He felt as if he hadn't slept at all. The sun still a distant thought in the early morning, Thomas rolled out of his blankets and followed the large shadow of the raptor with his eyes as it soared above him. The kestrel shrieked again, and Thomas smiled in return. He had been dreaming. He was still in the Highlands. The dark creature that had almost emptied the life from him was dead. Only a bad memory. Thomas closed his eyes and breathed deeply, enjoying the crispness of the air. A bolt of fear ran through him. His eyes popped open, and he looked down at his right hand, the Sword of the Highlands firmly in his grip. He didn't remember pulling the blade free from its scabbard when he woke. Had he done so in his sleep? An unnerving realization shot through him as he stared at the inscription that ran down the length of the steel: *"Strength and courage lead to freedom."* The fight against the dark creature had been a dream, of that he was certain, but what of the duel against the cowled figure? Had that been a dream as well? Or had it been real?

Thomas turned his gaze toward the north and the Charnel Mountains, which were only a smudge far off in the distance. Within those ash-covered peaks lay the Shadow Lord's lair. Blackstone. The seat of his adversary's power. He could feel the pull. It was growing stronger by the day, more insistent. He would need to go there one day soon. But not yet. Thankfully not yet. He needed to do something else first. If his plan worked as he hoped it would, he could do as he said when he spoke to the shadow with the blood-red eyes. Something that his enemy wouldn't expect.

2. RUMBLING DISSATISFACTION

A tall figure covered in misty, pitch-black robes stood in the center of his throne room lost in thought. If not for his fiercely burning blood-red eyes, he would have blended in perfectly with the natural gloom of the chamber. The symmetry of the alternating black and white tiles, all as large as a man's stride, usually pleased him, giving him a feeling of control. That everything could be put in its proper place. But not now. Not in this moment. Not when his mind drifted elsewhere. At first, fixated on the future, on what was yet to come, then just as much on the past, on what had come to pass. Finally, it was the present that drew him back from his mental wanderings.

The Shadow Lord listened to the roars that drifted into the circular room through the open doors. Normally the sound would have filled him with a sense of his own power, of what he could achieve when the time was right. Now it only reminded him of his failures. He glided out onto the balcony and looked down upon the immense courtyard below. Ogren raiding parties formed into ranks on the square, destined for the Highlands with the goal of creating an avenue into the Kingdoms that would allow his dark creatures to avoid the Breaker. The

Shadow Lord was certain that, if necessary, his Dark Horde could break through the Kingdoms' primary defense, scaling the massive wall built to keep him and his servants in the Charnel Mountains after the devastating conclusion of the Great War. But why take an unnecessary risk? Why not circumvent the inevitable delay that breaching such a barrier would create? Why not put in place a better strategy that would allow him to gain his objectives more quickly and easily?

With all that in mind, he had done so, cultivating and corrupting the current High King. The Shadow Lord had aided Rodric Tessaril during his rise to the throne of Armagh and the honorific of High King that went with the title. He had helped that inept scoundrel remove the uncle and cousin, giving that insipid yet temporarily useful fool a clear path to power. And with Rodric as High King, the Shadow Lord could use him to weaken the other Kingdoms, bringing to his side those willing to sell themselves for the riches and power he offered, and isolating or eliminating those foolish enough to ignore his entreaties. At first, the move had proved effective. Yet in the last few years, despite the time and effort that went into every single detail of his plans, the strategy, so long in the making, had begun to unravel.

As a result of the defeat of the Armaghian army in the Highlands, the High King Rodric Tessaril was on the run, risked losing his Kingdom, and had threatened the Shadow Lord's plans with collapse. With Rodric no longer a threat, the Marchers could turn their attention to protecting their northern border, making it harder for his Ogren raiding parties to gain control of the territory that he needed that would allow his Dark Horde, when the time was right, to avoid the Breaker and sweep into the Kingdoms unopposed. All his planning and scheming appeared to have been for nothing, his plan decades in the making now laying in tatters, thanks to an incompetent High King and an upstart boy. A boy who should have died a decade ago, but didn't, escaping the assassin's blade. A boy who should have died multiple times since then, but still lived.

Rodric, Killeran and Chertney all had been in a position to stick a knife between the boy's ribs, but failed to do so. Every Nightstalker and Shade sent against him had been defeated as well. Even Malachias had been found lacking in his efforts to eliminate the boy, and he was the most powerful of the Shadow Lord's servants. The one who had served him the longest and with the greatest success. Even the Wraith, the most dangerous of his assassins, had fallen short, at least initially. Perhaps the Wraith would succeed in time, only bested by the boy but not destroyed. But was it wise to count on the dark creature to complete its task having already failed once? Time and time again the boy had made a fool of him and his minions. That seemed to be the only constant.

The Shadow Lord's blood-red eyes burned like a raging fire as his fury began to consume him. So much at stake, all of it at risk, because of a boy. And now the boy was growing stronger and more dangerous by the day. The boy needed to be eliminated, yet he was surrounded by fools and incompetents and nothing he had tried in the past had proven successful.

As he drifted back into the chamber and came to a stop in its very center, the Shadow Lord struggled to control his temper as a tremor of unease flitted through his thoughts. Was he the boy of the prophecy? The one destined to stand before him on this very spot and engage him in a duel that would decide the fate of the Kingdoms? Maybe so. Maybe that was why the boy continued to escape the traps set for him. Maybe only he, the Shadow Lord, could kill the boy. If such was the case, then so be it. He would take great pleasure in sliding his blade into the boy's heart, for the Shadow Lord had no doubt how the duel would end. He was too skilled, too powerful, too treacherous to lose.

But it should never have come to this. It should have ended

long ago. Needing to release his anger, the Shadow Lord shot a bolt of black energy through the gloom, shattering the skylight that enclosed the top of the circular chamber. The Shadow Lord watched without emotion as the broken glass rained down around him, the sparkling shards covering the disc set in the very center of the hall and surrounded by the alternating black and white tile. Unexpectedly and much to his annoyance, a beam of sunshine blasted through the hole at the top of the chamber and shined down on the glass-covered stone disc just seconds after he had destroyed the skylight, the light revealing the intricate design carved into it.

Two figures emerged from the cuts in the block, done with such excellent workmanship that they appeared lifelike. The first resembled a young man with a blazing sword of light. Opposing him was a tall man with a cruel face wielding a sword that swallowed the light. They were locked blade to blade, their faces no more than a finger's breadth apart. The boy wore a look of determination, the man a grin of arrogance and sure victory. As the sun met the stone it grew warm, the light touching the broken glass and igniting a kaleidoscope of colors. A rumble began in the room, drifting out to the very edges of Blackstone, an occurrence that had become much more common in the Shadow Lord's city over the last few months. An event that suggested change could be coming. A happening that still worried the Shadow Lord despite his confidence in the likely result of the prophesied duel.

As the rumbling intensified so did the brightness of the beam of light, the dazzling colors dancing irregularly across the chamber's halls. Gaining more and more strength with each passing second, the sunlight blasted away the scraps of darkness and gloom that inhabited the throne room until the Shadow Lord had no choice but to turn away, the glare of the blazing, white light too strong even for him.

3. ANOTHER DEMAND

The tall man walked silently along the mountain trail, cloak drawn tightly across his shoulders, cowl pulled down to cover his head in a failed attempt to ward off the biting cold. Although it appeared that he wasn't paying attention, his senses were extended in all directions, attuned to everything around him. Dark creatures haunted the crevices, crags and shadows of these peaks, so his hand never strayed far from the short sword on his belt. Touches of darkness, of things terrifying and unnatural, of things better left in the jet-black of night, flitted across the extreme edge of his perception, but he knew that he wasn't in any immediate danger. If he hurried, he could reach the grotto that would offer him some protection and peace of mind as he settled in for the night.

Most people refused to enter the Charnel Mountains, and those who did rarely returned. Any who traveled within ten miles of the forbidding crests shrouded in ash could feel the evil lurking there, hidden away from the sight of man, but always present. Always watching, always lurking, always waiting for just the right moment to strike.

Some said that the Charnel Mountains were an abomination, caused by a tremendous magical battle between the forces of good and evil. Those who followed the light had won, but they could not destroy the dark, they could only hold it back. So instead they imprisoned their enemies in the mountains, sealing them away for eternity, or so they thought. Before the Shadow Lord came to be, the Charnel Mountains looked very much like the Highlands, the landscape defined by hidden valleys and lakes, the wind-swept peaks, towering evergreens and other conifers, and brambles and thickets hiding innumerable glades. But when the Shadow Lord took up residence there and began creating his servants — the Ogren, Shades, Fearhounds, as well as other beasts that were even more frightening and deadly — the mountains slowly transformed into what they are today. Barren. Desolate. Dead. Dark grey stone formed the stone spires, the very tips of the monstrous peaks a sooty black. What trees that remained were stunted and twisted, struggling to survive with their roots in an earth covered by a thick layer of ash and cinder.

The tallest of the mountains could not be seen completely, as fully a third of its mass rose up into the grey clouds. Known as Blackstone, that single peak had an even older name. Shadow's Reach. On certain winter days, when the sun was in just the right position, the shadow of Blackstone reached out across much of the Northern Steppes, turning day into night and, for those travelers caught in that empty land, life into a horror.

No one in their right mind scouted the Charnel Mountains on their own. Not if they wanted to live. Yet that was his task, so here he was, wandering the ravines and gullies, staying out of sight, tracking the dark creatures that sought to raid across the flat grassland to the south into the Highlands and perhaps into the Kingdoms beyond.

Having reached a steeper part of the narrow trail, the tall man began to pick his way carefully, wary of the scrabble beneath his feet. He reached out to the rocks lining the path, pulling himself up the more difficult sections. As he finally attained the level part of the path, he stopped short, his hand whipping the short sword out in front of him.

The blade glowed brightly as the scout infused it with the Talent. A mysterious man wrapped in black robes stood before him. Bald, his features sharp, he appeared almost skeletal. His sunken, dark eyes gave away no emotion. There was nothing in his eyes but a flinty hardness, a malevolent spark dancing within that sea of black and sending a shiver of fear through the scout.

"There are easier ways to arrange a meeting, Malachias. You don't need to play your games."

The Shadow Lord's servant examined the man before him, noting that the sword remained within his grasp, its white light pulsing along the length of steel. He ignored the comment.

"You dare to challenge me?" questioned Malachias with a smirk, his raspy voice sounding like metal sliding across stone.

The tall man stared at Malachias a moment longer, then sighed, acknowledging the power that he faced. Releasing his hold on the Talent, he sheathed his short sword. He knew that he didn't have the strength to defeat the Shadow Lord's right hand, so there was no point in continuing the show.

"I have another task for you."

The man shook his head in frustration. "I have done enough, more than enough. I have done everything that you have asked of me. This has to stop. No more tasks. No more assignments. I want to be free of this."

For the first time some little fragment of emotion drifted behind Malachias' eyes. He appeared to be amused.

"You believe that you can break the contract that you made with our master?" A scratchy laugh erupted from Malachias. "You knew full well the bargain you made, and what you were getting in return. Once you struck your bargain, the terms were set. Your fate was sealed. Your life was no longer your own. You belong to the Shadow Lord."

"I have done everything he's asked!" shouted the tall man, Malachias' words cutting to the very bone. He had been such a fool, thinking that he could find some way to escape the deal he had accepted. The compact that bore down on him like a ten-ton stone. "Everything. And many of the things I've done I'm desperate to forget, but I cannot. They stay with me, always there in the back of my mind. Please, I need to be free of this. I can't do it anymore."

Malachias' laughter died quickly, his eyes resembling granite once more. "Once you have committed yourself to the Shadow Lord, there is no turning back. There is no release, not even in death. You will do as commanded. Remember, there are always worse tasks that can be given to you. Tasks that will make the ones that plague your memory now seem pleasant in comparison."

The tall man closed his eyes in resignation, desperate to be free of the bindings on his soul, but acknowledging reluctantly that he had no power to remove them. Knowing that his one moment of weakness had turned his life into a waking nightmare.

"What would you have of me?"

Malachias stared at the man before him a bit longer, confirming for himself that the traitor understood the strength of the cage within which he had placed himself so long ago, a cage that would continue to hold him no matter what he tried to do to escape.

"Multiple plans have been set in motion to remove a thorn from the side of the Shadow Lord. But this thorn has proven most resilient and continues to prick our master, as you well know. This thorn has prevented us from using the Highlands to enter the Kingdoms. That cannot continue. We must be able to avoid the Breaker. Yes, the Kingdoms are weak. We can surmount the barrier. But it would cost us time and resources. Better to make the Highlands our staging point. If the Dark Horde can march through the Highlands, the Kingdoms are doomed before the battle even begins."

"And my role?"

"Put yourself in a position to remove this thorn, as you've done in the past. You should have no trouble getting close to him if circumstances demand it. But this time do what's required of you. Remove this thorn. Otherwise, the consequences will be severe."

"Who am I supposed to kill?" the tall man sighed with weariness, knowing the answer already but still needing to ask the question. A bolt of fear sent a shiver up his spine and jolted him from his growing melancholy. He had tried once before and failed, barely escaping with his life. His hand unconsciously moved to his chest, touching the silver amulet hanging around his neck, the silver amulet carved into the shape of the curled horn of a unicorn. It felt like an icicle against his body.

"The Highland Lord."

4. TAKING FLIGHT

Thomas Kestrel stood atop the Breaker wrapped in a thick, dark green cloak, ignoring the harsh, cold wind that buffeted him, seemingly trying to knock him from his perch on the battlements. Carved from massive blocks of granite, the Breaker rose well over three hundred feet in height and was one hundred feet wide, extending from the western Highlands to the coast and the Winter Sea. Its broad expanse gave the soldiers of the Kingdoms the space they needed to repel an attack by the Shadow Lord's dark creatures. But there were no defenders standing atop the parapet now, and there hadn't been for centuries. Because the Shadow Lord had faded from reality to myth in the minds of most in the Kingdoms, the Breaker was no longer viewed as a barrier, but rather just as an obstacle.

The first time the Shadow Lord had tried to conquer the Kingdoms, one thousand years in the past, the rulers of the different lands didn't perceive his evil as a serious threat then either, since he was far to the north and the Northern Steppes stood in the way. Consequently, only a small contingent of troops from the eastern Kingdoms went into the Northern

Peaks to fight. They did all that they could, not knowing what they truly faced until it was too late, as they were heavily outnumbered by the Ogren, Shades, Fearhounds and other hideous beasts that formed the Dark Horde that sought to invade the Kingdoms. The soldiers fought valiantly, yet could only disrupt the Shadow Lord's inevitable advance and hope that help would come.

The other Kingdoms finally realized the great threat presented by this new danger, that hard-earned wisdom built on the lives lost because of that initial ill-conceived stratagem, but it would take weeks for those Kingdoms to call together their armies and march to the north. At that time, druids still held sway over the land, and often served as advisors in the courts of the different monarchs. The chief druid, a woman named Athala, suggested that the Kingdoms send their best warriors to her, and under her leadership they would fight the Dark Horde until the massed armies of the Kingdoms could take the field ... or her small fighting force was destroyed.

The unprepared and rattled rulers balked at first, but several unexpected events finally convinced them to move forward with the proposal, and the greatest warriors of that time met Athala on the Northern Steppes in order to counter the Dark Horde, which was pushing hard for the south and would soon break out of the Northern Peaks onto the grasslands. When that happened, the Kingdoms would have little chance of stopping the dark creatures from flooding the Kingdoms. Athala called those who made up her small host of only several hundred Sylvan Warriors, naming these courageous fighters after a mythical band of soldiers who, the stories told, appeared in times of need and fought for those who had been wronged or protected the land when danger threatened.

The Sylvan Warriors met the Dark Horde at the southern border of the Northern Peaks, and there at a place called the Knife's Edge they battled for three days and three nights. The

Sylvana fought desperately to hold back the Shadow Lord's advance. In the end, after untold sacrifices and a bravery rarely seen on the battlefield, they succeeded. The small band of warriors forced the Dark Horde to retreat to the north. Before the Shadow Lord could recover and send his dark creatures south once more, the armies of the Kingdoms arrived and pushed him and his minions even deeper into what was then already being described as the Charnel Mountains.

But despite their best efforts the Sylvan Warriors and the combined might of the Kingdoms couldn't destroy the Shadow Lord. They could only defeat him. So the rulers of the Kingdoms again followed the advice of Athala and proclaimed the Sylvan Warriors a permanent fighting force with no ties of allegiance to any Kingdom. The sole purpose of this elite company was to fight the Shadow Lord and his servants, and they had done so ever since.

Yet even with the formation of the Sylvana and trusting in their skills and power, at the conclusion of the Great War the Kingdoms still feared the Shadow Lord's return, knowing that if their armies had not appeared when they did to aid Athala and her intrepid troop, the Dark Horde would have overrun the Kingdoms. Therefore, the monarchs of the Kingdoms banded together and built the Breaker and formed the First Guard, soldiers from the different Kingdoms charged with serving a year on the massive wall, watching, waiting, and preparing for the next attack so that when the Shadow Lord once more tried to conquer the Kingdoms, and all assumed that he would, the Kingdoms would be better prepared to defend themselves. But as time passed no attack had come, and the Kingdoms began sending fewer and fewer soldiers to serve in the First Guard until eventually no one stood atop the Breaker, leaving only the Sylvana to guard against the return of the Dark Horde.

Now, in a replay of events a millennium gone, many of the Kingdoms failed to recognize the danger or willingly ignored it, more worried about the happenings in their own Kingdom thanks to the machinations of the High King rather than, at least to their own eyes, a yet to be confirmed threat to the Kingdoms as a whole that appeared to remain more story than substance. Such short-sightedness could prove costly, Thomas knew, as it had in the past. Not very tall, the Lord of the Highlands still radiated a power and presence that few could project. Deep in thought, his green eyes flashed brightly as he stared to the north at the dark smudge of the Charnel Mountains that rose above the flat expanse of the Northern Steppes. He had needed to clear his mind, to get away, if only for the afternoon, from the crush of business that had fallen upon him now that the Marchers had expelled the High King and his army from the Highlands. Finally, after a decade of terror and anguish, of servitude and misery, his homeland was free. But for how long?

Attacks by the Shadow Lord's dark creatures continued in the northern Highlands. At first the raiding parties had predominantly been Ogren led by Shades, but now packs of Fearhounds and Mongrels also were attempting to carve a path through the peaks of his mountain homeland. The increased pace of these incursions could mean only one thing. Time was growing short. The Shadow Lord was stirring, and the Dark Horde would come again. But Thomas couldn't focus on that task just yet with the High King still running free.

Rodric Tessaril seemed to be able to slither out of closing traps with ease. Every time Thomas thought that he had the man responsible for his grandfather's murder within his grasp, he slipped away. Admittedly, the last time, just a few days before, Rodric's hidden ally had come to the fore and helped him, allowing the High King to flee back to Eamhain Mhacha, capital of Armagh, with his tail between his legs. Thomas couldn't let the High King enjoy his freedom for much longer. Rodric would only create more problems and intrigue, which would distract from what needed to be the primary focus – defending the Breaker and defeating the Shadow Lord. No, before anything else, the issue of the High King had to be addressed, once and for all. Rodric Tessaril needed to be removed from the playing board. Permanently.

Thomas turned to the northeast, facing Blackstone. Although he couldn't see the dead city situated among the Charnel Mountains, he could feel its pull. It was growing more insistent, more demanding. He knew that the prophesied time that he feared the most approached faster than he would have preferred. Just not yet, but soon. Very soon. Unable to take his mind away from that fact, his grandmother's favorite saying ran through his mind: *You must do what you must do.* Even if doing what you must came at a cost you didn't want to pay. Forcing that depressing thought from his mind, he turned to the west. He felt another pull, a fainter pull, very faint, but with each passing hour it was becoming more irritating, like an itch between his shoulder blades that he couldn't reach. This very vague tug reminded him of the time before he joined the Sylvan Warriors, when the pull of the Pinnacle had grown increasingly stronger as time went by. The same thing was happening now, this strengthening need for him to travel to the western coast of the Kingdoms. He wasn't certain, but he suspected that this new sensation was connected to the task that he dreaded. Should he follow it? Would whatever he discovered at the end of this nagging feeling give him a chance, however slim, of surviving his encounter with the Shadow Lord? He could think about it all he wanted, but there was only one way to find out.

The Shadow Lord. The High King. Two problems that continued to plague him. Separated, these two opponents tested him constantly. Combined, they could prove overwhelming. So better to cut away the High King and eliminate that threat as quickly as possible. When he returned to the Highlands, he would convince the other rulers of the course that needed to be taken.

That decision made, his mind began to wander. Was Kaylie Carlomin another issue that needed to be dealt with? The Princess of Fal Carrach had made her anger known when he had stepped within the dome of energy his grandparents had constructed with the Talent as they sought to contain the Hydra-like dark creature the Shadow Lord had set upon them during the final battle for the Highlands. Just thinking about her punch to his arm after he had destroyed the monster set his arm aching. The vehemence of her words continued to play through his mind: "Don't ever do that again." He could understand her anger, but what she had done next had left him stunned. Why had she kissed him after hitting him? Her action had surprised and confused him, leaving him standing there not knowing what to do. But the more he thought about the incident, the more he realized that there was more to her words and actions than met the eye, and that worried him. What was he to do? And knowing what his future held, should he do anything at all?

A shrill squawk that reverberated off the Breaker pulled his thoughts back to the present. The large kestrel settled itself onto the battlements just a few feet from Thomas, its sharp gaze seeking him out. Its strong wings spanned seven feet, and the white feathers speckled with grey on the bird's underside blended perfectly with the sky. When visible, the raptor was a dangerous predator. When hidden, it was deadly, shooting down through the thin air like an arrow, its sharp claws outstretched for the kill. The Highlands was the raptor's domain, now its only home. Once, not too many years before, raptors lived in every Kingdom from the Western Ocean to the Sea of Mist. But no more. Nobles and wealthy merchants paid dearly for the feathers of the mighty bird. Rumors of their magical powers abounded. Some believed the feathers, when ground down and mixed with a few select ingredients, served as an aphrodisiac. Others insisted that drinking the strange brew gave wisdom. Still others thought it brought riches. Though no one had ever proven the truth of these myths, the old beliefs died hard. As the years passed, so did these majestic birds, until none remained except those in the Highlands, protected by the harsh weather, the rough landscape and the Highlanders themselves, for the raptors held a special place in their hearts. Moreover, the kestrel was the namesake and the symbol of the Highland Lord.

Thomas knew this raptor, having met it several times before. It appeared almost as if this kestrel looked out for him. And with that knowledge, strange as it may seem, came a sense of comfort. Looking up into the cloudy sky, he picked out the four other raptors that circled above. Not a day went by that he didn't have four or five kestrels flying above him now, ever vigilant. Watching. Waiting. Protecting. The massive birds enjoyed the strong current of air gusting off the Charnel Mountains and flowing toward the Breaker, twisting and turning at the whim of the wind. He realized that circumstances had changed drastically when they dipped their wings at the same time to curl toward the blackened mountain peaks to the north.

Dots appeared in the sky, appearing larger with every heartbeat. The raptor that had landed on the Breaker nodded to him, then used its sharp claws to push off the weathered stone, beating its wings fiercely to catch up to its brethren. Thomas watched intently, a sense of dread settling in his stomach as those dots materialized into monstrous beasts. More than four times the size of the raptor, the Dragas was a significant threat. The flying dark creatures enjoyed a clear advantage over the kestrels, their scaled hides offering them additional protection though it did cost them the speed that the raptors put to such good use.

Five Dragas approached, roaring in fury upon seeing the

raptors. Normally, the kestrels would work together to take on just one of these massive dark creatures, seeking to dig their sharp claws into the soft underbelly of their mortal enemies. But they couldn't do so today. There were simply too many to fight. Yet that didn't stop the predators. The raptors dove from above, hurtling down toward the Dragas and trying to catch them by surprise. Although several of the kestrels did succeed in slicing into the unprotected undersides of a few Dragas, most failed, their sharp claws simply skittering off the hardened scales as the Dragas avoided the attack. The battle quickly denigrated into a game of cat and mouse, as the kestrels used their speed and tighter maneuverability to avoid the chasing Dragas, understanding the penalty if they were caught by the dark creatures' long, spike-like claws and sharp teeth.

Thomas watched the fight in the air begin, his anger growing, as he saw several of the raptors barely escape the Dragas, which were emboldened by the knowledge that though the dark creatures did not have the speed of the kestrels, they enjoyed greater stamina and strength. The longer the battle continued, the greater the chance of success for the dark creatures. Keeping all that in mind, Thomas took hold of the Talent. In a flash of bright white light, he took the shape of a kestrel, rapidly winging his way toward the aerial fray.

Quickly gaining height, Thomas surveyed the sky around him. One kestrel flew to his left, darting about, desperately trying to escape a Dragas that flew just a few feet behind its tail feathers. Tipping his wing, Thomas banked down and to the right, curling toward the raptor that struggled to dodge its pursuer. With a final burst of speed, Thomas shot right below the chasing Dragas, extending his claws and slicing across the dark creature's belly. The Dragas extended its wings, stopping its flight and hovering in the air, its attention now focused on Thomas as its black blood flowed freely from the long, deep gash that scored its underside. Ignoring the pain of its injury, the Dragas prepared to launch itself toward Thomas, who had flown back around in a tight circle with the hope of lining up another strike. The Dragas viewed his attacker as the primary target, realizing too late that Thomas had become the bait. Not sensing the danger, before the Dragas could propel itself toward its new quarry, the raptor it had chased slammed into it from behind, its deadly claws tearing through the Dragas' wings until the thin, loose skin had been shredded into a bloody mess. With a screech of anger and fear, the Dragas dropped from the sky, its broken and torn wings no longer able to support its weight.

Thomas and the other raptor didn't bother to watch the dark creature slam into the ground far below. Instead, they turned their attention to another Dragas, this one also pursuing a kestrel, so intent on its prey that the dark creature missed what had just occurred. Working together, Thomas and the other kestrel quickly dispatched the next Dragas in a similar fashion, Thomas focusing on the belly, the kestrel on the wings, both raptors so quick in their attack that they didn't have to worry about the Dragas' teeth or claws. Thomas and the kestrels built on his strategy, and as each Dragas fell from the sky, plummeting to the grassland far below, the kestrels, which had at first been the prey, quickly had become the predators. In just a few minutes, the skirmish came to a satisfying end for the kestrels. The sky clear of Dragas, the raptors screeched in triumph, exultant in their victory.

Thomas turned to the south and began winging his way toward the Highlands. Four of the raptors took up positions around him, much like points on a compass, while the fifth kestrel, the one that had tracked him since his time living in the Crag, dipped down from a higher altitude to fly next to him, its pride obvious in its sharp eyes. As Thomas and his escort neared the Highlands, the snow-covered peaks became more distinct as the raptors' powerful wings drew them ever closer.

Thomas resolved that he'd keep this latest incident to himself. Remembering her reaction to his taking on the dark creature sent by the Shadow Lord, he didn't want to risk angering Kaylie again. Who knew what she was capable of?

I hope you enjoyed the first four chapters. To keep reading *The Fight Against the Dark*, Book 8 of *The Sylvan Chronicles*, order your copy from my website at www.PeterWachtBooks.com or Amazon.

This short story is a prelude to the events in my series *The Tales of Caledonia* and is free to readers who receive my newsletter.

Join Peter's newsletter and get your FREE short story.
www.PeterWachtBooks.com